FURY
CALLING

A FURY UNBOUND NOVEL
BOOK 4

YASMINE
NEW YORK TIMES BESTSELLING AUTHOR
GALENORN

A Nightqueen Enterprises LLC Publication

Published by Yasmine Galenorn
PO Box 2037, Kirkland WA 98083-2037
FURY CALLING
A Fury Unbound Novel
Copyright © 2017 by Yasmine Galenorn
First Electronic Printing: 2017 Nightqueen Enterprises LLC
First Print Edition: 2017 Nightqueen Enterprises
Cover Art & Design: Ravven
Editor: Elizabeth Flynn
Map Design: Yasmine Galenorn
Map Layout: Samwise Galenorn

A Nightqueen Enterprises LLC Publication
Published in the United States of America

ACKNOWLEDGMENTS

And so we reach the end of the first story arc in Fury's world. I can't give you a specific date for the second arc, but I definitely plan to revisit Fury and her friends at some time. Meanwhile, I'm drawing this story arc to what I feel will be a comfortable close, leaving room for the world to grow in the future.

Thanks to my usual crew: Samwise, my husband, Andria and Jennifer—without their help, I'd be swamped—to the women who have helped me find my way in indie, you're all great, and to Fury herself—who started long ago as a glimmer of an idea, and who wasn't allowed out of her cage till I escaped from mine.

Also, my love to my furbles, who keep me happy. And most reverent devotion to Mielikki, Tapio, Ukko, Rauni, and Brighid, my spiritual guardians and guides.

If you wish to reach me, you can find me through my website at Galenorn.com and be sure to sign up for my newsletter to keep updated on all my latest releases!

Brightest Blessings,
~The Painted Panther~
~Yasmine Galenorn~

Welcome to Fury Calling

"Behold, Hecate the Crone Mother, the Mistress of Magic, the Keeper of the Cauldron of Change! Make a deal with me, and let me weave the threads of your web and your life!"

Standing there before me was an ancient crone, with hair as silver as the starlight, and her face a map of wrinkles so deep they were furrowed into her skin. Her eyes, though, were clear and brilliant and cruel, and she was dressed in a gown as black as the night with a silver belt and silver snakes that writhed around her arms.

I fell to my knees, afraid. I had never met this Hecate before, this ancient hag who embodied all the power of the night within her very essence. She was Queen of the Night, Queen of Nightmares and Dreams, Queen of the Dead, Queen of Phantoms, and around her, ghostly images flooded in, swirling like smoke rising from her hem. She caught hold of one and bit into it, draining the spirit dry as it screamed and fought against her.

"I am the Keeper of the Cauldron. Do you dare to make a deal with me? Or do you stay Fury, beloved of Hecate, the Goddess of the Crossroads?"

Map of the Seattle Area
Post-World Shift, Post Tsunami

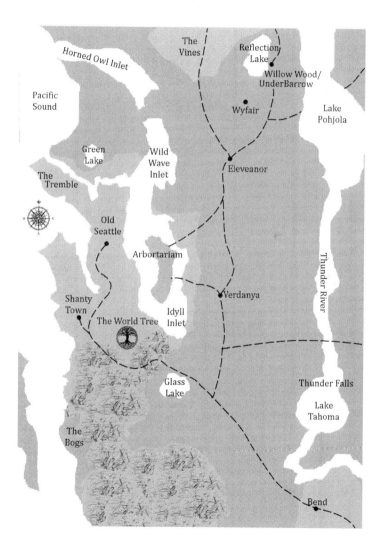

The Beginning

THE END OF civilization as we knew it arrived not with a whimper, but with a massive storm. When Gaia—the great mother and spirit of the Earth—finally woke from her slumber to discover the human race destroying the planet through a series of magical Weather Wars, she pitched a fit. The magical storm she unleashed change such as never before had been seen. The resulting gale ripped the doors on the World Tree wide open, including the doors to Pandoriam—where the Aboms—chaotic demons of shadow and darkness—live, and the doors to Elysium, where the Devani—ruthless agents of light—exist.

In that one cataclysmic moment, now known as the World Shift, life changed forever as creatures from our wildest dreams—and nightmares—began to pour through the open doors.

The old gods returned and set up shop. The Fae and the Weres came out from the shadows and took up their place among the humans. The Theosians began to appear. Technology integrated with magic, and now everything is all jumbled together. Nothing in the old order remained untouched. The world might appear to be similar to the way it was, but trust me—under that thin veneer of illusion, nothing has remained the same.

Chapter 1

My name is Kaeleen Donovan. They call me Fury. I walk in a pillar of flame, a circle of fire. As we rebuild after the fall of Seattle, the Wild Wood has become our sanctuary and home. And yet, the Order of the Black Mist is coming close to plunging the world into chaos. I have a vision that promises a chance to prevent this from happening…but is my sight illusion? Do we risk everything on a hope born in a smoke and flame?

"STEADY—HOLD IT steady. Don't let go just yet." Hecate's voice rang through the cloud of smoke and sparks surrounding me.

I couldn't see farther than my hand. My shoulder hurt. I had been holding my arm straight out in front of me for an hour, balancing the ball of flame on my fingertips, forcing myself to stand straight and not waver. That I was sitting on a boulder helped—at least my lower back and legs weren't aching. But I didn't dare waver more than an inch either way. If I lost control of this little ball of flame, it would rapidly grow into a flurry of sparks and shower hell all over the surrounding area. We had had a lot of rain lately, but the foliage was thick, and it would be easy to set off some of the wild patches of long grass and weeds that rose knee high in the clearing.

"How much longer?" I exhaled slowly, trying to steady my focus.

"Just because you asked, another half hour." Hecate laughed.

I stuck my tongue out in her direction, but said nothing. As I settled back against the boulder, I narrowed my attention. As my breathing grew deeper, I sank into deep trance.

The flame existed as an extension of myself. I was plugged into the elemental plane of fire and I was channeling the ball of fire directly from the source. It was different than drawing off my own power. Sourcing energy directly from the elemental planes made the magic flow easier and didn't drain my own energy. But the learning curve was steep, and it had been a challenge to narrow my focus as deeply as needed. At the beginning, I had struggled, but after I finally discovered the key—to coax the energy instead of forcing it—I had made a breakthrough. Within the span of six months I had gone from barely being able to tap into the primal energy to now, where I could hold the channel open for over an hour.

As I immersed myself in the flame, a faint laughter caught my attention. I followed the source, allowing my mind to wander through the billowing clouds of smoke and flame. The laughter beckoned seductively from a glowing cloud of golden light that appeared beside me. I reached out to touch the flame, wondering what it was.

"Fury! Fury? Let go, now!" Hecate's voice broke through my thoughts. "Don't touch that light. Back off now."

Reluctant—the golden light seemed so playful I wanted to stay—I obeyed. With a slow breath, I withdrew the flame, rolled it back out of my hand, and sent it home, managing to keep control of it. As the flame vanished, so did the smoke and sparks that had surrounded me, and I cautiously stretched, shaking my arm to clear the pins and needles out of it.

"What's wrong? Why did you have me stop?"

"You were on the edge of touching a fire elemental. They're dangerous and you won't have the ability to contain one for a very long time. If it decided to jump you, it would be free to raise havoc here. They're always hungry and of all the elementals, the most likely to take over the one who summons them."

I swallowed hard. "That doesn't sound like a good thing."

"It's not. I didn't think you'd encounter one on the outer edges of the plane, so I didn't even think to warn you. But you listened, and you acted as you should—easing the fire back. I'm proud of you. You're making quick progress." Hecate sat on a rock opposite me. She was watching me closely.

"Any aftereffects? How are you feeling?"

I ran down the checklist we had established. My body was still quivering from running the fire through me at such an extreme rate. My mind felt singed around the edges, but my heart was singing. The flames had charred me around the edges, burning the outer layer away, and while what it left exposed felt a little raw, it also felt clean, as if scrubbed clean by the universe itself.

"Good. A little shaky and my shoulder aches, but overall, I'm feeling good. At least this time I didn't lose control of it and we don't have any fires to put out." I kicked the ground toward the bushes nearby.

She laughed. "True, but just in case..." She whistled long and low, and a moment later a huge burly man with a wild beard came traipsing out from between a waist-high fern and a huckleberry bush. He was carrying a hammer that rivaled any weapon I'd ever seen.

"You rang?" Thor was massive, bigger than any man I'd ever met. He was nearly seven feet tall, and muscled in a thick, burly way. His hair was a shock of gold that flowed down his back, and his beard, a coppery color. He was gorgeous, in a gigantic sort of way.

"I think a light shower would be in order to make certain no sparks went astray. Fury kept control this time, but you never know." Hecate winked at me.

Thor let out a chuckle. "Oh, that's for certain. One shower, coming up." He closed his eyes, then hit the ground with his hammer. A sudden swirl of clouds began driving over our area, thick and heavy. The god of thunder and agriculture waited for a few seconds, then struck the ground again. This time, the reverberation sounded in a crack of thunder as the clouds opened up and the downpour began, the fat droplets soaking everything, including us.

I blinked, trying to see through the rain as it sluiced down my face from the sudden deluge. "Well, that should take care of any fires I may have accidentally kindled."

"Yes, and we should get back to the village. Lord Tam was asking for you, Fury. It seems news has come in off the grapevine and Verdanya has sent an envoy to discuss something happening in the south." The massive god motioned toward the trail leading into the wood.

As I gathered my things, the summer rain beat a steady tattoo against the firs and cedars. Without another word, the three of us headed back to UnderBarrow as the birds took up the refrain announcing the arrival of the surprise rainstorm.

UNDERBARROW WAS NOW more than just the Barrow of the Bonny Fae. UnderBarrow was a city proper. Or rather, the cornerstone of a village—Willow Wood, Tam had named it, for all of the weeping willows around the area.

Six months before, when Seattle fell to the zombies and the Order of the Black Mist, and then to the tsunami, which pretty much put a slam dunk on a trio of disasters, Tam had shifted the Barrow. He moved it adjacent to Reflection Lake north, in the Wild Wood. We were now located north of Wyfair, the village of the Frostlings, and we were in the process of establishing a strong foothold in the deep woods.

Over the past few months, a number of the Elder Gods had joined us. At first it had been just Hecate, Freya, Thor, Sif, and Athena. But then, more had arrived, and now the Finns, the Celts, the Norse, and the Greek pantheons were building new compounds nearby. The Peninsula of the Gods in Seattle sat abandoned, and though the gods didn't speak of it much, a pallor of sadness hung over the subject. Willow Wood had also attracted a number of Theosians who made their way through the Wild Wood, petitioning to join the village.

While only the Bonny Fae—and a few others, like me—actually lived *in* UnderBarrow, Tam opened the village to anyone who promised to comply with the rules. And so, for six months we had grown. Now, we were getting used to the rural life, and to the vastly different situation into which our world had been thrown.

HECATE AND THOR peeled off at the main hall of the gods—which they had named Gudarheim—and I followed the trail back into the village proper, then dashed toward UnderBarrow. I was soaked to the skin by the time the guards saw me coming. They bowed as I passed, opening the door for me without a word. They knew who I was—the lover and consort of Lord Tam, Prince of Under-Barrow.

I paused just inside, where one of the serving girls passing by handed me a towel from her laundry basket without a word. She asked no questions, just offered me a deep curtsey.

"Thank you," I said, wiping my face off and draping the towel around my shoulders. Whatever heat I had been running from keying into the elemental plane of fire was gone. The summer rains were cool, and while it was a balmy sixty-seven degrees out, the rain brought a chill to the woodland.

Heading toward my room, I realized I was starving. It felt like I hadn't eaten in days. Ever since Hecate had increased my training and started putting me through trials so advanced that I had never dreamed I'd be able to master them, my need for food had gone up. Magic burned calories, as did heat, and my appetite had shot up.

I was finally getting used to the labyrinth of the Barrow. The passages wound in a seemingly chaotic manner, but I soon realized that they were much like a web, with a central hub—the great hall—from which all passages snaked out. The passages wove and interwove, but I had finally convinced Tam to start labeling them like the Mudarani had in their underground chambers. The cat people who lived out on the Tremble had numbered each juncture of their subterranean lair, making it easier to identify

7

place points. While the Bonny Fae had an innate sense of direction, any visitors to UnderBarrow easily got lost. Tam had humored my request.

I finally came to the juncture that led to my room—number F451—and gratefully darted into the chamber, ringing the bell pull for Patrice. It had taken me awhile to get used to having a personal maid, but I was grateful for her help, and she seemed to enjoy her work. I tried to make her duties easy, but she assured me that everything was fine and that she liked working with me.

I peeled off my wet clothes and gingerly dropped them into the laundry hamper as she entered the room, curtseying when she saw me.

"Please draw me a hot bath. Thor's rain showers tend to be icy cold."

"Perhaps it's because he comes from the north," she said with a grin as she fiddled with the controls on the bathtub that stood behind a screen to the side. I still had no clue of how the Fae magic managed to produce hot and cold running water, but I didn't question it. I just enjoyed the results.

"Maybe he just likes cold showers?" I chose a bath wash—pumpkin cinnamon—and poured the last of it into the tub, sad to see it go. We'd have to send another raiding party into Seattle for supplies soon, and I made a note to ask them to plunder one of the devastated boutiques for bath wash, soaps, shampoos, and whatever else they could find. That was one downside to living in the Wild Wood. The things I had liked about civilization were no longer easily available, and pretty soon, I'd have to wean myself off a number of them as the supplies in the fallen city ran low or expired.

Patrice rummaged through my closet as I lowered myself into the steaming tub, sighing as the water permeated the aches and pains that ran though my muscles. Not only was I undergoing intense magical training, but my already rigorous workout schedule had been increased to five days a week, two hours each time. I rested my neck on the bath pillow and closed my eyes.

"What do you want to wear, milady?" Patrice popped her head out of the closet. "Something comfortable yet pretty, I would think?"

Formality was the way of the Bonny Fae, and while it still made me somewhat uncomfortable, I had forced myself to get used to it. As long as I was dating the Lord of UnderBarrow, I would play by the rules.

"I'm done with training for the day, so the green skirt and tank top. And my flats. I don't expect to be doing much running around the rest of the afternoon."

I slid under the water, dousing my hair. As I came up, I began lathering it up with the bath wash. I was about to duck and rinse when Patrice appeared at my side with a jug of water. Smiling at her—I knew the drill—I leaned forward and closed my eyes, holding my breath as the water cascaded through my hair, washing away the suds into the tub. She brought a second jug, and my hair was cleared of soap.

"Do you want to soak for a while, milady?"

"Yes, if I have time." I nodded. "How long till dinner?"

"Three hours."

My stomach rumbled. "All right. Would you bring me some bread and cheese? Also some berries and a cup of coffee? I'm starved, but I don't feel like getting out of the water just yet."

As Patrice curtseyed again and vanished, I wrapped my hair in a towel, then leaned back in the still-steaming water and closed my eyes. So much had happened in the past nine months. It felt like forever.

MY NAME IS Fury. Actually, it's Kaeleen Donovan, but there are days I almost forget I ever wore that name. I'm a Theosian—a minor goddess. When Gaia rained down her anger over how her body was being tormented, she stirred up a shit storm of magic, some of which permanently became embedded in areas of land. One of those places is the Sandspit—a two-hundred-acre wasteland in the city of Seattle where rogue magic wanders in the guise of clouds, permanently changing anybody it hits.

When Gaia struck the industrial district, creating the Sandspit, the very first World Tree rose from the ashes, a hundred-foot-tall oak, rising out of a crater almost as deep, and on this oak, doors to different realms and dimensions appeared. Creatures of all sorts came streaming through, including the Abominations who come from the realm of Pandoriam. Hecate trained me to hunt them—it's one of my natural abilities, and that's what I did until recently, when—battered and bruised—Seattle fell and we had to flee.

Anyway, one night my mother, Marlene, was taking a shortcut through the Sandspit. She was on her way home from the Metalworks, tired and pregnant with me, when she was hit by a patch of rogue magic. *Boom*, my DNA was changed and I was born a Theosian. There are a number of us, and we're all mutants. We aren't human any longer, but our own separate race, yet all incredibly different. My powers came in flame and fire, and so I was bound to Hecate, the Elder Goddess of the Crossroads. I belong to her, forever, until this life passes.

Long story short, the government fell into a corporatocracy, ruled over by ruthless, greedy men. But a magical society rose, one bent on engendering as much anarchy into the world order as possible. They're known as the Order of the Black Mist, and they are a worldwide threat, seeking to yank open the portal on the World Tree leading to the Elder Gods of Chaos. If they manage it, life will become problematic, and Gaia will go to war again. I was after Lyon, the leader of the local Order of the Black Mist, but things got out of hand and he helped engineer the fall of Seattle. We haven't worked out how to stop them yet. But time is ticking, and if they find the portal before we put a stop to them, then all bets are off.

FINALLY WARM, I toweled dry and asked Patrice to braid my hair back. I had recovered fully from all the injuries that I had sustained in our flight from Seattle, but still bore a few of the scars. They paled in the brilliance of the tattoos that marked the milestones in my life with Hecate. Along my left leg, trailing down the outer thigh and calf, was a flaming whip, and when I needed a weapon, all I had to do was slap my hand against the handle and the whip came off my leg, ready to use. A quick slap against my leg and it returned to its inked state on my skin. Hecate had inked it on me herself, the night she branded me with my name.

My neck tattoo—three entwined snakes on my neck—came much earlier, when I reached puberty. It was almost like a baptism, even though I had been bound to her shortly after my birth. And the third, an ornate *F* in the middle of a heart with flames trailing off each side, rested against my tailbone. Hecate had given it to me six months ago, when I made a choice that seemed more difficult than it was, actually.

I had always been fit—sturdy and muscled. I had to be, given how strenuous hunting down Aboms could be, but after six months of a highly rigorous training schedule I now felt hard and chiseled. I was still solid, but I could move like the wind and I could bring down an opponent three times my size.

I slipped into my clothes—the green plaid skirt was mid-thigh length, leaving my leg free so I could easily get to my whip. The tank top was a

V-neck and it was a loose gauzy cotton. I slipped on my shoes as Patrice entered the room again, carrying a tray with my coffee, a couple of rolls, a small round of aged cheddar, and a bowl of mixed berries. Most of our food was simple, but hearty and nutritious.

We had—and by "we" I mean the village—had tilled about five acres of land in a clearing. The herbalists spent a lot of energy infusing the soil with elemental earth energy, charging it so that the crops were growing huge and bountiful.

"Lord Tam is requesting your presence at a meeting in thirty minutes," Patrice said, dipping into a quick curtsey. We kept clocks from the outer world in UnderBarrow, to keep track of the relative time, since the days moved differently inside a Fae Barrow.

"Oh?" I hadn't seen him since breakfast. As Lord of UnderBarrow, he had a great many responsibilities, especially with the establishment of the village. We spent most nights together, and we tried to eat dinner and breakfast together, and we claimed half a day once a week, but some days were more problematic than others.

"Apparently, the runners brought news and he's called a meeting of the Sea-Council." Patrice kept her ear to the ground a lot. She was an excellent maid-slash-spy.

"Really?" I nibbled on one of the rolls, slicing a piece of cheese to go with it. We had formed the Sea-Council after settling Willow Wood. Most of us had been forced out of Seattle during the zombie invasion, though we had added a few members since then. Tam, me, Jason, Elan, Laren, Hans, Greta, Kendall, and Tyrell were all members, as well as Sarinka—a healer from Seattle who had joined us. We also invited Damh Varias to join. He was Tam's main advisor. We hadn't met for about a month, so if runners had brought news, Lyon was probably on the move again and we needed to find out why.

"I assume that Hecate, Thor, and Freya have been notified?" The Elder Gods didn't always sit in on our meetings, but we made sure they were always informed about whatever we learned.

"Yes, milady, I believe so." Patrice finished tidying up after my bath. "Is there anything else you require?"

"Have you seen my notebook?" During the past six months, we had had to learn to do without technology. The cell towers were faulty and few and far between, and all our lovely gadgets were so much flotsam and jetsam. But we had concentrated a few raids specifically on things like paper products of all sorts, and anything that didn't require electricity to work. We were set for a number of years and by the time we ran out of scavenged goods, we'd be firmly set up to carry on. At least, we *hoped* we would.

"Here it is, along with your pencils." She handed them to me.

I slipped them into my tote bag and slung it over my shoulder. Purses were useless out here, but a good leather tote was a goddess-send. "All right, I guess I'm ready. I'll be back later—I don't know if we'll go straight in to dinner afterward. It depends on how long our meeting runs." And with that, I headed out.

AS I ENTERED the council chamber, I saw that Jason had arrived early, along with Elan. They were finding their way as a couple, and they seemed to be doing well. Jason and I had a rough spot that lasted a couple months when I discovered that he had had an affair with my mother before I was born, but we had gotten past it. Although things were different, we were back on steady ground as friends.

Tam rose, holding out his arms. The Prince of UnderBarrow looked more in his element than ever. The Wild Wood agreed with him, even though he missed his beloved computers and gadgets. Tall and lanky, he was sinuous, and the Bonny Fae charm oozed out of him. His hair was a mass of raven curls that tumbled down his back, and his eyes were silver, ringed with black. He had an exotic look, almost alien, but it only heightened his sex appeal.

I took his hands and he planted a firm but decorous kiss on my lips. We were cautious about our public displays of affection, taking care never to overstep the boundaries of what was acceptable among the Bonny Fae. Tam's people were very sexual, but never sloppy.

"Love, how was your day?" He led me to the chair next to his and held it for me.

"Hard. Hecate is really pushing me, but I'm making progress. It's amazing what I can do now with the fire. Tomorrow morning, she says she's got a special surprise for me. I'm not sure whether to be excited or scared." I laughed, then took my seat.

Jason and Elan were listening, and Jason winked. He had taken care of me as I grew up, after I landed on his doorstep when a serial killer murdered my mother. A hawk-shifter, he had owned a magic shop back in Seattle. We had plundered everything we could from it when we left and he had set up an apothecary shop in the village. Dream Wardens might not be the same size or scope as before, but it lived on.

"I'd be scared," he said. "When the gods talk about a surprise, I'm pretty sure they aren't talking birthday party."

"I'm afraid you're right. So, how are things at the shop?" Until we fled the city, I had a secondary business—a psychic cleaning company—that I ran out of Dream Wardens. I missed it, but right now my training was so intense that I didn't have any time to spare.

"Good. Laren is actually helping me in between boat runs. He's handy and the clients like him." Jason gave me a long look, almost smug, as though he were hiding a secret.

"What are you up to?" I asked, narrowing my eyes. "I can read your face, you know."

"Oh, nothing."

Elan elbowed him and he shut up as the others trickled in. When we were all assembled, Tam cleared his throat.

"Hello, and thank you all for attending on such short notice. I have news from Seattle and the surrounding areas. Runners came in this morning, and Damh Varias and I have been in conference with them most of the afternoon." He paused.

I didn't waste any time. "Do you have news about Lyon?"

He nodded. "Of a sort. The Devani now seem to be working with the Order of the Black Mist—an odd pairing given how ordered the former are, and how chaotic the latter is. But whatever the case, from what our intelligence can gather, Lyon's searching for the portal on the World Tree that will lead to the realm of Chaos. The Abominations are running unchecked through the remains of the city, if you can call what's left a city. Seattle's pretty much gone. All the Order of the Black Mist is ruling over is a ghost town."

The last was hard to hear, though not unexpected. "Do we know how many people are still living there?" It was hard to think about the number of dead. At least one hundred thousand had perished during the zombie attack. And then, an unknown toll from the tsunami. While a number of the survivors had fled the city before the waves hit, there must have been tens of thousands who had been still trapped when the waters came rushing through.

"I don't know, but reports are that the Junk Yard was swept away. The survivors have created a small compound they're calling Shanty Town. The Sandspit seems to be a playground for Abominations, but the creatures are moving out into the wilds. They're traveling out of the city for some reason—probably because of the lack of ready victims."

The whip on my leg itched as the urge to go play hunt-and-seek hit me. But I kept quiet.

Tam tossed the papers he was holding on the table. "But we have even more disturbing news. We've managed to gather a few reports from the rest of the country. The Conglomerate is gone. The country has fallen into chaos—there is no more Americex Corporatocracy. The Order of the Black Mist may have taken Atlantea, but there's been nothing but radio silence from there. We have no idea of whether they're managing or not."

"What about the rest of the world?" Greta was furiously taking notes.

Tam shuffled through his papers till he found the one he was looking for. "The Canadian Empire is standing, but it's closed its borders. The same with Bifrost and a few of the other countries over-seas. Other than that, we don't know. We *do* know that the Asiatic Empire, New London, and Paris are all gone. Even the Kiwi Nation is lost. Most of this is due directly to the Order of the Black Mist."

"And Lyon is *still* trying to rip open the portals. I wonder if they're attempting the same thing on the World Trees around the world. It would make sense. And if that's the case, then stopping Lyon isn't going to stop them from achieving their goal." I was beginning to wonder if we should just cut our losses and enjoy what time we had left until they managed to bring back the Elder Gods of Chaos.

"That, I can't tell you. It would make sense. But if it's true, they haven't had any better luck than Lyon has." Tam leaned his elbows on the table. "As things go, there's not much we can do right now. With the Devani supporting Lyon, we don't have the force necessary to go up against him unless the Elder Gods step in, and so far, they've given us no sign they're going to do so."

A knock on the door stopped the conversation. As one of the guards peeked inside, Tam motioned for him to enter. "What is it?"

"Lord Tam, we have reports from the south side of the village. An Abomination has been spotted near the town. The guards wondered if you would help." He paused, looking directly at me.

I jumped up. "I'm on my way. Let me go change."

That ended the meeting. As I raced back to my room, I called for Queet, the spirit guide to whom I was bound. He appeared in a whirl of mist.

"Come on, Queet. We have a job." And as much as I hated to admit it, I was glad for the diversion. It made life feel somewhat normal again.

Chapter 2

PATRICE CAME RUNNING when I pulled the bell three times, which meant "I need you *now*!" I was already shrugging out of my clothes when she burst through the door.

"I need leather shorts and bustier, my leather jacket, my Briggs boots, and my sword and dagger. Abom coming toward the village." My hair was already braided back and I quickly pulled it into a chignon and used a barrette to firmly clip it in place. She handed me my clothes and I shoved my feet through the legs of the shorts, easing them up and zipping them. As I put on the bustier, she helped me adjust it and I zipped it up the front.

I sat on the bed to slide on my boots—they were calf high with sturdy block heels, and they laced up. She began lacing one while I laced the other. As soon as my bootlaces were tied, I fastened my belt and slid my dagger neatly into the sheath.

Then I draped Xan—my sword—over my head to rest against my back for easy access. I could reach over my shoulder and smoothly draw her within seconds. All in all, it took me less than ten minutes and I was ready to rumble. Patrice handed me a pair of leather, fingerless gloves and I slid my hands into them as she strapped the wristbands, making sure it was firm and snug.

"I'm out." I waved at her and dashed to the door, where I found Tam and Jason waiting for me. Jason was dressed to go with me. Tam couldn't, being Lord of UnderBarrow—not unless it was an active military decision.

"Come on, dude. Let's rumble." I planted a quick kiss on Tam's lips. "Don't worry, we'll get him."

"I will always worry about you," he said softly as Jason and I took off.

The guards cleared the way as we headed toward the entrance of UnderBarrow, darting through the crowds. They parted to the sides like unfolding wings. Everybody knew who I was, and seeing me racing for the door with my sword, dressed for action, was clue enough to get out of the way.

Jason and I met the guard who had seen the Abomination. He was already seated on his horse, waiting with two more in tow. They were ready to ride, with weapons and small shovels and hoes strapped to their sides. There was good reason for the gardening tools. If I needed to use fire, they would have to make certain it didn't catch a spark in any dry vegetation.

We mounted the steeds as the horses whinnied, excited for the chase.

My horse was special. He was another Theosian. Captain Varga was bound to Poseidon. When he was on land, he immediately transformed into one of Poseidon's white stallions. After the fall of Seattle, he had chosen to remain in horse form, and we had bonded with a loyal and unfailing attachment.

"Come on, Varga, let's go. Abomination to the south," I whispered to him.

He shook his head, his glorious mane shimmering under the late afternoon sun, and proudly swung around to follow the guard. I patted him on the side of the neck and we took off, loping through the trees on the narrow footpath that a number of villagers had spent several weeks clearing.

Jason rode behind me, ready to offer whatever backup I needed.

And Queet—Queet was a swirl of mist in an already misty forest. The spirit was my partner in chasing Aboms, bound to me by Hecate. He and I had had some rocky times, but we had come to appreciate one another.

Sunset wasn't far away and the air had cooled dramatically. It was about sixty degrees now, and thin tendrils of fog began to roll along the forest floor. Varga wove in and out of the trees, following the lead of the guard. It helped that Varga was a fully sentient Theosian—I could talk to him and he would understand. I just wished that he could talk back. I wanted to ask him why he chose to stay in his stallion form, rather than go back to the sea where he could become human again. I wanted to know what had happened to his boat. But he couldn't tell me, and if anybody else knew, it remained a secret.

We rode in silence, weaving through the fir and cedar. The forest was interspersed with oak and maple, but the trees were mostly coniferous. Tall, straight, birch trees shone with their white trunks at various points throughout the forest, and ferns—waist high—covered the ground along with huckleberries, and Wandering Ivy, and Honey Sickle. The latter was a derivation of honeysuckle— beautiful flowers with sweet nectar, long trailing vines, and sharp thorns that were mildly poisonous. They wouldn't kill you, unless you got trapped in a patch. Then they would pierce their victim with hundreds of thorns and slowly kill them for the nutrients the body provided the soil.

As we approached the southern side of the borders of Willow Wood, I brought up my Trace screen. I could spot Aboms with it and pinpoint their whereabouts if they were within a certain range. It was like having an internal GPS focused on one enemy only.

Nothing...nothing...and then, *there he was.* About a hundred yards to the left, off the main trail. I signaled to Varga and he slowed to a walk, then stopped. Behind me, Jason also came to a halt, as did the guard in front of me. I motioned to them for silence and quietly dismounted, assessing the undergrowth between me and the stand of trees where the Abom stood.

Queet, can you go see if he's in a human vehicle?

Sure, Fury. I'm on it.

Queet whisked away. At first he had resented being tied to me. He still complained, but the complaints were fewer and farther between, and we had finally developed a rapport over the years. I was thirty-one now, and he seemed to accept that being my guide and guardian was his destiny, just as destroying Abominations was mine.

Within a few seconds, he was back. He worked fast, that was for sure.

Fury, he's big and he's hungry. He's in a human vehicle, all right—a zombie, which means he's made his way over from Seattle.

Crap. I had only had to deal with one Abom who was in zombie form, and he had been a rough take-down. The Abom maintained a greater control over the body than the zombie's innate need to feed did. And they were harder to kill, for that very reason— the zombies continued until they were torn to bits. And far worse, the soul-holes—an energy nexus on the vehicle where the Abom attached to the host— shrank. If they vanished altogether, then I couldn't send the Abom back to Pandoriam. I could destroy the vehicle, but the Abom would then be free to find another. And killing an Abom who wasn't in a vehicle? Ten times harder.

I quickly turned to Jason and the guard. "I'll need to take him over to the Crossroads. He's driving a zombie."

Jason's response was immediate. "What do you need us to do?"

"I need you to create an intersection here while I lure him over." Another reason for the shovels and hoes. "I can't get to the Crossroads without one. It doesn't have to be big, but it needs to be apparent. I'll go lure him back this way. You get busy."

As the men immediately pulled the hoes and shovels off their horses and set to work without another word, I darted off trail, into the undergrowth. I wasn't going on horseback because it would be tricky to maneuver through the thick foliage, and the last thing I wanted was for Varga to hurt himself.

The mist was almost knee-deep now, rolling through the undergrowth like fingers of smoke. I couldn't see where I was walking and these woods were rife with tree roots and detritus—mulch thick with decaying leaves and fallen limbs. A large tree trunk—waist high—blocked my way. The nurse log was covered with velvety moss and toadstools growing out of the emerald patches. Keeping my Trace up, I placed one hand on the log and lightly swung myself over. I wasn't sure if the Abom could sense me yet. They usually picked up on me when I got within a hundred feet or so.

Queet? Can you distract him so I can sneak up on him?

Sure thing, Fury. I'm like a tasty snack to them. Pure energy.

I couldn't move at blur speed, so when I did catch the Abom's attention, I was going to have to keep out of his reach until we reached the intersection the boys were creating back at the road. Luckily, zombies moved slower than the living. Not so luckily, they weren't detoured by impediments. If there was a way over or around or through something, they'd find it. They could trip and break an ankle and still chase you, as long as there was any possible way.

The forest had gone very still. The animals sensed the Abom and they wanted no part of him. I had finally gotten used to the incessant sound of birds and creatures in the undergrowth. Back in the city, all the sounds of traffic and people hadn't fazed me, but it took me awhile to get into a comfort zone out here in the woodlands.

Now, I noticed when something was off. The creatures of the forest were a great early warning system if you trained yourself to pay attention.

I circled around, wanting to give Jason and the guard time to create an intersection for me. Good news? They were experienced at it by now. The bad news was it would be small and I would have to lure the Abom into close contact in order to take him over to the Crossroads.

Fury, you better hurry. There's someone nearby and he's picked up on them.

Oh, hell. I couldn't let him attack—the zombie would eat the victim's flesh, while the Abom ate their soul. Not a pretty picture and depending on who got their appetite on first, it could be terribly painful.

I grabbed a stick and broke it as loudly as I could. There was another sudden hush and then, there was the sound of something trampling through the bushes, coming my way.

He heard you.

I meant him to.

I paced myself, breathing softly. I couldn't use my flame in such tight quarters—even with the incessant rain, there was too much chance of hitting dry kindling and sending the forest up in a blaze of fire. My whip would get entangled by the foliage. And my sword—well, it would be unwieldy in such tight quarters. I slowly drew my dagger, waiting for the Abom to break through the trees. I would do what I could to keep him here for a few minutes, giving Jason and the guard time to create the intersection, then head back for the trail.

A moment later and the creature appeared from behind a towering fir tree. As per their usual tricks, the Abom had chosen a massively muscled man. They always chose the toughest, biggest vehicles they could find. But the man was obviously dead. His complexion was mottled, and he looked like he had been dead for a long, long time. Zombies didn't lose all their flesh, not unless they were starving, and then they became gaunt and sallow, but they did bloat up, like any decaying body, and in no sense of the word did they look like a normal person.

"Yo, you! I see you. You know what I am, don't you? I destroy your kind." I waved my dagger at him, laughing. The Aboms could sense my ability to take them down.

Where's his soul-hole, Queet?

Right at the base of his tailbone. Odd how it varies when they choose a zombie over a living body.

Yeah, we could speculate all day on why that is, but right now is not the time. Okay, he's big enough, and with the fact that he's a zombie, I'm definitely going to have to take him to the Cross-

roads. He must have been a B-ball player in life.

Either that or he made a living changing light-rings for people who couldn't reach the ceiling without a ladder.

The Abom began moving in my direction. He was actually faster than I expected, not a good thing. And he had a cunning, speculative look in his eyes—another not-so-good thing. I darted a few steps back, my dagger firmly in hand. I stared at him for a moment, gauging just how long it would take Jason to finish my intersection.

To my surprise and dismay, the Abom suddenly picked up speed. He wasn't running, but he was moving faster than any zombie I had ever encountered. I stumbled, caught myself, and took off racing toward the nurse log. As I cleared it in one jump, I glanced over my shoulder to see where the Abom was. He was gaining on me. I couldn't run at blur speed with all the trees in the way, although I was far faster than the average human. But he was catching up and that was never a good thing.

I began shouting as I neared the road. "Incoming! Abom on my tail. I hope you have that intersection handy!"

"One more minute," came the echoing reply.

I began to weave, to give them the extra time they needed. I darted to my left behind a big cedar, then swung a hard right when the Abom veered to follow me. Then another sharp left when he was behind another tree. Finally, I had to take him out of the woods or I'd be too far from the intersection when I hit the road. I sucked in a deep breath and forced myself on, driving my legs at a frantic pace as leaf and branch whipped against them. I was almost to the trail when a vine lunged out and wrapped itself around my ankle.

Oh crap! Wandering Ivy!

I tripped before I could stop myself. The vine was holding onto my ankle. As I rolled to a sitting position, I saw the Abom closing in. With one swift slice, I brought my dagger down to cut through the vine and it lashed at me, angry and in pain. I scrambled to my feet and, jumping over the patch of ivy, landed at the edge of the road.

Jason and the guard had moved to the side. They had cleared enough of the vegetation to create a small intersection and I said nothing, just raced into it and jammed my dagger into my sheath, bringing my hands overhead as I waited for the Abom to join me. He rumbled out of the woods, eyes focused on me. I shouted at him, taunting him so that he wouldn't change direction and go after the others or the horses.

The Abom turned to me and began striding in my direction. He was lurching—zombies lurched— but then he was in the intersection. As he reached for me, I clasped my hands together, whispering the words that would take me to the Crossroads.

THE CROSSROADS. A place of mist and fog, all intersections met here, and the gods of the Crossroads made their homes. Hecate ruled here, and Papa Legba, the master of Voudoun. The messengers of the gods traveled from world to world via the Crossroads. Mercury and Hermes were frequent visitors, passing through as they carried their missives from the other gods. Janus, two-faced god of gateways and doors, lurked in the shadows, and all the others who ruled over decisions and turning points.

The Crossroads was a vast realm of scrub trees and fallow fields, of undergrowth and scattered rocks and long plains of whispering grasses. Perpetually cloaked in mist, the realm existed in perpetual shadow, neither day nor night, and the roads wove a labyrinth of passages as far as the eye could see.

I always landed at the same spot—near Hecate's cauldron. It sat at a Y-juncture, with a signboard next to it that read:

Stand at the Crossroads
State your claim
To seal the deal,
Strike the flame.

I had never kindled the cauldron's flame—I already had my deal in place, simply by right of being born. But there were those who sought Hecate's services, and they would come here by way of spell or prayer to make a deal with the Elder Goddess via her cauldron.

A bench sat beneath a tree that was either yew or elder—I hadn't determined which yet. I often would rest there and think when I wasn't fighting Aboms. But at this moment, I had no time to waste. The Abom appeared with me and, as I set foot on the crossroads, I danced back out of reach so that it couldn't catch hold of me.

Queet, are you here?

I'm here, Fury. No worries that.

Soul-hole at the tailbone, you said?

Yes. I'll go around and see if I can get him to turn so you can see.

Queet could take substantial form on the Crossroads when he chose to, and now he swung around in back of the Abomination and solidified into a foggy, glowing figure.

The Abom sensed him and whirled, looking for an easy meal. As he turned, I was able to see the glowing hole that indicated his connection to both the vehicle and the physical realm. All I had to do was give a good swipe at the soul-hole and land true, and the Abom would be sent home to Pandoriam. Most people wouldn't be able to see the hole, or manage to land a direct hit even if they did. Hence, most people who met Aboms became their victims.

I eyed the hole, watching as it started to close. Somehow, being in a zombie vehicle gave them more of an immunity to being attacked—and a better chance to roam our realm.

I can't hold him forever, Fury. He's coming at me! Queet danced back, trying to keep the Abom's attention while staying out of reach.

I slapped my thigh, bringing my whip up to bear. I was far more accurate with it than I was with my sword because it was easier to direct the length from a distance. I whipped the flaming whip around my head. The sound of its crack brought a swell of joy to my heart and I smiled. I loved the pulse of power that rippled through my hand. I eyed the tailbone of the Abom and the ever-shrinking soul-hole, and let loose with the whip, bringing the fall down to lash against the opening.

The flames from my whip flared to life as the fall hit square on point, slicing it wide. The Abom screamed as the soul-hole stopped closing, flaring as it began to split open, a shimmer of light spilling out. The sickly green light bled out into the astral. The bleeding intensified as the viscous pool of life-energy hemorrhaged out. Then, with one last shudder, the Abom vanished, screeching as he was dragged back to Pandoriam. The force of his departure blasted me, sending me reeling back as he disappeared.

Usually, that would be the end of the fight and I could collapse. Altercations with Aboms on the Crossroads left me wiped. But the zombie remained upright. Last time, Hecate had been here to help me corral both menaces. This time, I was facing him on my own. Which meant, as tired as I was, I had to take him down.

I slapped my whip back on my leg. It wouldn't do much for me against the zombie itself. I started to reach for my sword, but then something whispered, "No—use your flame."

I backed away, amazed that I could still stand. As I turned, I held out my hand and reached for the connection to the primal flame. I sought for the nexus point where my fire touched the elemental source of unlimited fuel. And then, there it was—a tiny spark in the distance. I focused on it, beckoning it closer, coaxing it until it was all around me.

The spark became a flame became a blaze and I was in the middle of it. I remembered what Hecate had taught me—*Don't lose yourself in it, keep control of your thoughts or you will burn forever in the warmth and welcome of the brilliant flames.*

I kept hold of my name. *I'm Fury. I'm of the fire and yet separate from it. I can exist in the fire and yet outside of it. I connect with the fire without becoming the fire.*

Another beat, and I was back to myself, the connection steady enough to open my eyes. Resting on my hand was a ball of flame crackling with a ghostly heat. I intensified it, willing it to grow, enlarging it as I stood there. And then, when it was big enough and strong enough, I aimed it at the approaching zombie and let go.

The flame surrounded him, engulfing him. Within seconds, his tattered clothing was alight, and then his skin, blistering and burning as the fire consumed him, gobbling him up in a blaze of delight and hunger.

The passion of the flames terrified me, but I struggled to control my fear. Fear would negate the connection. Fear would short-circuit the attack.

Horrified by the joy I felt in watching the zombie burn, I forced myself to remember that he was already dead. Whoever the man was, his spirit had fled his body when he died. Finally, I quit resisting and gave into the delight. Leaning my head back, I laughed as he danced like a puppet on a string. In another moment, the zombie was on the ground, and in another, only the bones remained, scorched clean. As I watched, the primal force ate through them, too, and there was nothing left but a pile of ashes.

I tried to pull out of the trance, but something was tugging me deeper. At first I thought it was the flames, but then I realized that some other force was dragging me down. I collapsed.

Fury? Fury? What's wrong? Queet swirled around me.

But I couldn't answer. I was too deep in my trance. The force holding me didn't feel dangerous, but it was wide and expansive, and I wanted to follow it. I knew I should get off the Crossroads, but I couldn't let go. After a moment, I surrendered and let it take me where it wanted me to go.

I WAS STANDING at the base of the World Tree. I looked up to see a giant of a woman—standing tall over the Sandspit, far taller than the skyscrapers. She was a swirl of stars, of trees and leaves. Her body was the curvature of the earth, her hair ran in waterfalls that cascaded down her back. Her breasts were mountains, her stomach a plain of blowing grass. Her thighs were thunderous, tree trunks so big that they could hold up a city. As she reached out, her arms extended into tendrils and vines that encircled the world. No one needed to tell me who she was. Her energy was clear, her name rang from every pore of her body.

"Gaia," I whispered.

Gaia, the wind sang as it whipped around me.

She pointed to the World Tree.

The original…

Her voice thundered in a quake that rocked the earth.

The first.

Again, a cacophony as the ground rumbled beneath my feet.

I stared at the World Tree, understanding dawning. "This was the first one you created? This was the first World Tree?"

The mother of them all.

She sang and the world responded. Boulders crashed down her shoulders, shaking the ground as they fell around me.

This is the key.

I nodded, trying to understand. As I watched the tree, the portals blazed on it—gateways to all realms shimmering like vortexes. I walked over to the trunk and began to climb it, taking the steps that led a circular path up the tree trunk.

As I passed by each portal, I could feel the energy emanating from it. Some were tempting—they felt like a long, luxurious vacation or a respite from worry. Still others were darker, like storm clouds and snails under wet boards that had been lying around too long.

I was high on the tree when I realized that there was one portal I hadn't noticed before. It was a kaleidoscope of colors, ugly and mottled, and I found myself focused on it. Among the hundreds of junctures, it had been invisible, at least to me, but now it began to shimmer into view. The symbol on it was a spiral, but this was no ordinary spiral. It looped in on itself, in a crazy swirl that made no sense when I tried to look at it. Every time I looked away, I could see it as plain as day, but when I turned my attention to it directly, it vanished and became a chaotic jumble of unnerving energies wrapping around themselves, like a skein of yarn that had been all tangled up.

Gaia pointed toward the portal, her finger as thick as the World Tree's trunk.

This is the mother. Destroy this, you destroy all of them on all of the trees.

I tried to register what she was saying. I understood the words, but the meaning was escaping me.

"Destroy what? The portal?"

Yes.

"Destroying this portal will destroy all portals on all World Trees?" But even as I said it, I knew that wasn't the right answer. "Destroy this one and all identical portals will be destroyed on all of the World Trees?"

And the realm will be locked away from this world, and from those who seek to open it.

Gaia's voice flooded my thoughts with images. Dark turmoil, the winds of war raging across the land, nebulous shadows of terror and darkness, chaos unbound all came whirling through my mind as I watched the figures—so huge that I couldn't even comprehend how big they were— ravaged the world, plunging it into one big vat of madness.

And then I knew. I knew where the portal led.

"This is the way into the realm of Chaos. This is the door Lyon's seeking."

He cannot see it, not yet. The way remains hidden. But eventually, he will find it. Destroy this, you destroy all chances.

I reeled. The answer to the worst of our problems was in front of me. The portal writhed with long tendrils that reminded me of worms. The Elder Gods of Chaos were madness incarnate and despair, and to see this gate opened would rain down horror on the world. Lyon had no clue what he was trying to undertake. But he would continue trying until he found a way because he was either stupid or demented.

"What do I do? What can I do?"

Destroy the gate. Seek Heimdall, with his horn resounding. Gjallarhorn will sound once again, signify the beginning, or the end of things.

And with that, Gaia vanished along with the World Tree, and I was curled on the ground, stuck in the Crossroads, too sick to move.

Chapter 3

"FURY? FURY?" A woman's voice penetrated the fog encasing my head. I blinked against the brightness, then realized it was candlelight and even that was hurting my head. I tried to sit up, but Elan pushed me back. Hecate was standing in back of her, staring at me with a concerned look on her face.

"Elan...where am I?"

"You're in your room, at UnderBarrow. Queet summoned Hecate to your aid, and she brought you here. Can you sit up yet, or do you need to lie back down?" Elan bathed my forehead with a cool cloth, and I closed my eyes, enjoying the feeling of water against my skin.

I felt like I had been burned raw by the fire, and I probably had, at least on an auric level. I knew that I wasn't hurt physically—at least no more than when I took down an Abom. But psychically, I felt

39

like a piece of raw meat. I drifted as she continued to wash my head.

"Fury?" Hecate's voice brought me to attention. I could ignore the others, but I couldn't ignore her.

"Yes?" I croaked out, my throat feeling scratchy.

"If you can sit up and tell us what happened, please do. We'll help you." She was firm, but caring, yet it was a demand rather than a request.

I groaned, but let Elan and Tam roll me to a sitting position. Patrice padded the headboard with pillows so I was propped up when they lay me back.

I squinted. The light didn't seem so bad this time. "I'm thirsty. What time is it?"

"It's almost dawn. You've been out for a long time. Here, drink this." Tam held a cup to my lips.

I took a drink and sighed again. It was mint tea and honey, soothing to the senses as well as to the throat. I drank again, and then another sip before he took it away.

"You don't want to drink too much, too fast, or you might throw up," he said, stroking my hair back from my face. He sat down on the bed and leaned in.

"No, you don't want to take this on—"

Tam's kiss could heal. He could take on my pain and sweep it away from me with a touch or a kiss. I didn't want him to know just how rough I was feeling, but he pushed aside my protests and pressed his lips to mine, kissing me deeply.

As the kiss intensified, the weariness began to drain out of my joints and muscles, and the fire that still burned in my thoughts vanished under a wave of cool, calm water that rolled in like the tide. I kissed him back then, drawing more strength from him. He could handle it, and I reveled as the scorched and blackened sensation began to wash away. Finally, I pulled away.

Tam held my chin, staring deep into my eyes. "My love, I'm so sorry. I'm so, so sorry. You were burning like the desert sun. So much pain..."

"I'm all right now, thanks to you. And thanks to Hecate, whom I assume brought me back off the Crossroads." And it was true—I felt much better. Tired and hungry, and deeply thirsty, but I didn't feel charred to the bone anymore.

Hecate moved over to sit by my bed. Tam scooched away to give her room. He crawled over me to sit beside me and wrapped his arm around my shoulders. Elan handed him the cup of tea. He held it to my lips, even though I was strong enough to take the glass myself, and I drained it dry. The mint and honey ran through me like a sweet balm.

"Tell us what you saw." Hecate looked strained. "I know it was something powerful, but I can't quite grasp what it was."

I cleared my throat as the images flooded back. "I went into the fire. I had to in order to destroy the zombie the Abom had co-opted. After I burned him to ashes, the flame drew me deeper. There was something else there—it wasn't just the flame, but a deep, dark force that welcomed me. I tried to resist but finally, I gave up and let it take me where it wanted."

"That sounds like the edge of Vision, the chasm that most oracles come to, and they have to willingly drop into it in order to activate the sight. I didn't know you had that ability."

"I didn't either. Anyway, I let it take me. When I opened my eyes, I was standing in front of the World Tree. And Gaia was there. She was so massive she blotted out the sky." I couldn't help it, as I spoke of the Great Mother, I was caught up in the wonder again, and I paused, closing my eyes to drift in her immensity once more.

"Gaia…" It wasn't a question, but more of a whisper. Hecate leaned forward, staring at me. "The Earth Mother came to you? What did she say?"

I described her, and then what had happened. "She showed me where to find the gate to the realm of Chaos, and she told me who to go to in order to destroy it. When we destroy this gate, all the other gates to Chaos on all the other World Trees will vanish. The Order of the Black Mist won't be able to open the doors no matter what they do."

Everybody in the room was silent, including Hecate. I finally turned to her. "Do you know Heimdall?"

She shook her head. "No, but Thor and Freya do. I think he's out here with them at New Valhalla—the temple they're building out in the woods." After a pause, she added, "I'm both stunned and grateful. But Fury, if Gaia came to you, then she's been watching the course of events. If we don't stop Lyon, you can guarantee she'll take it into her own hands, and when Gaia moves, everybody stands a chance to lose."

"Which means we don't have a choice. She offered me the solution. We have to try it." I shifted, fully awake now. Even though I was tired and hungry, I felt strangely alive, as if every cell in my body was vibrating. "I want to get up."

"You should rest a little longer—" Tam started to say, but I pushed back the covers and shooed him off the bed.

"No, we have things to do." I realized I was in a nightgown. "Patrice, can you get me one of my gauze skirts and a tank top?" To the others, I said, "I'm getting dressed. You can stay or wait outside."

Jason and Elan quickly withdrew from the room. Hecate also. Tam stayed while Patrice helped me dress. My body was stiff, but a lot less stiff than it used to be, even with taking down an Abom. All my training sessions were paying off.

"Patrice, in a while, after we've talked, I'll need a massage."

"Yes, milady." She was as good of a masseuse as any other I'd had. "Just let me know when." She hung my nightgown over the clothing rack. "Are you hungry? Should I bring you some breakfast?"

I glanced at Tam. "We should hold a meeting of the Sea-Council this morning."

"I can gather people in an hour. That will give you a chance to eat. Patrice, please get my Fury some breakfast. I think fruit, eggs, and bread would be best after what she went through." He pulled me to him as Patrice discreetly withdrew. When she had shut the door behind her, he leaned in, kissing me deeply as his hands caressed my back. "Oh, Fury, I was so worried. I know it's your job, but I always fear for you when you chase after the Abominations. They could drain your soul if they catch you."

"I know what they can do, love." I burrowed into his embrace. "But I'm growing stronger every day, and my training with Hecate is increasing my power." I rested my head on his shoulder. "I am afraid, though. Going back into Seattle to destroy the portal to the realm of Chaos isn't going to be easy. You know Lyon will have his men swarming the tree, looking for it. That's why we have to move, and move fast."

"I will send an army with you to protect you, if it comes to it." Tam paused, then—his hands on my shoulders—pushed me back a few steps. "Fury, six months ago, when we started on our way here, I told you that I had something to ask you. Well, I waited. I waited because we were in the midst of so many things. But I realize that there will never be a time where we're in a lull. So now, I'm ready."

My breath caught in my throat.

He took my hand in his. "Fury, Kaeleen Donovan. In the past six months, you've come to mean more to me than anyone has in a thousand years. In my world this seems quick, but I don't have to wait. I want to marry you. I'm the Lord of Under-Barrow, and I want you to be my queen and rule over the Barrow with me."

I stared at him. We had a quiet sort of love—but it ran deep and passionate. There were few arguments, and when there were, we resolved them and moved on. Tam wasn't mired in angst, or uncertainty, and he was the most secure man I had ever met. When we came together, I had been totally taken unaware, but we quickly found our niche, and from the start, it had felt so right that I couldn't understand why it hadn't happened sooner, except for the fact that I had been carrying a torch for Jason at the time.

"Will your people accept me?"

He shrugged. "Those who will, already do. Those who won't, can find another place to live. The Bonny Fae have long sought wives and husbands outside of our race to keep from inbreeding. While I am not half-human, or any other mix, many of our people are. The Fae side breeds true in the blood. You are not an anomaly, though I doubt we have had any Theosians join the Barrow."

That was true enough. And I had encountered very little ill will in the months Tam and I had been together. I searched my heart, wanting to make certain I had no doubts or regrets, but then I realized—I didn't need to. My only concern was in getting Hecate's approval. Technically, she could stop me from doing anything, and I owed her my allegiance first. My thoughts must have shown on my face, because Tam lifted my hands and pressed them against his heart.

"I know you have to get Hecate's permission. I understand that you will always and forever be bound to her first. She has your loyalty and devotion. I simply want your heart." The sincerity in his voice reverberated through the room.

"As long as Hecate gives her approval, I will be your wife. I will live with you in UnderBarrow and join your people." And as I spoke, the realization that I was pledging myself to this man who was so alien and yet so familiar broke through my reserve and I broke out laughing. For a moment, I shoved aside all thoughts of Aboms and duty and the Order of the Black Mist and simply reveled in the knowledge that Tam loved me, and that I loved him.

EVERYBODY MANAGED TO make the meeting. I pulled Hecate aside before we began. She had brought Freya, Thor, and Athena with her. Thor had also dug up Heimdall from somewhere. The god was tall and fair-haired and looked too yummy to be real.

We stepped out of the council room and I fidgeted a bit. We had been spending a lot of time together since my training intensified, but I had no idea how she was going to respond.

"What's going on? Are you all right?"

"Yeah, I'm fine. I just have something to ask you." I didn't realize how nervous I had been that she might say "No." But my heart started to pound, and my knees were shaking as I shifted from one foot to the other.

"For heaven's sake, just spit it out. Something's obviously bothering you." Her eyes narrowed, and a concerned look washed across her face.

"Tam...he asked me...we want to..." I froze.

"Did he ask you to marry him?"

That broke me free. "Yes, he wants to marry me. I would like your permission. I love him, Hecate.

I've never felt the way about anyone the way I do about him. I thought I was in love with Jason for years, but this is love. Jason, he was an infatuation."

For a moment I thought she wasn't going to respond but then she broke into a wide smile and leaned down to kiss my forehead. "You have my blessing as long as you remember: your oath always comes to me first. But I will do my best not to let it interfere with your life with him. You'll still be fighting Abominations, and you'll still be training with me, you understand?"

"Of course. I wouldn't want it any other way. Though I wouldn't mind if the Aboms went back to where they came from willingly. But I'm used to being active. I wouldn't make a very good lady who only sits on her throne and never does anything." And then the realization that she had given us her blessing hit me and I hugged myself, smiling uncontrollably. "Even though we're facing some stiff odds, I'm so happy right now."

"As you should be, Fury. You have to learn to take celebration where you can find it. If you don't, life would be pretty sour indeed. Now come, let's get to the meeting." She opened the door and stood back, waiting for me to enter.

I ran over to Tam and whispered, "She said yes."

He glanced at Hecate, who winked at him, and then grabbed me around the waist, pulling me snug to his side before quickly letting go.

As we gathered around the table, Tam stood, motioning for silence. "First, before any grave discussions, Fury and I have an announcement to make." He gestured for me to stand. As I did, he took my hand. "We want to announce that we're getting married. Fury will be my queen. Please say nothing outside of this room until we make the official announcement. Damh Varias, you will see to that, please. Don't wait—notify the people today."

Everybody in the room applauded. I looked over at Jason and he gave me a soft smile, and I knew that our relationship had just shifted from guardian and ward to one on equal footing.

As the chatter died down, Jason stood. "I hope we don't seem like we're upstaging you, but Elan and I also have an announcement. We were going to tell you yesterday but it got lost in the fray. But we need to say something now because Elan's duties need to be cut short. You see, she's pregnant. I'm the father."

I almost choked on the muffin I had just bitten into. "*A baby?*"

They beamed. However, given how traditional the hawk-shifters could be, I was surprised they hadn't announced an engagement while they were at it.

"Congratulations," Tam said. "Elan, I order you to immediately stand down from your duties as my bodyguard. We'll find something safer for you to do here while you're with child. Damh, get on that as well. For now, sit in on the meetings, but you won't be going out to help on anything more laborious than a berry-picking expedition."

Elan started to protest, but stopped as he held up his hand. "Now, with two happy announcements out of the way, we should move on to the reason for the meeting. Last night, Fury took down an Abomination that was heading for the village. Fury, I turn it over to you."

I outlined everything that had happened, and when I was done, the room was silent.

"I have to go back to Seattle, to the World Tree. Lyon's looking for the gate. I have to find it before he does."

"We can't go in until we figure out exactly what we're doing. Also, remember that since UnderBarrow moved, there won't be any secret entrances like there were before—not from here." Tam waved his hands at the others. "We need ideas. Don't be shy. We need to brainstorm."

"With the Devani aligning forces with the Order of the Black Mist, isn't this pretty much a suicide run? They'll be watching the World Tree." Tyrell didn't look that impressed. He was a Theosian, bound to Dagda, the father of the Tuatha de Dannan.

"We can't very well let that stop us. The world won't be worth living in if they break open that gate," I said. "Do you realize what happens if they find it?"

"Of course I do," he said, sounding grumpy. "What I mean is—can't we go in from another country? Isn't there any way to contact Bifrost and have them send out someone there? They have World Trees over there, too, and if destroying a gate on one takes care of all of them, then why not leave this to somebody with more chance of getting through?" Tyrell was a good guy, but we had discovered, over the past few months, that he tended to get blustery when he thought that he was right. And not just blustery—downright belligerent at times.

I decided to nip the argument in the bud. "No, we can't. The World Tree in Seattle is the mother tree—it's the original. The portals can only be closed down on a worldwide basis from there. Not from any other tree."

"So where is the gate on the tree?" Tyrell stared at me.

I shook my head. "I can't tell you. I won't be able to pinpoint it until I'm on the tree itself."

He shrugged. "Do you have a plan yet?"

I shook my head. "Nope. Obviously, we need to do something before Lyon finds the portal and opens it. There's no way of knowing when that will be, so the sooner the better." I turned to Heimdall. "What did Gaia mean about seeking you out? And what's Gjallarhorn?"

The Elder God looked a little unsettled. I had a feeling he wasn't used to hanging out with the non-divine brigade. But after a quick, whispered consult with Thor, the stately Norse god answered. "Gjallarhorn is the Horn Resounding. Its sound can crumble any wall, destroy any edifice. But it can only be used when it agrees to be used. However, with a little of its power, I can fashion you a magical explosive to implode the portal and per-manently close it."

My eyes must have brightened because he held up his hand.

"Be aware, there are numerous dangers. You cannot set it off from this side of the gate. Someone will need to cross through the vortex and set the explosives there. They'll have only a short time to escape. So you see, if things go right, it's not a problem. If things go wrong..."

I nodded, seeing what he meant. "If things go wrong, it's a suicide mission. How long will it take you to make this? And I suppose I should first ask, are you willing to help us?"

At that, Heimdall laughed. "Oh, ye of the fiery crown. I will help you, yes. As to how long it will take me to make the explosive? One month. So you'd better pray your enemy doesn't find the portal before then, because there's no way of hurrying up the process."

"Then I guess we don't have to make our plan in a hurry." And with that, the meeting ended and everyone gathered around Tam and me, and Elan and Jason, to wish us all the best.

ELAN WALKED ME back to my room. Tam had given Damh Varias instructions to call a special session of the Court so that we could announce our wedding plans. We didn't even have a date, but he wanted people to get used to the idea.

"So, big day for both of us," I finally said as we neared the door to my room. I wasn't sure just how much she would want to talk, but I wanted to give her the option.

She paused, then asked, "May I come in?"

I invited her in. Patrice was there, sorting

through my clothes, and I asked her to bring us tea. She curtseyed and left.

"So." I motioned for Elan to take a seat at the table. "A baby?"

"Yeah. We were surprised, too. I thought the cycle drugs I was taking worked, but apparently, only with men from my own people." She blushed. "I wouldn't have chosen this route so early, but Jason and I talked about it and decided that we want to make a go of it. And we want to give this child a chance to grow up. I thought about the options and while, with a stranger I probably wouldn't choose this route, Jason..." She paused.

By now, I knew just how reserved the Woodland Fae could be. "You love Jason."

Elan blinked. "I suppose I do. And I think he loves me. We have similar backgrounds, even though he's a hawk-shifter. Our people are much alike." She paused for a moment, searching my face. "Fury, how do you feel about this? I know it may not have been his story to tell, but in a way it was. He told me about your mother. How he and she..."

I let out a long breath. "Let's not play games, Elan. I consider you a good friend, and so is Jason, though I admit our friendship almost broke over that. I still believe he should have told me early on. I spent a long time crushing on him and I felt like a fool. But in the long run, it doesn't matter. We never would have worked as a couple. Tam—Tam's different from anybody I ever expected to fall in love with. We mesh in a way that I can't explain. I knew him for most of my life and never once looked at him as a prospective lover. Husband. Partner. Whatever you choose to call it. But the first time he kissed me, it felt as natural as breathing. I fell into him, you might say. He surrounded me with his energy and I not only felt safe, but right at home."

I stopped, frustrated. I felt like I was talking around the subject, trying to find the right words. "I love Tam in a way that I didn't think I could love anybody. He has my heart."

She brightened. "Then, you're okay with Jason and me? And with me being pregnant?"

"I'm more than okay with it. I think you'll be good for him. And maybe becoming a father will pull him out of that pit of angst he so regularly dives into. He gets into his head and forgets his heart at times. I think you and the baby may put a stop to that." I smiled and reached out to take her hand. "You do realize that, because Jason brought me up and took care of me, we'll be family. Maybe not by blood, but by spirit."

The bright look blossomed to fill her face and I realized just how beautiful she was. The fair maiden with golden hair. She should be a princess in a fairytale. But instead, *I* was going to be the princess of the Fae Barrow. The world worked in strange and unusual ways.

"I like that." She squeezed my hand. "I know that my people are reserved, but I just want to tell you that I appreciate your friendship, and I'm never going to take Jason away from you." She bit her lip. "Do you think Shevron will approve?"

Shevron was Jason's actual sister, and for the

past six months she and her son Leonard had been living in Verdanya, Elan's home city. Leonard was sixteen with anger management issues. Or rather, discipline issues. His father had been human, and the hawk-shifter blood hadn't bred into him. He felt like he belonged nowhere—not among the Cast—the hawk-shifter clan—or among humans. It tore at his sense of identity, and he had been acting out. But we all were hoping that a year living and working with the Woodland Fae would straighten him out.

"I think she'll be happy. I love Shevron. She was like a mother to me."

"Good, because they're coming to visit in a few days. We got word last night. We haven't told them about the baby yet, but I'm hoping that she won't be upset." Elan paused. "I haven't asked Jason about it, but what can I expect for my child among his people? Our people are insular, but I have the feeling that the hawk-shifters make us look like we have open arms."

I sighed. This was a whole 'nother ball of wax. "The Cast are a rigid people. I won't pussyfoot around it. They weren't thrilled when Jason took me in, to be honest. But because he didn't attempt to bring me into the Cast, they didn't say any-thing. I was Theosian and had my own path, so I never minded. But Leonard's had a rough time. He was brought up to be part of the Cast, and yet he is no more hawk-shifter than I am. His father's blood bred true. He feels lacking, constantly, and that's where his behavior springs from. Jason and Shevron just don't understand. He has all of the responsibilities of a Cast member, but none of the perks. And the other kids teased him horribly about it."

I stopped, realizing I had just painted Jason and Shevron in a pretty unflattering light. But it was also the truth, and I wasn't going to lie to Elan.

"I think you should do your best to impart your lineage to your baby. Never make him—or her—feel like the mixed blood makes them lacking. That way, your child will always have a sense of lineage and self that Leonard is lacking. You see, his father ran off when he was born. Shevron only had the Cast to back her, and they did. Make no mistake about that. But Leonard has never been fully accepted, even though they pay lip service to him."

As I finished, I sat back and took a long breath. Jason would probably be pissed I had said so much. He was a stickler for the rules of the Cast. But Elan had a right to know what kind of culture he came from. I was surprised she hadn't asked him already.

She was silent for a moment as Patrice returned with the tea. After pouring for us, she exited the room again, giving us privacy.

"Thank you for telling me. I know it seems odd that Jason and I haven't discussed this, but we only realized that I was pregnant last week. And we've both been in shock." She propped her elbow on the table and leaned her chin on her hand.

"Are you going to get married?" I was beginning to get the feeling that Jason and Elan were in over their heads.

"I don't know. I love Jason and I know he loves

me, but...it's such a big step." She glanced over at me. "I envy you. I can hear the surety in your voice when you talk about Tam. You belong together and it's obvious from watching you. But I don't know if Jason and I are meant for the long run. We want to give it a try, but neither one of us has even mentioned marriage yet. And I don't want to marry unless we're sure."

"That's probably a good idea." I thought for a moment, trying to figure out the best approach to what I was about to say. "Maybe your first decision should be how the child will be raised—as hawk-shifter or Fae. But I suppose that depends on whose lineage breeds through."

Most of those with intermixed heritages followed either the mother or the father. A few would have traits from both, but usually, one lineage dominated.

"Whatever the case, I'm grateful for your support. You set my mind at ease, at least about you and Jason. As to everything else, I'm just not sure." Her voice trembled and I realized that the usually stalwart Elan was actually frightened.

I swept around the table and wrapped my arms around her shoulders. Her people might be reserved, but she needed a hug.

"It will be all right," I whispered. "You'll have a lovely child, and you and Jason will make wonderful parents."

And that seemed to be just the thing Elan needed to hear.

Chapter 4

THREE DAYS LATER I was out in the woods, patrolling. While the guards officially kept watch, I wanted to keep an eye out for Aboms. The fact that one had made it up to us was unnerving enough. I had told Tam I was going out for a walk, but really I was scanning the area with my inner Trace, watching for any telltale blips. I had scoured the perimeter of the village, finding nothing beyond a few scattered rabbits and foxes, when I heard a commotion coming from the checkpoints. I hurried over. The guards, seeing me coming, bowed, then quickly returned to their posts.

"What's going on?"

"Visitors coming through, milady. The scouts ahead sent word via a gravely bird."

Gravely birds were somewhat intelligent, and they could talk with a limited vocabulary. They were highly useful if you could win them over to working for you.

"What kind of visitors?"

"We're not sure. But they come on horseback and they're flying a pennant."

That didn't sound too terribly bad. "Weapons?"

"Some, but that's all I could get out of the damned bird."

For the millionth time, I realized just how much I missed having a phone. The first few months of living out in the woods had been all about establishing the village, building homes, and figuring out routines. Now that we were somewhat settled, the lack of luxuries from civilization were beginning to make themselves felt.

"I'll wait with you." I searched my Trace, but no Aboms.

"Begging your pardon, milady, but the queen-to-be should not be out here in front where danger might befall her," one of the guards said.

I let out a snort. "The queen-to-be fights Abominations and has taken more than one beating and kept going, boys. I think you need to realize that I'm not a fragile flower to be locked away in the Barrow. And Lord Tam already knows this."

That quieted them down. Whatever they were thinking didn't matter—only that they listened to me and didn't try to stop me from doing what came naturally.

"As you wish, milady," was the only thing the guard said.

Another ten minutes and we heard noises coming through the undergrowth. Then, a party of seven horses came clopping around the bend and I let out a cry.

"Shevron! Leonard!" I raced up to the party. I didn't recognize the others traveling with them, but I would know Jason's sister anywhere. She was as tall as Jason and far more pale. Her son was shorter, with warm, brown skin. Both slid off their horses the moment they saw me.

"Fury! I can't believe you're out here to meet us!" Shevron threw her arms around me, hugging me so tight I could barely breathe. Len piled on top.

After they let go, I stood back, looking them over. Shevron may not have gotten any color from the sun, but she was wearing a tunic and trousers, and looked stronger than I had ever seen her. There was a glint in her eye that hadn't been there when we left them in Verdanya. As for Leonard, he was dressed in the same style, and a hunting knife hung at his side. He had a bow and a quiver of arrows over his shoulder, and the sullen look I remembered had been replaced with a brilliant smile.

"Look at you two. You both look good." I motioned to their companions. "Introduce us?"

Shevron motioned to two of the riders—a woman and man who looked a lot alike. "Fury, meet Idyn and Var. They're cousins to Elan and Laren, and twins like them. And our guards, Ket, Traves, and Vilma. This is Fury, Hecate's Theosian."

All five of the Woodland Fae nodded, touching their hats.

I motioned to the guards behind me. "Farnes and Zed."

Zed stepped forward. "Please, allow me, milady." He turned to Shevron. "The Lady Fury is no longer simply your friend. She is queen-to-be, betrothed of Lord Tam of UnderBarrow."

I blushed, but realized that the guards were just doing their duty. It was their responsibility to make certain I was treated appropriately.

Shevron gasped as her companions dropped to one knee.

"You're getting married?"

"Yeah, that's the long and short of it. Tam asked me to marry him a few days ago, and I said yes. Come now, though, let's get back to UnderBarrow. There are so many things we need to tell you." I glanced at Idyn and Var. "Stand, please. I'm so glad to meet you. Elan and Laren are good friends. I'm sure they'll be thrilled to see you."

"Thank you, milady Fury," Idyn—the woman— said. "We have much to discuss as well. There are dark tidings from the east. If you and Lord Tam will grant us an audience as soon as possible, it would be safest."

And on that note, we returned to the village.

UNDERBARROW PROPER WAS a thriving community, and Willow Wood was also thriving. We had about four hundred people living in the village now, most of whom were refugees from Seattle. A few had moved here from Eleveanor— a small Fae village to the south—but mostly, the people we had taken in were humans and Supes who had fled the city when the tsunami came through. We had very little trouble, and anybody who decided to cause havoc was exiled.

The permanent houses were mostly log cabins, or built of stone from the rubble of past cities found in the woodland, and numerous temporary shelters had been erected as we struggled to make sure everybody would have a sturdy lodging come winter.

We had established several viable wells throughout the town and were on the edge of Reflection Lake, which offered plentiful fish for the taking as well as reeds for basket weaving, and other resources. While our raiding parties had brought in massive amounts of goods that would serve well for years to come—pots and pans, plastic tubs with lids, furniture and canned foods, books and supplies—we all knew there would come a day when the relics from our recent past would give way to those we could create ourselves. So we rationed out what we found, and everyone in the village was required to learn a useful skill that could carry through to the future. Even the children, besides their book learning, were being taught how to hunt and garden and build and sew.

As we rode into the village, Shevron's eyes widened.

"You've built a world already, Fury."

"Not personally, but yes, we've worked hard to establish Willow Wood. UnderBarrow is off limits to anyone not of the Court, at least to live in. So we needed to create a viable town for those who found their way to us. So much has happened in the past six months that I don't even know where to begin."

"Fury, are you still chasing Abominations?" Shevron's voice dropped and she slipped off her horse, leading him by the reins.

"Yes. Why? I haven't found many out here, but earlier this week I took down one in a zombie vehicle."

"Because Verdanya is being overrun by them. We can destroy their bodies, but they jump hosts. Until they get someone like you down there, the city has closed its gates and the magicians are using force fields to prevent anybody entering who isn't vetted first." She shook her head. "There have been at least two or three a week that try to break through."

"That's not good. I wish...I wonder." It occurred to me that perhaps there was some way I could train others to hunt them. It would take a special type of person—someone who had a way of seeing the Aboms' soul-holes, but maybe it was a viable thought. "I'll talk to Hecate and see what we can do. I can't take care of all of them myself, but maybe we can figure out something."

"I think Idyn and Var are here to ask for help. I'm not sure what else—they don't keep me informed, but I know that's become one of Verdanya's chief concerns right now." She slipped one arm around my waist. "I've missed you, and Jason. How are things going?"

I bit my lip. I didn't think that she knew about the fight I had with Jason. "In the times Jason's contacted you since you've been in Verdanya, did he tell you that I found out about him and my mother?"

The puzzled look on her face told me that he had not. In fact, I was taken by surprise when she said, "What about Jason and your mother?"

I tilted my head, trying to read into the question. Did she really not know, or was she just being careful not to say the wrong thing?

"About Jason and my mother's affair. You knew, right? That he slept with my mother for a while before I was born?"

"Oh, hell." She blanched. "I had no clue. Nor did our parents. They would have beat his backside for that. Oh, Fury. I can't imagine how you must have felt." Shevron had known that I carried a torch for Jason. She had been my shoulder more than once when I waxed mournful over the fact that he was engaged.

"I didn't take it very well, that's for sure. But it's done and over with. And it cured me of any remaining doubt that Jason's just my friend." I bit my tongue as I was about to add, "Especially now because of the baby." But that wasn't my news to tell.

"So you and Tam are engaged?" Shevron wisely shifted the subject. Hawk-shifters were pretty good about picking up on touchy subjects.

"And I'm thrilled. Leonard seems a lot happier. Has it been rough, living in Verdanya?"

"Their ways are not so different than those of the Cast. And Leonard seems to feel more accepted there. Var has been teaching him to hunt and skin animals, and how to track in the forest. He has a natural bent for it, and he has grown very attached to Var and Idyn, though I wish he'd quit hinting about wanting to join the guard. I don't like the thought of him being a soldier."

"That's what he wants to do?"

She snorted. "How can he possibly know what he wants? He isn't even seventeen yet. But I'll tell you, he started out belligerent, but after a month or so of being assigned wood-chopping and kitchen duties when he fucked up, he came to his senses. Once he realized they were willing to teach him *if* he followed the rules, he stopped screwing around. I'm proud of him."

We arrived at UnderBarrow, where one of the guards summoned grooms for the horses, and I led Shevron, Leonard, Idyn, and Var into the depths of the Barrow after sending word ahead to Tam and Jason that we had company.

I led them to the council chamber, figuring some visits were best made in private than in public. Tam, Jason, Elan, and Laren were there. Elan flashed me a nervous glance, but I shook my head and smiled at her.

Jason and Shevron hugged, briefly, and then he clapped Len on the back. "You're looking good. You know how to use that bow?"

"Yes, Uncle J." Len sounded a lot more respectful than he had before.

"Good. Be sure you keep up the practice. It's not an easy skill." He turned to Shevron. "I'm so glad you decided to visit. We have news."

"I don't think this—" Elan started, but Jason took her hand and pulled her to his side.

"Nonsense. This is happy news. Elan and I are going to become parents."

I groaned, softly but loud enough so Tam heard it. He flashed me a bemused look, then nodded me over to his side. I joined him, watching as the look on Shevron's face turned from one of disbelief to startled worry. She paused, just a beat but enough for everybody to feel the awkwardness of the silence, then broke out in a wide smile.

"Congratulations! You hear that, Leonard? You're going to have a cousin."

"Well, I didn't expect that." Len cast a quick glance at me, and I winked at him. He followed his mother's suit and hugged both Jason and Elan, but there was a certain strained feel to the situation and I was glad that it wasn't me involved.

"Well met, cousin," Idyn said when there was a lull in the chatter.

Laren broke in. "It's been too long. Please, sit down. We can catch up later. I assume you have official business with Lord Tam?"

"True enough." Idyn slid into a chair. Jason led Elan to her chair, then sat down. Shevron and Len sat near him. Laren sat near his cousins, and Tam led me to the chair next to his.

"I see there's much to catch up on, but first, Idyn, Var, welcome to UnderBarrow. Why don't we get official business out of the way, first?" Tam knew how to take hold of the situation, that was for sure. I really found myself glad I wouldn't have to sit in on the family reunion that I foresaw coming up. Congratulations aside, I had the feeling that it wasn't going to be as hunky-dory as it might seem on the surface.

Idyn spoke for the group. "You surmise correctly. We came as escorts for Shevron and Leonard, yes, but more than that. Verdanya is under siege from Abominations. We are keeping them out via gate and force field, but something must be done. Far too many are wandering in the woodlands now."

I stepped in. "Shevron mentioned your problem. I'm willing to ask Hecate if there's any way we might be able to train those with the natural talent to fight and destroy them. It's one thing to destroy their vehicle, but unless you send them back to their realm, they'll just drift till they find another vessel they can take over, which puts anybody fighting them at risk. If, say, a guard manages to destroy the body, it's all too easy for the Abom to jump the guard afterward."

"It's happened. We've seen it. We need help. If there's anything you can do, we beg you to try." Idyn looked tired. I had the feeling Verdanya wasn't faring as well as we were.

Tam must have picked up on the same thing because he asked, "What else is happening to the south? I have a sense that there's more at stake than just fighting Aboms."

"There is," Var said. "Two pieces of information. First, Lord Tres is dying."

Elan and Laren froze.

"He was taken with a wasting disease and nobody can figure out how to treat it. They've given him two months to live unless something can be done, but there's little chance of that." Idyn turned to me. "Lord Tres is the lord of Verdanya. Like Lord Tam runs UnderBarrow."

"Then he's your king?"

Elan nodded, but it was Laren who spoke. "He's also our uncle. Idyn and Var's father."

I scanned their faces. They all looked grave, but I never would have guessed he was such a close relation if they hadn't told me. The Woodland Fae were even more reserved than the hawk-shifters. Maybe it *would* work out between Elan and Jason.

"Who ascends to the throne if he dies?" Laren said. "You or Var?"

"There's the catch. Neither of us. Your father will become the Lord of Verdanya. He's the next in line. I thought you knew that." Idyn waited a beat as the news sank in.

Elan and Laren broke out talking at the same time.

"Father? But that means—"

"You really mean it? I thought sure the throne—"

Var held up his hand. "No, it's been so long since Verdanya has had a new king that we actually had to research the passages relating to who is heir. Last time was before Bifrost was its own country, long before the World Shift."

"Back when Eire was UnderBarrow's home," Tam said softly. "This means you and Laren should return home."

Elan froze, glancing over at Jason. "Perhaps Uncle Tres will recover. We can hope."

"I would not waste much time on wishing. The oracle says he will not, and whatever disease has riddled his body, it's not likely to leave him breathing." A cloud covered Var's face and he stared at the table. "The best direction to take is to prepare for the transition of power. Your father concurs, as does ours. He's making preparations now to invest Uncle Kesbet with the crown. But we *do* have a problem. Shay. You know his and Tera's father passed away a few years back?"

"We hadn't heard," Elan said, frowning. Shay was a subject we left alone, after sending him back to Verdanya for punishment.

"Excuse me, but how do he and Tera fit into the picture?" I wanted to make sure I was following this carefully.

"Tera is our youngest cousin," Idyn said. "And Shay's younger sister. Their father was the youngest brother of Lord Tres and Kesbet. I'm next in line for the throne after Uncle Kesbet, then Var. After that, Elan, Laren, and then Shay. But given he's incarcerated, he's no longer considered suitable material. But that's the other matter we came to discuss. Shay's escaped."

I rubbed my head. Tam had warned me that we should execute him for his crimes, but I couldn't do it and I didn't want him to, either. Now, Shay was out and probably looking to take revenge on Tera.

"Are you on your way to warn Tera, then?" I asked.

"We already have. We're going to loop back to Eleveanor and make certain she's all right before we head back home to Verdanya." Var's dark look told me just how much he thought of Shay. "When we catch him—if we catch him—he'll never escape again."

I wanted to ask what that meant, but decided perhaps I was better off not knowing. The Fae could be ruthless, whether Woodland or Bonny, and they all lived to strict codes of honor. That honor might not always match what humans or Theosians acted on, but they still had a code of ethics they were expected to abide by.

"How's she doing?" Elan asked. "Dare I ask about her daughter, Sara?"

"Yet another tragedy. Sara killed herself shortly after her marriage. Apparently, she cursed Shay as she did so, and you know how family curses can be." Idyn's eyes were luminous and she looked as though she might cry, but I also knew that most of the Fae didn't cry easily.

"Great Mother of the World," Elan whispered. "Poor Tera. She must be a wreck."

"She is. When she found out Shay was on the loose, she went into seclusion. I think she's petitioning Artemis to release her from her curse. She wants his blood, and she's hungry for it. If he even gets near Eleveanor, he'll be shot on sight. The guards have orders to catch him, whether dead or alive doesn't matter."

"It would do the world good to have him out of the gene pool," Tam said. "He was a monstrous man and responsible for a great deal of harm. If we see him, we will capture him and return him to... should we take him to Tera or to Verdanya?"

Without missing a beat, Idyn said, "Technically, he should be returned to Verdanya. But if you capture him and he still lives, my thought is a stop in Eleveanor wouldn't be amiss." She caught Tam's gaze and I read the unspoken message in her eyes. If Shay showed up anywhere around here, or Eleveanor, he was a dead man walking.

"Very well. So, Elan and Laren, it sounds like you should prepare for a trip back to Verdanya. You must pay your respects to your uncle before he passes." Tam glanced at Jason. "We need you here, Jason. At least for now. With what we have coming up, we need every member of the Sea-Council we can muster."

"I don't have to go," Elan said. "Laren can go for me."

"No, you *must* come. Your father has ordered both of you to return home for the vigil and wake, and then you must be there for the investiture when your father ascends to the throne. After that, you'll be expected to take up duties as the king's daughter." Idyn's tone was firm.

"What? But this is my home—"

Idyn shook her head. "You cannot go against a direct order from your father, Elan. No matter how much you want to. Your post here was agreed on with the explicit ruling that it not supersede your duties to Verdanya. You know that."

Elan pressed her lips together, looking ready to boil.

Jason shook his head. "With the baby coming, I don't want to be apart from Elan."

Idyn, Var, and Shevron froze.

Elan turned to Jason. It was hard to read what she was thinking. "I wanted to tell them in my own way, but I guess now's as good a time as any."

She glanced back at Idyn and Var. "He's right. I'm pregnant."

"When's the wedding?" was the first thing out of Idyn's mouth.

"We can make it part of the investiture. Your father can preside," Var said. "This doesn't give us much time to prepare, you know. But the wedding of a princess of Verdanya will have to be quite an affair. We'll need to rush invitations to the other Fae clans."

Jason looked like a deer caught in the headlights. "I didn't ask her. But we haven't even agreed whether we want to get married." He gulped.

Right then, I knew he was in trouble. That was the wrong thing to say to the mother of your child when her relatives were pressuring her, even if it was the truth.

Idyn turned to him, fixing him with a steely-eyed gaze. "Oh, you *will* be married. Any child coming into the royal line of Verdanya must have legitimate parentage. There's simply no question of it. Elan knows this."

Elan gulped. "Laren, help?"

Laren shrugged. "You didn't even tell me. I may not be one for tradition, but Elan, there's nothing I can do to help you get out of this. The minute you conceived that child, you engendered an heir to the throne and the heir *must* have bona fide parentage. You know full well Father won't entertain any arguments on the subject. He won't let the family be shamed, and neither will you." He turned to Jason, eying him with a friendly but sober look.

"Welcome to the family, brother, whether or not you want to be one of us. If you refuse to marry Elan, you'll be disgracing her in the eyes of our people."

Tam reached under the table and took my hand, squeezing it. I swallowed the lump rising in my throat. It was one thing to make a decision to have a child, and another to have the world suddenly arranging your life and marrying you off. Elan looked like a spooked deer, and Jason had walled himself up. I recognized that look. He was back in his head, trying to analyze the best response.

"I need to be near the water," Elan said, suddenly pushing back her chair in a panic. "I really need to get some air." Elan was an otter-shifter, something I usually forgot because most of her shifting was done in private.

I pushed back my chair as Idyn and Var continued to yammer at her. "Come on. The rest of you just hush. We'll be back in a while." I grabbed Elan's hand and headed out the door. Shevron followed. "Will shifting hurt the baby?"

Elan blinked, looking confused. "What?"

"If you shift, will it hurt your child?"

"Oh, no. It's fine."

"Then come along." I motioned to a couple of the guards. "We need to go down to the lake. Bring several guards to keep watch for us." I swept out of the Barrow, Elan in the middle and Shevron on her other side. Elan was crying by now.

UnderBarrow wasn't far from the lake. It took us ten minutes to reach there. I glanced behind us to make sure no one but the guards were following, but I suspected Tam was keeping everybody occupied, giving us time to help Elan adjust to all the changes being thrown at her. Not only was she pregnant and not certain of her relationship, but now her family was trying to marry her off.

Reflection Lake was aptly named. The water was glassy, reflecting the surrounding trees and mountains in its mirrored surface. The afternoon was warm, and sun peeked out from behind a few lazy clouds drifting by. While the guards took up their stations, I walked over to the shore of the lake and stretched.

"Come on, let's get a swim in." I motioned to Shevron.

"Oh, yes. That sounds lovely." She didn't sound terribly enthusiastic, but she stripped off her clothes alongside me. Elan silently followed suit. When we were naked, Elan and I dove into the lake. I had learned to swim when I was fifteen— Shevron had taken me out to a pool and taught me. I had taken to it well. Shevron gingerly waded into the lake until she was up to her waist, and then she stopped.

"Is something wrong?" I asked.

"No, I'm just trying to wrap my head around the fact that I'm going to be an aunt. I'm thrilled, Elan, but with what just went on in there, I admit I'm floundering a little."

"I wish he hadn't told them! I wasn't going to, not for a while. Not until we figured out what we wanted to do. If we decided not to marry, I wasn't going to tell my family who the father was, just to prevent something like this from happening." Elan buried her face in her hands. "I'm so stressed."

"That's not good for the baby. Now you just breathe and shift if you need to. Swim around, play. We've got plenty of time. Nobody's going to force you to the altar right now." I motioned to a nearby log that was floating by. "Go for it."

The worried look began to melt as she eyed the log. "Thanks, Fury. I owe you one."

"No, you don't. Just get busy. Meanwhile, I'm going to get some of my workout today in swimming a few laps."

Without a word, Elan shifted into her otter self. This was the first time I had seen her up close as an otter. She was a river otter with tawny fur, darkening into a deep brown near her feet and tail, and her eyes were luminous and loving. She dove beneath the water, surfacing to float on her back, and as she splashed around the shore, all of a sudden she did a barrel roll and began to swim in earnest.

Seeing she was all right, I pushed off, heading toward to the right. The lake had several little inlets where the shore came to rest, and the nearest was about a quarter mile. It was still within range of our village territory that we had claimed, and I swam between there and here to build up endurance. I took long strokes, moving my head from side to side as I powered my way along. Behind me, Shevron had found a place to sit so she was up to her chest in the water, and she was leaning back, closing her eyes as the warmth of the sun broke through what clouds there were and showered down on us.

I put in three miles before I decided that was enough for the moment, and I swam back to Shevron, who was watching Elan play in the water. I leaned back next to her, my hair plastered to my back.

"How do you really feel about this?" I kept my voice low. Elan might be in otter shape but there was nothing wrong with her hearing.

"I don't know. I'm happy, I suppose. I like Elan well enough, and I think she could fit into the Cast, but it seems to be a question of will Jason fit into their world? I don't like to think of losing him to the Woodland Fae, but it's not my call."

I sought for words, trying to figure out a way to say what I had to say without offending her. "Thing is, if she came into your world, her family would be losing her. And even if it is a distant chance, she's heir to a throne. Can you reasonably ask her to give that all up to just be Jason's wife?" I swatted at a little fish that decided to take a nibble on my arm. It flickered away so quickly I almost thought it was an illusion.

"No, I guess not. The Cast is very insular. That's why we seldom took you to meetings."

"I'm glad you didn't. I have the feeling that anybody who's any sort of an outsider is always and forever going to be kept outside. Isn't that true? Look at what it's done to Leonard."

"He's Cast…" Shevron stopped. "No, you're right. He's not Cast and he never will be. Even if he were to do everything the way they wanted, he'll never be Cast because he doesn't know what it is to fly. To be up there, soaring over the earth. It's a freedom that you can't begin to understand until you have it."

I wrapped my arms around my knees. "Shevron, you'll pardon me but I think that you forget, there are other freedoms in the world. Look at Elan—she can dive, she can travel in the water, she swims in a way neither you nor I ever will. And me—I have the freedom to shift over to the Crossroads. Granted, it's usually to fight, but it's something that you can't understand until you do it. Hawk-shifters are no more special than anybody else who has a unique talent. The Cast may be your world, but it's not the only world."

Shevron blinked. She was about to answer when one of the guards behind us called out.

"Milady Fury! Come quickly! Lord Tam needs you. Something's happening back at UnderBarrow."

As I scrambled out of the water, I prayed an Abom hadn't gotten loose in UnderBarrow, because that would be a nasty fight, and in close quarters, there was so much damage he could do. I called back that we were coming and, leaving Shevron to watch Elan, I grabbed my clothes and put them on at a run.

Chapter 5

TWO OF THE guards and I hurried back to UnderBarrow, leaving Shevron, Elan, and the other guards to watch them. Nobody could tell me what was happening, just that the alarm had been sounded.

I brought up my Trace but saw no sign of any Abom, so it had to be something else. Oh cripes, had Shay made it this far? But as we entered the village proper, I saw it was something else entirely. There was a brawl in the middle of the village green. At least fifty people were involved, and the guards were wading in, trying to quell the disturbance.

Tam was standing to one side, motioning to me. I raced over to him, taking his hand as he pulled me close. "Love, we have to bring everybody in. Something's going on and it's not just hot tempers run amok."

"Elan and Shevron! They're still at the lake."

Tam turned to a couple of guards who were waiting for his command. "Get them back here safely."

The men raced off toward the shore.

I scanned the crowd. "What happened?"

"I don't know. One of the guards came to tell us that there was a fracas going on, and by the time we got out here, it had escalated. As you can see, it's not just men, and they can't all be drunk."

Sometimes the Bonny Fae got a little out of hand when they had too much to drink. It seemed to coordinate with full moons, so I thought that maybe Tam's race was a little more moonstruck than normal. But we weren't near the full moon yet—we hadn't even reached first quarter—so that couldn't be it. And these were village folk—mostly human.

There were a lot of shouts and catcalls. The guards responded in Gaelia, the language of the Bonny Fae. I was beginning to pick up the language but it was going to take me some time. And it wasn't just one main cluster. There were several groups of people tussling. As Tam said, it wasn't just the men, but women too. And in one corner, four kids were going at it.

"What the hell started this?" I looked around, trying to find some central theme, but when I couldn't understand the language, it didn't make for good deduction.

Tam shook his head. "I have no clue. They're screaming insults at each other, and I've heard a few accusations—*You slept with my wife, you stole my money, you destroyed my bucket*...this is absolutely confounding."

"What do they all have in common?"

"They all live in Willow Wood. Seriously? I don't know." Tam and I watched as the guards waded through, pulling them apart, cuffing them to various posts far enough apart so they couldn't go at it with their feet. Everybody was snarling, cursing, frothing at the mouth. Part of me wanted to laugh—it seemed so ridiculous, but then I sobered. Whatever was happening was serious. There had been bloodshed, and medics were trying to treat scratches, black eyes, and broken bones.

Sarinka came running up. She was an incredible healer, Theosian by nature, and she was bound to Brighid. She was a certified mender back in Seattle, but that meant nothing now. What mattered was that she could get the job done, she could work with herbs and not just the medications doled out by the Conglomerate.

"I think I've figured out what's going on. I've seen this before, on a much smaller scale. I'll need to do a few blood tests, but I have the necessary reagents. I think they've been poisoned by Tripwater."

"Tripwater?" I'd never heard of it. I must have looked clueless, and Tam looked about as confused as I felt, because Sarinka cleared her throat.

"Tripwater is a powder that, when introduced to water, can trigger aggressive behavior. It causes the victim to become angry over any perceived slight and sends them into a mindless rage. There must have been a few petty—or perhaps not so petty—grievances floating around for this much fallout. But that's human nature." She pointed to the general mercantile where two more men were still going at it, even as the guards were pulling them apart. "It affects more men than women, because testosterone already makes them tend more to violence."

"Okay, so we've had someone poison the water supply. Can you cure it? Can you find out if all of the wells have been tainted with Tripwater?"

She nodded. "Yes and yes. But nobody should drink any more well water right now. Don't even try to boil it or touch it. Have everybody who hasn't been affected start hauling in lake water until I can find out what's going on. I'll need some volunteers. Thank the gods I managed to find a huge supply of medical gloves on the last raid." She turned to me. "Can you round up a few herbalists? I'll need a specific subset of herbs and they're not easily identified. I need gatherers."

I nodded, then paused. "How long does it take to affect someone with Tripwater?"

"Oh, two hours? Maybe less. It works quickly." Sarinka stopped. "I see where you're going with this. The water had to have been tainted within the past couple hours or the entire town would already have been at each other's throats. Nobody living in the Barrow will be affected because we source our water there."

I turned to Tam. "Gather the guards who haven't drunk any water in the past three hours—add an hour to be safe—and have them start questioning everyone who can think as to whether they've seen any strangers in the area, especially around the wells. Meanwhile, I'll go talk to Memy Pendrake about the herbalists. She'll know more than I will."

Memy Pendrake was an old, old woman and she looked it—her face a wrinkled map of her life, showing every journey she had ever taken. That she was Bonny Fae meant that she was far older than any of us could fathom, even Tam. She was an herbalist and healer, although she now preferred sitting in the sun or by the fire, dreaming away the days. But when you asked her a question, she was sharp as a tack. We had become friends over the past few months.

I raced back to UnderBarrow, through the labyrinth of passages to her door. When she answered, it was with a smile on her face, and a plate of cookies in hand. She was wearing a long flowing dress, and her hair was braided, down to her knees. It was the color of spun silver, gleaming as brightly as a full moon on a clear night.

"I had a feeling you were coming to call on me, child. I don't know why—the vision comes and goes these days—but I sensed you near."

I accepted one of her cookies. They were always excellent and I also had no wish to offend her. "Thank you. Memy, I need a favor and I need it quickly. We have an emergency and I need the names of all of the herbalists you know. Sarinka needs them."

Memy motioned for me to follow her into her chamber. UnderBarrow was a labyrinth of chambers, some spacious like Memy's, with two or three rooms to the apartment. Others were more utilitarian. The sitting room wasn't large, but it was homey and comfortable. Two armchairs sat kitty-corner the fireplace, and a desk rested against one wall. A small table and chairs were positioned near a wood cook stove where a kettle was whistling. A china teapot rested on the counter, next to a sheet pan of freshly baked cookies.

"You might as well stop for a moment. It will take me a few moments to gather the information for Sarinka. Pour the tea, child, and I'll be with you." She motioned toward the kettle. While she hunted down the names, I poured the water into the teapot and carried it to the table. Then I moved the cookies off the cookie sheet onto the plate and carried them over to sit near the teapot. Finally, I found the teacups and saucers in an upper cupboard, and brought them, along with the honey and lemon, to the table. By the time she was finished looking through her desk, tea was ready and I was pouring.

Memy returned to the table. She was carrying a list of names, and she settled herself opposite me. "Drink while I go over these. What does Sarinka need them for?"

"She needs to make something to counter Tripwater and said she needed herbalists who will recognize some rare plants."

"Tripwater?" Memy looked up from her paper. "I haven't heard of that being used in a long while. Who on earth could have done this?"

"We don't know, but somebody poisoned at least one of the wells with it. Perhaps all of them. Sarinka says she can make an antidote, but it will take some time and she'll need help. A lot of people have already been affected." I added lemon and honey to my cup. I didn't like tea much, but I was learning because it was the drink of choice among the Bonny Fae.

"Then that gives me a good idea of which herbalists won't be of much use. She'll need those with the most experience, because some of those herbs can be very tricky. Campwort looks a lot like knuckleberry bush, but knuckleberry bush is deadly, whereas campwort tends to be a cure-all. Let me see, Minda would be of great help, and Luisa, but not Hanny." She went down the list, crossing off some names and adding a couple more. Finally, she handed the paper to me. "You get those twelve together and they'll help her fix things right up."

"Where do I find them? I don't see any apartment or chamber numbers here." I stared at the list of names, feeling like an idiot. I had basically lived in UnderBarrow for six months and still felt like a total stranger.

"No worries there, child. Do you know who Dame Ferrika is?"

I knew the name, but not the person. "I've heard of her."

"Ask Damh Varias to introduce you. She knows where everyone in UnderBarrow lives. She's the Head Mistress of the UnderBarrow staff. She can send someone to fetch all the herbalists for you a lot faster than you can look them up yourself." Memy gave me a satisfied wink and sipped her tea. "Fury, one of these days I'll teach you to pour a proper tea. This...will do, but you will have to learn if you're to be our new queen."

I glanced at her. Damh Varias had released the official announcement and I had been getting congratulations from all sides, but it still took me by surprise.

She must have read my expression, because she laughed. "Don't think old Memy doesn't see everything that happens in the Barrow. Now, about that tea—we'll get you straightened out."

I blushed, feeling foolish all over again. "I'm sorry."

"No, don't go on about it. You aren't used to our ways, and that is not a fault, it's simply a fact. But when you take your place on the throne with Lord Tam, you're going to have to know a bit more about the culture here. You come to me after this crisis is over. Hecate may teach you how to fight and track the creatures you do, but I can teach you how to navigate the polite vagaries of UnderBarrow nobility. And that is a lesson you will truly need, my dear." She waved to the door. "Now go. I know you're in a hurry. Take another cookie. You look like you can use the extra energy."

As I quickly thanked her, I grabbed a cookie and the list and headed out to find Damh Varias.

TWENTY MINUTES LATER, I had met Dame Ferrika, who was almost as daunting as the Elder Gods. She was a tall woman, thin and gaunt, and she wore her hair in a braid wrapped around her head. She was polite, but icy, and I had the feeling that nobody ever rose to her standards. Which was probably why she had the job she did—exacting expectations led to high-quality workmanship.

She sent me packing with a promise that she would have the herbalists gather at Sarinka's within the hour. I hurried away with Damh Varias, grateful to be out of her sight.

"She's strict, isn't she?"

"She's more than strict, Fury. She keeps Under-Barrow in line, and she's also an aunt to Lord Tam. She'll be one of your relatives, my dear." Damh Varias grinned at me, a twinkle in his eye. I had the feeling he was taking delight in scaring me silly.

"His aunt?" I paused, then asked a question I had been wondering about for some time. "Where are Ta—Lord Tam's parents?"

"His mother and father rule over a Barrow back in Eire. You might say UnderBarrow is a hive off that one. Once, long ago, they were known as the Winter King and Queen. Now, the Winter Court is known as the Bonny Fae Court, and the Summer Court is known as the Woodland Fae Court. Perhaps one day we'll return to the old nomenclatures, but until that day, Bonny Fae we remain."

I stared at him. So Tam's parents were still alive? For some reason, I had never thought about it before, but now it made me nervous.

"Does Lord Tam keep contact with them?"

Damh Varias inclined his head. "He does. When you marry, they'll be here to welcome you into the family."

I froze. The bigwigs of the Bonny Fae world

were going to be my in-laws. For some reason, it hadn't registered that I would be dealing not just with Tam's people, but with Tam's actual *people*. I would have a mother-in-law, and a father-in-law, and they would be looking me over like a prize horse. What would they think about having a Theosian for a daughter-in-law? At least the Bonny Fae seemed more open to integrated marriages than some other races, but still, I had no mother or father for them to meet, and what I did wasn't exactly suitable for Court business.

Damh Varias must have seen the fear on my face, because he laughed and clapped me on the shoulder—a rarity, given how proper he was. "Oh, Fury. I wouldn't worry too much. If you were marrying the Lord of Verdanya, you might have a problem, but with the Bonny Fae Court? They'll be honest, but they'll also be thrilled. We are darker than the Woodland Fae, and the High Court will appreciate your occupation and nature."

"I hope so," I muttered. "I don't think I realized what a big deal marrying Lord Tam is. To me, he's always just been 'Tam.' But now I'm in his world and it's a whole different game."

"You're right, it *is* a different game. And there are a lot of rules to learn, and nuances that won't come easy. But you'll work through it with our help. I, for one, welcome your presence. We've been wanting his Lordship to marry and settle in for some time, but after..." He paused.

"I sense a story behind that. After what?"

Damh Varias shook his head. "Best he tell you himself."

"What? Is he already married? Is there someone I have to worry about?"

"Only ghosts and memories, Fury. Come, let's check on Sarinka." He escorted me to the front of UnderBarrow and out. I wanted to push him into telling me what he meant, but the Bonny Fae could be cagey, and if Damh Varias didn't want to say anything, he wouldn't.

Outside, there were a few more brawls going on with the guards breaking them up, but Sarinka was standing in the middle of the town square over a massive cauldron. She was flanked by two women, whom I assumed were also herbalists. They were Bonny Fae by the look of them, and they were feeding herbs into the cauldron on her cue. Another woman raced back from the trail into the forest, her basket overflowing with a plant that I recognized, but had no clue what the name was.

"I see the herbalists found you," I said as we approached.

"They did. Thank you kindly. I've got four of them out in the woodlands searching for the other herbs I need. These are the ones that are easier to find. Thank the gods that it's summer and not winter, or we'd be up the stream without a paddle." She motioned to the woman on her left. "Those go in now. Mind you, don't add the flowers—just the roots."

"How long till you finish with the antidote?" Damh Varias asked.

"At least till sundown. Then it has to steep overnight. Tomorrow morning it should be ready for use. Until then, we're sedating all of those who were hit by the Tripwater. Also," Sarinka said, wiping her hands on her apron and resting them on her hips, "we discovered that they tainted two out of the four wells. So I'm making a massive batch because we'll have to pour at least two gallons of the antidote into each well. I'm pouring it in the other ones as well, to make certain that we didn't miss anything. And you'd best post guards on each well for now, till we figure out how this happened and who did it."

She wiped her forehead with her apron—the day was warming up, and she had been standing over a roaring fire for quite some time—and turned back to her work. "Go on with you, now. I need to focus."

We left her be. I crossed my arms, hugging myself. I was impatient and wanted to be doing something *now*, but Sarinka's antidote would take time, and so would Heimdall's explosive.

"I feel so helpless. There's nothing I can do right now."

Damh Varias started to answer, then closed his mouth, gesturing over my shoulder. I turned to see Hecate standing there.

"There is something you can do right now. Come with me." She nodded to Damh Varias and turned, motioning for me to follow her.

We made our way through the narrow trail leading to the encampment where the gods had set up shop. Several hundred yards to the north was the new Temple Valhalla. While Hecate, Athena, and Artemis hadn't created a new version of Naós ton Theón, they had erected a plaza and enclosed gazebo. To the west, the Celts were creating their temple—the Temple of the Sylvan Woodland. The Finns had set up a temporary camp to the northeast until they could build a new settlement on the edge of the lake.

The Greek gazebo was actually quite spectacular, for being so hastily cobbled together. While not the gleaming marble of the temple back on the Peninsula of the Gods, the pillars were made of birch logs, and the roof was thatched from cedar boughs. The sides were colorful tapestries from the old temple that they had rescued, and inside, it was big enough for three rooms—one for each of the goddesses. Other Greek gods had also trickled into the woods, but so far, no permanent plans had been made.

Hecate lifted the curtain that they were using as a door and motioned for me to join her in her "office." I slipped inside, taking a seat. No leather couches here, but simple wooden benches with cushions on them. And her desk was a plank of wood atop four cedar stumps.

"Sit. Rest for a moment before we talk." She paused, then at my skeptical look, added, "It's nothing urgent. Don't worry."

So I sat, closing my eyes. Instead of the sounds of air conditioning and office machines, we listened to birdsong and the wind through the trees. Slowly, I began to relax. As I drifted, the currents of the wind caught my attention. Even though the tapestries kept them at bay, I could feel the direction they were blowing. The warmth had penetrated the forest enough to make me drowsy as I lingered in the moment. I took a deep breath, held it, and then slowly exhaled, the tension and worry streaming out on my breath.

Finally, I opened my eyes and straightened my shoulders. Hecate was watching me, a bemused smile on her face.

"What did you want to talk to me about?"

"Nothing," she said. "Everything. I want to ask you a question, and you aren't to answer now. I want you to seriously think about it for a while."

"All right," I said. Whenever anybody asked me to think over something "for a while," it usually meant that whatever they were asking was pretty big. "Ask away."

"A simple question. Are you happier out here than you were in Seattle? That simple. Think about it. Dissect it if you will. But come back when you truly know the answer in your heart." She leaned back in her chair, stretching as she yawned.

I blinked. "That's it? That's the big question?"

"Yes, but you need to really think about it because your answer affects a great deal. Well, yours and several other answers combined."

I nodded. When Hecate said "Don't answer now," she meant it. "About the village and whoever poisoned the wells. Do you have any idea of who did it?"

Hecate's easy smile faded. "No, but I wish I did. Thor's poking around now, looking into it. I wouldn't want him on my bad side, especially if I were human. That much I'll tell you."

I leaned forward, resting my elbows on my knees and clasping my hands. "I'm not sure what to do,

Hecate."

"What do you mean?" She looked perplexed. "The herbalists are concocting an antidote. That will help those who were afflicted."

"Not about the wells. Just in general." I stood, stretching, and began to pace. "Back in the city it was go-go-go. When I wasn't chasing after Abominations, I was working on a psychic cleansing. Or visiting Jason. Or hanging out at Dream Wardens. Here, the whole routine is gone. I don't have many Aboms to chase. There aren't really any psychic cleansings for me to tackle. It's not the same. I could hang out at Dream Wardens here, I suppose, but..."

"I understand. You've been uprooted. Fury, your whole life was spent in the city. Most of your friends are much older than you and they've gone through a number of significant changes in their lives, including living situations. Don't be surprised if you feel like they're handling this better than you are."

I lifted a corner of the tapestry nearest me and peered outside. There were no windows—without the tapestries the entire gazebo would be open to the elements. She was right. I had been feeling like I wasn't picking this up as fast as everybody else. Jason had adapted. Tam adapted. Of course, he still lived in UnderBarrow, but the Barrow hadn't been moved in thousands of years and now, it seemed that the time in Seattle had never existed. Even Greta and Hans were adapting. Of course, Greta was steeped in her training with Freya to a point even I couldn't quite fathom.

I turned back to Hecate. "You nailed it. Really, I think that's part of my problem. I don't know how to change easily. My life was thrown into a tailspin when I was thirteen. And when Jason took me in, it pretty much settled into a pattern. Even after I moved out and into my own apartment, it stayed the same. I cherished the routine because, after Marlene died, change seemed like an enemy. I need to learn how to adapt."

"Your days are fuller than you think. You train with me three times a week. You train your body six days a week. But now, it's time to train your mind."

"What do you mean? Go back to school?"

"In a way," she said, laughing as she shook her head. "Fury, you've agreed to marry the Lord of UnderBarrow. Don't you think it's time you started learning about the people and the history of the world you're going to enter? You can't just stay like this after your marriage. Yes, you'll always be bound to me, and your work with me comes first. But that leaves a large chunk of your life that you'll need to devote to the Bonny Fae. You owe it to Tam to embrace his world and make it your own, as well."

I stared at her. "I plan on learning the language—"

"Girl, don't be dense. You'll need to know the customs, the laws, the rules, the history. It's like marching into Olympus and expecting everybody to adapt to you instead of the other way around. You'd be tossed off the mountain quicker than you could blink. Tam is Lord of his people. You owe it to him to know how to act, to be able to communicate. To not be a disruption in his kingdom."

Hecate stood beside me. She lifted back the tapestry and tied it so that we had a good view of the forest. "Look out there. It's a whole different world than Seattle. And UnderBarrow is, as well. You've been a guest, but now you're going to be their queen. You must understand what that means."

I stared at the thicket of cedar and fir that surrounded the gazebo, and as the bustling sounds of the woods filtered in, the realization that Seattle had well and truly fallen crashed into me like a Monotrain derailing off the tracks. A longing for my old life welled up, and I burst into tears, surprising even myself. I leaned against one of the pillars supporting the thatched roof and cried.

"I loved the city. Even with the Corp-Rats and the Devani and all the bogeys, I loved it. It's all I've ever known. I'm not sure what I have to offer out here."

Hecate opened her arms and I fell into her embrace as she held me against her shoulder. She was incredibly tall, and I found myself nestled against her breasts, which seemed weird at first, but the warmth of her hug wedged a crack in the barricade I had erected. My fear and worry came flooding out in the wash of tears and she let me cry until the sobs began to subside on their own. After a few minutes, I stood back and she handed me a handkerchief.

I wiped my eyes, noting that my makeup truly *was* waterproof, and blew my nose. "Thanks. I'm sorry. I didn't realize that I was so upset."

"That's one of the reasons I wanted to talk to you. The first few months of any new situation, especially one as drastic as the one we came out of, are always a blur. We had to escape, then set up a new way of life, manage through the rest of the winter, all of that. Now, things are slowing down. We have time to breathe. And to think. I figured it was about time for a meltdown." She winked, taking the sting off her words.

"I suppose it was." I inhaled a deep breath, then let it slowly whistle through my teeth, taking the edge off the raw feeling that was irritating my lungs. Hiccupping, I let out one last choked sob, and sighed. "You asked me how I feel out here. I guess I feel like I'm a lot less useful than I was in the city."

"I figured you did. But go beyond that, Fury. Sit down, breathe, let everything settle."

I did as she asked. After a moment, I closed my eyes and once again I leaned back. This time, I could hear the chirping of birds, the susurration of wind through the tree boughs, the rustle of bushes. I could hear the forest around me, taking a deep breath and letting it out. There was a heartbeat to the land, I realized, just like there was a heartbeat to the city. Time here was based on the sun and the moon more than on lights and clocks. The rhythms were different, but they still existed. I just had to learn to settle into a new pace.

A few minutes later, I opened my eyes and sat up. "The silence out here has made me nervous. I can hear myself think, and that's sometimes a scary thing. I can get used to it, though. And my lungs appreciate the cleaner air, that I do know. I don't feel as rushed. And as long as I'm with Tam, I'm happy."

"Then you have your answer. Home isn't a place, so much as a state of mind."

I nodded, biting my lip. Then something jogged my memory and I recalled my conversation with Shevron. I straightened. "I was talking with Jason's sister. Verdanya is getting hit by Abominations. They have no one who knows how to fight them. Is there some way that we can train others who have the talent to see a soul-hole? To fight them, I mean?"

Hecate tilted her head, looking at me with a curious light in her eye. "I hadn't thought about that, but you're right on several counts. They're closer to the city and the World Tree. They'd be far more vulnerable to Aboms. And they need a way to fight them. Perhaps you have something there, Fury. Let me think about it. Meanwhile, why don't you go back to the village and see how they're coming with the antidote. I'll check with Thor on whether he's discovered anything."

I nodded. As I exited the gazebo, I thought about everything she had said. My life was changing and I had to run with that. Seattle was gone, and everything we had done there was in the past. While I would always carry my past there with me, it was time for the next chapter. And Hecate was right about another thing. I owed it to Tam to learn his culture, to learn his ways, and to become part of the world I was about to join.

I sucked in a deep breath, feeling the wind stirring again. New beginnings were on the horizon. Regardless of Lyon, regardless of Aboms, I was entering a new phase of my life. Ready to tackle my future head-on, I returned to Willow Wood, and to UnderBarrow.

Chapter 6

BY THE NEXT morning, Sarinka and the other herbalists had countered the Tripwater and Willow Wood's water supply was safe again. I was sitting at a long picnic table with Tam, Kendall, Jason, Elan, Greta, Hans, and Tyrell while Thor roasted his goat Tanngrisnir over the fire. We had eaten this goat a dozen times in the past six months, mostly during the winter when meat was scarce, and each time, I still couldn't get over how the next morning, the creature would be bouncing around camp with his brother Tanngnióstr, knocking over stuff like nothing had happened. Every time we had a special meeting, the god of thunder seemed to delight in providing fresh goat flesh. It almost seemed sadistic, but he was very careful to kill the goats quickly and he got them drunk first so the pain could be minimal. Both goats had a taste for booze that rivaled even Thor's.

"Did you find anything in your search for the culprit who poisoned the water?" Hecate asked. It seemed odd to see her leaning back on a bench against another big picnic table, legs crossed, dressed in jeans and a polo shirt. Her boots were exquisite, though, and I coveted them like Thor was eyeing the kegger that was sitting by the edge of the glen.

We were sitting next to the area where the Norse gods were building the new Temple Valhalla. At least, the ones who had stayed. When Seattle crashed and the world governments started to flounder, some of the Elder Gods chose to withdraw back to their respective realms, while some stayed here, deciding to back humanity.

"I found traces of Tripwater in a puddle to the south. It looks like whoever it was might have tested it out there on somebody. But no, I don't know who did it yet. I do have some news, though." Thor straightened up at the fire where he had been turning the immense spit containing the body of poor Tanngrisnir.

"As do I," Hecate said. "You first."

"We've received a notice from Odin. He's been thinking it over and he's decided that Midgard has always been a place we vowed to watch over. He—along with all those who went back to Asgard—are returning. Unfortunately, that includes my brother Loki, but beggars can't be choosers." He prodded the carcass and a whiff of the fragrant meat drifted past. I had to admit, dear old Tanngrisnir was smelling pretty good by now.

Hecate clapped her hands. "Wonderful! That's

about the extent of my news, as well. Zeus and Hera are bored back in Olympus, so everybody's returning."

I exchanged glances with Elan. That meant a full house of gods. What the other pantheons would decide was hard to say. The Finns had stayed, as had the Celts.

"Does that mean they agree to help humans?" I asked.

The original rift had been twofold—one, the fall of Seattle included the fall of the Peninsula of the Gods. Tsunamis didn't differentiate between human and Elder God. And two—those who determined they didn't want any part in interfering in human affairs once the going got rough had packed up and left.

"It will be like the old days," Athena said. "Back in Greece, our temples weren't filled with office equipment and gadgetry. Though I admit, I'm going to miss air conditioning."

"You're going to miss it," Hans said. "We're going to miss it too. We already do. Though this summer's not so bad yet, and living in the forest instead of in the city makes a big difference."

"Is it true, then?" Kendall asked. "Is Seattle beyond saving?"

"Yes, it is." I let out a long sigh. "I'm still surprised that Lyon thinks he's holding on to anything important. Except for the fact that the World Tree is in Seattle. Once Heimdall is finished with the explosive, we'll take care of that and then, I guess we're still back to a simpler way of life." I tapped my fingers on the table, thinking about what Hecate had said the day before. "I want to make a run into Seattle, though. We should replenish supplies."

"You aren't going anywhere, not until we have the explosive ready," Tam said. He gave me a long look. "Fury, we can't chance losing you since you're the only one who can see the portal on the World Tree."

"Tam is correct," Hecate said. "Send a different crew. I'm sorry, Fury, but you're too important to go gallivanting off on a run like that. Stay here."

As the meat crisped up and the tables filled with breads and fruits and cheese, I once again realized that my world was changing. But at least the Elder Gods were returning. At least we had that.

NOT QUITE TWO weeks later, I was sitting outside with Tam. I had just finished an hour with a language tutor that Damh Varias had found for me. I was studying Gaelia for an hour a day, and then customs and history for an hour a day with yet another tutor.

Tam was ecstatic. "You are making real progress," he said, wrapping his arm around me.

We had finally sat down and established some acceptable perimeters for public affection. The Bonny Fae were quite promiscuous, but it was mostly in private, and there was a truly stark juxtaposition between their nature and their public behavior. It was what it was, and I had learned to accept it. But Tam and I had come to an agreement so I wouldn't make a mistake that could embarrass the Court. Hand-holding was acceptable when we weren't in an official Court setting, or when we were leaving rooms. As were kisses, as long as lips were closed. Hugging was acceptable, as long as it wasn't drawn out, and he could put his arm around me, or vice versa, when we were out strolling or just hanging out.

"I'm trying." I frowned. "I'm having some trouble with the fact that you have a gazillion words for emotions. You don't just love, you love your spouse, you love your lover, you love your children, you love your sword, and each one has a different word for it."

"We love a great deal," Tam said, laughing. "We love so many ways we need a hundred words to describe it. Tell me you love me, in Gaelia." He flicked my nose, gently, and winked.

I bit my lip, running over the pronunciation in my head first. "*Iya eser ovair fre saswen.*"

He kissed me slowly. The warmth of his lips against mine made me shiver and I took his hand and stood.

"Iya eser ungar fre saswen."

"I'm hungry for you too," he whispered. "Let's do something about that." And with that, he led me into UnderBarrow.

TAM'S BEDROOM WAS four times the size of

mine. A giant four-poster bed rested against one wall, with covers woven in the colors of the aurora, shimmering with metallic threads that sparkled like stars in the muted light. The bed frame was made from walnut or mahogany, along with a matching set of dressers and nightstands. A sitting area held a sofa upholstered in a black and blue pattern, and two armchairs sat facing a fireplace built of white brick. The floor was a cool marble, and the ceiling was high—at least twelve feet. A door to the back led into a private bath that could rival any day spa.

I stared at the bed. When we were married, I'd be sharing this chamber with him, just like I'd be sharing his life. Over the past week or so, the realization of what marriage entailed had begun to dawn on me. We were joining lives, not just moving in together.

"When do you want to set the date?" I slowly began to undress, musing over the fact that we were talking about this at all. If someone had told me a year ago I'd be marrying Tam, I would have laughed them out of my apartment.

Tam shed his clothes. He stretched, his lanky, taut muscles rippling. He sauntered over to the bed. "Come here, woman."

I laughed, slipping out of my underwear. "All right, but we have to start making decisions because I'm already getting asked about the wedding."

As I jumped onto the bed, landing in the center of it, Tam sprawled, stretching out his arm. I snuggled into the crook, feeling once again safe and loved. He rolled over on his side, running his hand down my stomach, placing it flat right below my belly button.

"I want to talk to you about something else," he said, staring down into my eyes.

"All right." A flicker of worry raced through me that he might say sorry, let's call it off. This was the only serious relationship I had ever had. Every other man had been wrong for me in one way or another, and even though I had had a crush on Jason at the time I was dating all the others, I knew in my heart they weren't right.

"Love, you know my people are open about sexuality. We generally marry out of expectation, and take lovers as we will. But I want to reassure you—to make you a promise—that I'm not doing that. I'm promising my faithfulness to you."

I caught my breath. I had wondered when we would come to this discussion, and I had steeled myself in case Tam wanted to follow tradition. I hadn't decided how I would handle it if he said he wasn't cut out for monogamy, but I knew that the talk had to come. When he proposed, I had blanked it out of my mind—I had been too excited.

I rolled to a sitting position, turning to him. "Are you sure? Don't make promises you can't keep. The one thing I can't abide is lying."

"I know that, my love, and I promise you—if there ever is a day when I feel I can't resist, we'll talk first and decide how to proceed. But I don't anticipate that day. You make me feel alive. There's something about you that I can't explain, my lovely goddess."

"Don't call me that," I said. "I'm not a goddess."

"But you *are*. You're a Theosian. You are a goddess, minor or otherwise, whether or not you want to face facts. You may be bound to the Elder Gods, but you aren't mortal, my love. Not in the way humans are. Not the way your parents were." He took my hands in his. "How do you feel? I never asked you. Do you want to be monogamous? Do you want to take lovers? I suppose I should have asked before making my declaration."

I stumbled over my words, feeling both awkward and yet strangely free. Tam and I were discussing the building blocks of our future, and everything seemed suddenly real.

"Oh gods, no. I'm far too busy for more than one man. You are the only one I want to be with. Honestly, I've never been one to hand out my heart—or my body—easily. And now that you have both, I want to reserve them for you. To get to know you in that way very, very old couples know each other. Every curve, every corner, every mood...I don't think you can do that when you're juggling a bunch of paramours."

"Then it's settled. We cleave to each other." He kissed my fingers, one by one. "Now, as to setting a date. Perhaps the Winter Solstice? When the snows are thick on the ground and the holly berries are brilliant red, will you marry me?"

"That sounds perfect. By then, we'll..." I started to say we'd have taken care of Lyon, but I didn't want to jinx it so I just said, "That will give us time to prepare for the wedding. Yes, Winter Solstice is perfect."

"Then Damh Varias will bring in a wedding planner and we can discuss your dress and the service. We'll have to have a court wedding, love, tradition demands it." He sounded wary, as if he thought I'd object.

"I don't mind. As long as we're together." Secretly, I had hoped for something small and intimate, but I had learned enough about the traditions of the Bonny Fae to know that was a pipe dream. We would be married as royalty. "Now, make love to me. Hold me, touch me, remind me I'm yours."

And he did.

WE WERE TANGLED on the bed together, basking in the afterglow, when there was a knock at the door. Tam pulled his robe on, and strode over. Outside, the guards were posted to keep anybody out who wasn't invited and they knew better than interrupt for anything trivial. So it had to be important.

"Yes?" Tam opened the door a crack while I quickly began to dress over by the bed.

"Your Majesty, there's an envoy waiting for you in the throne room. It seems important." The guard's voice traveled back to where I was standing.

"Envoy? From where?"

"Eleveanor. A messenger from a Mistress Tera."

"Tera!" I hurried over, shoving my feet in my shoes. "I wonder if Shay is bothering them."

"I don't know. Take them into one of the private meeting rooms," Tam said to the guard. "The Blue room. We'll be there in a moment." He closed the door and quickly dressed. "I hope to hell he hasn't managed to cause problems for her again. I knew he'd be better off dead, but hindsight is always easiest. Let's hope that everything's all right."

"Well, it can't be all right, can it? Not with Sara killing herself. Tera's probably at her wits' end from that alone. If Shay has returned to Eleveanor, there's no way for a good ending there."

I waited impatiently as Tam finished dressing and brushing his hair. He was the Prince of Under-Barrow. He couldn't afford to go anywhere un-kempt unless it was the middle of battle.

We hurried down the hall, accompanied by two of his bodyguards. All the time we had hung out at Dream Wardens in Seattle, none of us had a clue that he was actually the leader of UnderBarrow. He had ditched his guards, never showing up with them, and we had all thought he was just Tam, one of the Bonny Fae.

We arrived at the Blue room—a private meeting chamber. It was decked out in soothing blues and ivory, like clouds against the sky, and Tam used it for meetings that might prove volatile, trying to calm the temperaments involved. As we entered, we saw one of the guards waiting with the visitor. It was Bryn, Tera's new beau and the man helping her run Eleveanor. He looked exhausted, and I im-mediately knew that—whatever the news was—it wasn't good.

"Bryn! What happened?" Tam clasped his hand

and shook it. I seconded the action.

Bryn, a hefty man—tall and muscled and strong as an ox—slumped back in his chair. He looked defeated. "I'm coming to you to ask a great favor. Please know, we don't expect you to say yes."

"Tell us what happened." Tam settled at the table.

Bryn ducked his head, staring at the floor. "Eleveanor is devastated. Shay returned, and he found the cull-fire magician and together, they rained fire down on the village. There are numerous injuries, and many of the houses burned to the ground. Luckily, we managed to prevent the flames from spreading through the forest."

"Tera—is Tera..."

Bryn pressed his lips together. "She's been injured, but she'll live. Fire was raining from the sky and it clings like glue. We can't move all the injured to Verdanya—not the ones in most need, at least. I was wondering if we could bring them here?"

"Of course," Tam said. "We'll send people to help you. What of Shay?"

"He's dead. I caught him and broke his neck." Bryn made a satisfied smacking sound. "He's done his last and best to destroy his sister. I hope he rots in whatever afterlife awaits him."

Tam motioned to the guard. "Summon Damh Varias immediately."

"How many are seriously injured?"

"At least fifty are burned seriously enough that we'll be lucky if they make the journey here. Another twenty-five with burns that are severe but not life-threatening unless they get infected. Numerous victims of minor burns and injuries, from collapsing houses and so forth."

I turned to Tam. "Maybe we should marshal some healers to go to Eleveanor instead of forcing them to come to us? At least, they could prepare the injured for travel."

"Good idea. What's the state of your village?" Tam asked.

Bryn shrugged. "Seventy percent burned to the ground, or can't be salvaged from all the smoke damage and the water magic that our mages threw at the flames."

"Are you going to rebuild? I know it's early to ask."

"No, I think we're done. A number of people are already on the move back to Verdanya. I estimate about one hundred want to join your village. They like this area and they wouldn't mind being near the Elder Gods again."

Tam and I glanced at one another. Tam paused, then said, "They will have to follow the rules in Willow Wood and if they do not, they will be forced to leave. And they must be made aware they're moving to Willow Wood, but they will be under the rule of UnderBarrow."

"I don't think any of them will have a problem with that," Bryn said. "Most who want to stay up this way are good with the bow and arrow, solid hunters and farmers. If they went back to Verdanya, they'd just be absorbed again by the city. They like being out in the middle of the forest, with solid work that feels important."

Tam nodded as the door opened and Damh Varias entered. Tam quickly explained the situation to him. "Gather a handful of healers who are willing to make the trip, and take supplies for stretchers, so carts will be a necessity. Ask Laren to lead them, since Tera's his cousin. Elan shouldn't go. I don't want any duties to compromise her pregnancy."

Cars couldn't make it through this area of the Wild Wood and we had gone back to a healthy reliance on horses and carts.

"As you will, Your Majesty. I'll make the preparations. Meanwhile, our guest might like to take a bath and rest for a bit. I'll have a late lunch sent to you, sir."

Bryn gave the advisor a grateful smile. "Thank you. I really need sleep. I've been on my feet for days, it feels like." As one of the guards showed him out, we sat in silence. After they were gone, Damh Varias sat down at the table with us.

"Your Majesty. Have you thought about what an influx of this size might do to the town's dynamics? I'm not sure if it's best to allow so many to come at once."

"I thought about that, but how can we say no? They're in need. We have plenty and we can offer them help. But assign several assistants to get them settled. Treat them like immigrants—insist they take a few classes in village etiquette. Find them jobs. Do what you can to make them feel welcome and yet remind them, they need to be on their best behavior. Keep them busy."

"As you will, Sire." Damh Varias turned to me. "Milady, a welcoming speech from the Lady of the

Land might be a nice touch. I'm sure that Patrice can find you something appropriate to wear."

I blinked. This was the first time he ever said anything about my clothes. But then I thought back to my lessons. He had impressed on me that my position would *not* be a token one—I wasn't going to be a figurehead. I would be queen of this realm. *Or princess.* I hadn't figured out yet quite how Tam was considered both the king and the prince of UnderBarrow. Either way, I was heading into a position of power and I needed to handle it correctly. If that meant giving a speech to welcome newcomers, then I would do it.

"Will you help me write it? I'm not sure what to say and I don't want to get off on the wrong foot. Most of my speeches start out with 'Die sucker' or 'You're going down.' And then I attack the creature I made the speech to." I had never had to give a public speech. Even reading fortunes and clearing houses was easier. Most of the time, I had my cards there to base my answers from. And with the ghosts, I wasn't there to befriend them. If I was a spokesperson, it was to deliver a ticket out of town.

Damh Varias held my gaze for a moment, and I thought I detected a sense of respect as he said, "Of course, milady. I'd be honored to help you."

"I want to make sure I do this right." I glanced at Tam. "I'm taking this marriage seriously. I don't ever want to be responsible for messing things up, and I'm overwhelmed. So I'm learning the language and customs and I'm having fun, actually. But making my first speech to a bunch of refugees? It feels huge. It scares me more than fighting an

Abomination because I *know* how to do that and I'm good at my job."

Ignoring our agreement, Tam pulled me into his arms in front of Damh Varias and gave me a long kiss. Damh politely turned away.

"Fury, my love. You will be a wonderful queen. And I'm so touched that you're this worried, but never feel like you have to change who you are. I love Fury, the chosen of Hecate. I'm not looking for you to turn into a great lady—" Tam stopped abruptly. He glanced over at his advisor, who gave him a warning shake of the head. Tam turned back at me. "You're right, though. Both of you. My people—soon to be *our* people—will expect you to know these things. You see more clearly than I do."

Damh motioned to me. "Milady, if you would follow me, we'll talk about your speech. Events like this will most certainly fall under your domain in the future."

And so, I followed, continuing my training.

FOUR DAYS LATER, the village was back to normal as far as the Tripwater went, but we still weren't sure who had sabotaged the wells. I wanted to know, but all Tam's investigations had led to nothing and it wasn't like we could pound on doors and demand the truth.

The herbalists had left with Bryn, and they were expected back the next day with the injured in tow, along with those able-bodied who wanted to join the village. Damh Varias had helped me write a speech. He had asked me to first write what I felt would be appropriate, and then he went over it, explaining why a few sentences set the wrong nuance, and why others needed refining. But the gist of it, he liked, which made me feel better.

Hecate had been laying off my training for a while, which surprised me, but as she put it, in the past six months I had come a long way and it would do me good to focus on something else until Heimdall finished the explosive he was making. Part of me wanted to poke around Temple Valhalla, nudging him to see if he could hurry it up, but I knew better. If he said it would take a month, it would take a month.

Patrice was helping me try on the dress in which I would greet our new villagers. It was actually a lot more comfortable than I thought, and I was startled to find that Damh had ordered it modified so I could still reach my whip if I needed to. The top was a fitted corset, which I liked, and the skirt flowed out, with a slit up to my right hipbone. The outfit was gauzy and light, in a midnight blue weave with metallic stars racing through the material.

The dress felt odd to me, only because I couldn't help but think about how quickly it would get shredded, and how little of it would protect me in case of an attack. I happened to mention that to Damh Varias, but he laughed and asked if I expected to be constantly ready for action when I was queen.

"I'm not sure, shouldn't I be?" I had said.

"Only during wartime, milady. There's no war right now—oh, I do not speak of the greater battle against the Order of the Black Mist, but UnderBarrow is peaceful and we are in a time of growth." He had winked at me, then headed back to discuss Barrow business with Tam.

"Are you sure it's secure?" I asked Patrice. I shimmied, trying to see if my breasts were in danger of falling out of the strapless corset. But when I bent over, even though they spilled over the top, no nipple escaped. I stood up again, appreciating the fit that had gone into the leather piece. Unlike the skirt, the blue leather was sturdy and tailored.

"Yes, milady. No worries. You won't be giving our new guests a peep show." Patrice tugged at the skirt and it stayed put. "You look lovely, milady. Let me brush your hair."

I sat down at my vanity and she began to brush my hair.

"Hecate stained your tresses with the crimson, right?"

I started to nod but realized that would hurt with the brush working through my hair. "Right. My hair would have been solid black, but the night she took me under her wing, she streaked it with the crimson."

As she plaited it back into a long braid, there was a knock on the door. Patrice answered. It was Elan. We hadn't had much time to talk in the past week or so, and I knew that her cousins were still in the Barrow.

"Patrice, you may go. I'll ring when I need you."

"Yes, milady." She dipped into a quick curtsey

and then excused herself. When the door closed, Elan turned to me and burst into tears.

"I didn't know who else to talk to. I can't talk to Laren about this, or Jason." She hugged her stomach. I had never seen her so upset. I quickly hustled her into a chair.

"Is this about you moving back to Verdanya? About your cousins telling you that you'll have to marry Jason?"

She hesitated, then nodded. "Yes. I left my home because I wanted to make my own way in the world, and do things my way. I knew I didn't want a life like everybody else's. I wanted to make my own decisions, whether or not they were the right ones. You don't understand how strict the Woodland Fae are."

"I get the impression that they're pretty rigid."

"That's an understatement. You're moving into the Bonny Fae Court, but life in Verdanya is nothing like this. Everything is structured. What you do, who you marry, how many children you have, when you have them. Everything depends on your parents. I finally convinced them to let me leave, but they only agreed if Laren came with me. Now, with Father taking the throne, I'll never get away. I'll never be able to live the life that I want."

She pressed her lips together.

"What happens if you don't go back? If you tell them you don't want to?" Sometimes I was almost grateful that I didn't have a family. Oh, my friends were my family, but we were all pretty much autonomous. *That's going to change, though*, a voice inside said.

Elan wiped her eyes on her sleeve. "My parents would disown me. I'd never be able to return home. If you're an heir to the throne—anywhere near the crown—you have to live in Verdanya. If I refuse to return, they'll cast me out."

She seemed so distraught that I could only think that her people were harsher than their supposedly darker cousins. "I'm going to ask you a question and I mean nothing cruel by it. Would that be such a terrible thing? It seems that if you return, you're going to be unhappy. There's no way to win in this situation without losing something. Return home and you lose your independence. Stay and you lose your family."

Elan leaned back in her chair, contemplating my question for a long moment before she spoke. "That's cutting to the chase. But you're correct. Either way, I lose a part of myself. It all comes down to what means the most to me. My chosen life, or my family?" She paused for a moment. "Fury, you're giving up things too. How do you feel?"

I shrugged. "To be honest, I gave up the biggest one by force—Seattle. I gave up the life that I knew but it wasn't because of Tam. It was taken from me by Lyon. So really, I'm giving up nothing. Am I taking on a new culture? Yes, but I'm not giving up anything except the freedom to wander around looking for a new place to live. When I think about it, I've always been a nomad. I don't have to give up Hecate, or hunting Aboms. I'm just taking on more."

Elan nodded. "In my case, I'd have to give up my job here. I'd have to give up the freedom to do what I want. It's a big enough change knowing I'm going to be a mother. Having everything turned on its ear is another matter."

A knock interrupted us. I answered the door. It was a guard. "Milady, Lord Tam requests you and Elan join him in the conference room. It's urgent."

"What's going on?" I could tell from the guard's face that he knew what was happening.

"Milady, we didn't feel it in here because we're in UnderBarrow, but there's been an earthquake. The village has been damaged."

"Cripes. Come on." I motioned to Elan. As we ran toward the conference room, I knew in my heart that the Order of the Black Mist was behind this, and if we didn't stop them, they'd continue trying to plunge the world into a chaotic nightmare.

Chapter 7

BY THE TIME we reached the door leading out of UnderBarrow, Jason, Tam, and a number of others were with us. I was muttering under my breath, hoping the body count was low. Not only did I *not* want to see people hurt, but too many of our healers were still out of the village, off to help Bryn with the injured in Eleveanor. Our resources to cope with a lot of injured were low.

We stepped out of the Barrow and jogged along the short path to the village square.

On first look, it was obvious there was a lot of damage. When we had first settled Willow Wood, all the houses we erected were makeshift. Over the past four or five months, those handy with tools had joined together to build homes, one after another. They were slowly working their way through the village, building tidy cottages to replace the hastily improvised shelters. The cottages had withstood the damage. The shelters, however, had collapsed.

People were milling around the village, some simply dazed, others with blood dripping down from head wounds, or obviously broken arms. Children whimpered by their parents' sides, and everywhere, there were cries coming as people stumbled out from beneath the thatched roofs that had fallen in on the shelters.

Tam motioned to his guards. "Mobilize every-one who can walk to search for the injured. Start a bucket brigade and find water witches to extin-guish the fires that might have started." He turned to me. "Fury, Elan, please marshal any healers you can find and take them to the Grand Ballroom in UnderBarrow. We'll set up an emergency hospital there. We could be in for aftershocks and I don't want the injured still out here."

I nodded, heading back to UnderBarrow. I led Elan to Memy Pendrake's rooms. As the elderly Fae invited me to come in, I shook my head.

"Memy, there's been an earthquake out in the village. I need a list of *all* the healers in UnderBar-row—doesn't matter how experienced. We're going to need everybody on board to help."

"And so many off on the trip to Eleveanor." She *tsk*ed her way over to the table. "Come in, children. You may not have time to sit and chat, but the names will take me a moment to gather."

As she worked her way through several journals, I glanced at Elan. "You all right?"

She nodded. "Yes, if anything, this helps me make up my mind. In Verdanya, all of this—helping out, finding healers, searching for the lost—everything would be left to the guards and servants. Our culture is so much more structured than the Bonny Fae. And neither Verdanya nor UnderBarrow are the High Courts of our people."

"So I recently learned."

"Well, it's even worse the higher up you go. I want to be useful. Not a decoration. That's what it comes down to. I want to be useful and productive, and back in Verdanya, as the king's daughter, I'd be kept on the sidelines, especially since I'm pregnant. I'd be a figurehead."

I gave her a long look. "Are you sure about this?"

"Yes, I am. I'm going to stay in UnderBarrow. Here, I have a purpose, and friends, and Jason. If he came back to Verdanya with me, he would end up resenting both me and our child. It's not easy to fit in with a different culture. He probably could, but he'd be a prince by marriage. A minor noble expected to keep to his place and to never make waves." She stopped as Memy Pendrake returned, a piece of paper in hand.

"Here's a list of all the healers in UnderBarrow. I checked off those who are currently on loan to Eleveanor. You might check with the Celtic temple, as well. The Lady Brighid has a number of healers in her service."

We took the page, thanked Memy, and headed out. After looking up Dame Ferrika and asking her to gather all the healers on the list in the Grand Ballroom, Elan and I headed back to the village. As we stepped out of UnderBarrow, we found ourselves caught in the wave of an aftershock. While it wasn't mild, it didn't send us reeling to the ground, which was a blessing.

"What the fuck does Lyon have hold of this time?" I muttered as we crossed the village at a slow jog, heading into the woods. The new Temple of the Sylvan Woodland was southeast of the village, about a ten-minute walk from UnderBarrow.

"Are you sure Lyon caused this?"

"How could it not be him?"

Elan shrugged. "This entire area is riddled with fault lines. They were here long before the World Shift. Earthquakes are common here, compared to some areas of the country." She paused as we hurried along the trail. "Do you realize that there is no more *country*? It just hit me—the Conglomerate is dead. The Corporatocracy has fallen. Nobody's in charge and we're all on our own. I never prepared for this day. In some ways it's frightening, but in some ways I feel liberated."

"Yeah, I've been thinking a lot about that. We get a second chance to do it right. Or a third. The World Shift gave people a second chance, and we got it right by forbidding weather magic and putting a stop to the wars that ensued from the misuse of that power. But I think we've been at war since then—the battles have just been economic. A battle of money against money, and damned be those who fell through the cracks. Life in Dark-town wasn't easy. I felt for all those families who were caught up in one tax law after another, tethered to the government because of their debts. But the men at the top? They never went hungry, they didn't work sixteen-hour days trying to scratch out a living."

"I guess sometimes you need a revolution, but the price is always going to be steep." Elan pointed to the bend ahead. "Around that curve is the temple."

We kept to the center of the trail. Even though workers were constantly clearing out patches of Wandering Ivy and Thunder Root and Venus Traps, the carnivorous, sentient plants were invasive and they constantly tried to take over the endemic vegetation.

"I gather up north where the Greens used to be, the Wandering Ivy has taken over and pretty much absorbed the area. It grew like wildfire the past six months and choked out the regular vegetation." The thought of having to trek through a jungle of the plants gave me the creeps.

"The Bogs have expanded too, thanks to the thousands of dead bodies in Seattle. But they've extended to the south. The dead produced so much fertilizer and mulch that the Bogs and Sandspit pretty much swallowed up most of the corpses down there. I dunno what's happened in Seattle proper, but I'm not anxious to find out."

"I'll be forced to, once Heimdall creates the explosive. I have to make it to the World Tree. I wonder just how hard that's going to be. I'm not sure if I'm more afraid of Lyon, or what's risen out of the ruins of Seattle."

There were probably still zombies running around, and who knew how many spirits might be lodged within the city. Lyon's zombie attack had decimated Seattle, and the tsunami shortly after that had finished the job. The thought of the Bogs swallowing up the city was horrible, but in some ways, it seemed a fitting end to the devastation that had been wrought.

"I'm thinking that it's going to be a long, long time before civilization returns to what it was," Elan said.

"I doubt that it ever will. Hecate finally helped me understand that life won't ever go back to what it was. Took me awhile to understand that. You and Laren and Tam…even Jason and Shevron… you have all seen a lot of changes in your lives. But I'm only thirty-one. I only ever knew the life I had." I pointed at the sturdy building up ahead. A well sat in front of it. *Of course* the Celts would have a sacred well, and I had no doubt that Brighid had claimed it.

"Here we are."

Tyrell met us in the Temple of the Sylvan Woodland. A Theosian like me, he was bound to the Dagda, and he had journeyed out of Seattle with us when we first fled the zombies.

"We need healers, Tyrell. Can you ask the Lady Brighid to send them to the village?"

"Why don't you ask me yourself?" The voice was melodious, graceful like a flute on the wind.

We turned to see a tall woman standing near the well, wearing a long green dress. She had flame red hair that burned as brightly as my fire, and she wore a golden torc around her neck and a circlet that also looked to be made of gold.

"I'm Lady Brighid. What is it you need?" She crossed toward us, so effortlessly that it seemed as though she glided over the ground.

I blinked, wanting to melt into a puddle. Some of the Elder Gods could do that to you—their presence was so graceful, so embracing that it wrapped around you like a warm blanket.

"Your...Lady..." I paused, trying to find my words. "Lord Tam bids that we gather as many healers as we can to help out in the village. The quake..." I drifted off, hoping I had made some sort of sense.

She smiled then, and the sun smiled with her. "Of course. I'll send my healers over to the village as soon as I can gather them up."

As she turned away, I watched her retreat, a warmth filling my heart. Sometimes, the gods were more gracious than I ever expected. As she disappeared, I glanced over at Tyrell, who was watching me.

"Lady Brighid affects everybody that way at first. She's grace incarnate, and yet she's stronger than you'd ever think possible. I'll be there shortly with as many as I can gather up. You must need help with the search and rescue. That quake was big."

"It's not just that," I told him. "We're expecting a big party of injured in from Eleveanor." I filled him in on what Bryn had told us. "So Shay's dead, but their village has been trounced. I know they said they're not rebuilding but my guess is, after the shock wears off, people will drift back to their homes, wanting to rebuild. Now, it's more important than ever to establish good relationships with other villages and towns."

"You're right about that," Tyrell said. "Because

for every village like Willow Wood or Eleveanor, there's going to be a village of malcontents, looking to expand and conquer. It's the way of the world. Best to gather our allies while we can."

Tyrell's point was valid. Given the nature of people, if we didn't establish allies, eventually we might be facing them as enemies. Eleveanor could have easily been our enemy had we allowed Shay to stay in control. He had been out for his interests only, and he had manipulated others to suit his own needs. He had led an entire village of people astray. Shay might be dead now, but he had hurt a lot of people and been responsible for his niece's suicide. I hoped he rotted, wherever he was in the afterlife.

"I'll talk to Tam. I'm sure he's thought of this, but it can't hurt to remind them." As Elan and I turned to head back to Willow Wood, Tyrell caught up to us.

"At least the gods are building quarters near us. But that means their Theosians will be making the journey here from all over the country. The Dagda told me that they don't want to spread themselves too thin. So they're calling all the minor gods to them. We're going to be a powerhouse area, which means we'll be a major target. You might tell Tam that as well."

"Yeah, you're right." I mulled over the thought as Elan and I headed back to the village.

THE QUAKE HAD destroyed about four hundred shelters, but luckily, we only had two fatalities, and both of those had been heart attacks in older village members. There were hundreds of injuries, however. Several of them were major. The healers were out in force, setting up triage stations to attend to the worst hurt first.

A couple aftershocks hit as Elan and I wandered through the clusters of people. The guards had marshaled all able-bodied men to start clearing out some of the makeshift houses, while Tam had ordered not only the Grand Ballroom but several other large areas of UnderBarrow to be turned into shelters for the homeless until enough tents could be raised to protect everyone. Luckily, with the heat of summer, there hadn't been much in the way of fire damage. A lot of cooking was still done at the community ovens and grills rather than in shelters.

I finally spotted a chance to talk to Tam alone, and—with Elan, Jason, Hans, and Greta behind me—I closed in on Tam before anybody else could drag away his attention.

"Lady Brighid is sending healers to the village. Also, Tyrell told us something." I repeated the conversation, helped by Elan. "It occurs to me that we're going to become a focal point."

"I hadn't yet realized the gods were deciding to make this their home base. At least what... four? Five pantheons? Which means a number of Theosians will be filtering into the area within the next few months." He paused, then turned to me. "Perhaps we should marry sooner than later? We need to establish a strong foothold here. As soon as you're done with the gate on the World Tree, we can go ahead."

I was about to say something—a winter wedding had appealed to me—but then stopped. Tam wouldn't rush things just to be obnoxious. He'd have a good reason and we could discuss it later.

"I think we'll be fine if we keep the date the same." I paused as one of the guards appeared. I recognized him. He was from the front gate—figuratively speaking. We didn't exactly have gates or walls, but he was from one of the main outposts that watched to the southwest.

"Your Majesty." He knelt before Tam, who motioned him to his feet.

"Yes?"

"The injured from Eleveanor are coming. They'll be here in about twenty minutes. I ran ahead to tell you."

I groaned, a thought tapping me on the shoulder. "You do realize, with as many injured as we have, we'll be prime targets for any large party of lycanthropes who can smell blood."

"Good point. Double the guards on duty, and start patrolling the lines between the watchtowers." Tam turned to me. "I know this isn't the best time, but go get dressed. We need to greet them as though we have this entire situation in hand. We can't let them feel as though we're not capable of handling disaster."

He spoke in low tones, but Elan still heard him. "Lord Tam, I'll escort Fury to her room."

"Very good." He brushed her off like the bodyguard she had once been, but she didn't look hurt. In fact, as we hustled toward UnderBarrow, she motioned for me to walk in back.

"Best they see you acting like a queen now, because before long, you'll be one."

I started to protest, but once again, realized that I knew very little of formality—especially when it came to court manners. I had to learn, and learn fast.

PATRICE WAS WAITING with the corset and skirt. I had no clue how she knew ahead of time that I needed to change, but she helped me into the outfit. I shifted my breasts in my corset, grateful that it didn't restrict my breathing. The laces were firm, but they weren't laced to restrict movement, only for support. I decided that I should wear my dagger. Tam wore a ceremonial sword when he held court. I wasn't going to be any different just because I was female.

"Bring me my dagger and the belt for it, please." Usually I wore it on my thigh, but I also had a belt specifically designed to hold the sheath.

Patrice hesitated. "My lady, shouldn't you wear a more ornate belt? I know where I can find one and it will be better suited toward your outfit."

"Quickly, then."

As she hurried out of the room, I ran over the speech in my mind, hoping that I wouldn't forget anything. I was a quick study, but given the quake my mind was elsewhere and I wasn't sure how I was going to fare.

Elan tapped me on the arm. "Practice on me."

I grinned, grateful she had picked up on my nervousness. I took a deep breath and began my speech. I stumbled a few times, but by the time I was halfway through, my nerves had calmed down, and I realized that I had this. By the time Patrice returned with an ornate belt that matched my outfit, I was ready. I buckled it around my waist, strapping on the sheath with my dagger. With one final look in the mirror, I let out a long, slow breath, and gave myself a decisive nod.

"Okay, I'm ready. Elan, walk with me, please."

She smiled. "You're going to be a wonderful queen. Perfect for UnderBarrow."

"I still haven't figured out if I'm going to be a princess or a queen. Every time I ask Tam, he's just says, 'It's complicated.' I'm confused."

"He's right. It *is* complicated. Among the Fae there are the High Courts, and the regional courts. UnderBarrow is a regional court. Tam's parents are the King and Queen of the High Court and he's the prince to the entire Bonny Fae realm. But he's King of UnderBarrow."

That wasn't too difficult to understand. "I wonder why he just didn't tell me that. It makes sense. So I'll be the queen of UnderBarrow...and... *Oh*. You mean I'll be a princess in the High Courts, as well?"

"That's about the size of it. Since you're married to Tam, if he were to ever take the throne over all the Bonny Fae, you would ascend with him as queen of the realm, so to speak."

I blinked. That had never even occurred to me. "I sure hope his parents like me."

As we approached the doors leading out into the village, Elan laughed. "Don't count on it. I say this with the utmost love, but no woman will ever be good enough for their son. Trust me. It's always the way among nobility."

And with her "encouragement" ringing in my ears, I stepped out of UnderBarrow to greet our visitors.

ONE LOOK AT the injured and my words died on my lips. They didn't need a *Rah-rah-welcome-to-the-fold* speech. They needed comfort, food, and pain relief. The majority were sporting bandages wrapped around various body parts, but here and there, the bandages had come off or been nonexistent. Gaping patches of raw skin and burns slick with pus made me queasy. The smell of charred flesh hung heavy over the group, and my anger toward Shay flared. How *could* he have done this to people who had trusted him and followed him for so many years?

As our guards led them in and they gathered in the town square with our own injured, I cleared my throat.

"My name is Fury, and I'm the queen-to-be, betrothed to Lord Tam. I'm here to welcome you to our village. I had a speech all prepared, but you look weary and in pain, and hungry, so I'll save my speech for later. For now, please follow the instructions of the healers and guards, and be welcome. We'll do our best to help."

With that, I instructed the guards and healers to get them settled, and turned away.

Elan motioned for me to head back to Under-Barrow with her. "You did right. They don't need a formal speech, they need painkillers. Some of those burns look horrible. I hope the healers and menders can ease them. Burns hurt worse than just about anything."

Part of me wanted to stay put and help, but there wasn't much I could do that wouldn't have me in the way. I had no training in healing. As we re-entered the Barrow, I hoped Damh Varias wouldn't be upset by the change in plans.

I thought longingly of my phone, wishing the cell towers still worked. But last time we had tried, there had been no signal—not for miles around. Seattle was reporting as dark. Our raiding parties said there weren't any lights left on in the city. What people were still there hid when our scouts came through. Zombies wandered the ruins, and the smell of mold and decay were still heavy, made worse by the warm, wet weather.

Elan and I found a bench near the door and sat down. "Some days this seems a wonderful adventure, and then we see this—" she nodded toward the door— "and I wonder how any of us managed to live to adulthood."

I leaned forward, my elbows on my thighs, clasping my hands between my knees. "I wonder if we should. Some days, I understand why Gaia went so ape-shit crazy on the world. We can't even keep from destroying ourselves, let alone everything else. It's a scary-assed life."

"I've seen worse. I've seen far worse," Elan said, but when I prompted her to tell me what, she shook her head. "No, not today. There's too much pain already. I suppose we should gather some of the servants and get them busy ferrying food and blankets out to the wounded. I'm sure the healers don't have the time to think about that, as well as tending to wounds."

"Let's go talk to Dame Ferrika. She can manage it much better than we can." With a sigh, I stood and held out my hand to Elan. She let me pull her to her feet and, discouraged and out of sorts, we headed into the depths of UnderBarrow.

TWO DAYS LATER, a surprise visitor arrived. Tam and I were walking through the encampment of the wounded when one of our guards from the watchtowers escorted a familiar—and welcome—face into the village.

"Tigra!" I let go of Tam's hand and raced over to the weretiger, grabbing her and hugging her before she could get out a word. "I'm so glad to see you!"

Tigra was a lovely woman, tall and muscular, sturdy as most weretigers were. Her skin was a pale yellow and she had faint black chevrons running up her arms and legs. Her hair was tawny blond, with black highlights. We had last seen each other over six months before. I glanced beyond her to see that her brother, Carson, was following her into camp. He looked winded, whereas Tigra was fresh and peppy.

"You brought your brother—" I paused. "Does that mean that Bend's gone?" Last we had seen Carson, he had been living in Bend. He was a research scientist for an independent laboratory, and the Corp-Rats had tried to shut them down but never managed.

"No, Bend still stands, but the company he worked for is gone. No more electricity. At least not right now. And anybody even suspected to have worked for the government is being driven out. Carson never worked for the Conglomerate, but people mistakenly thought so." The look in Tigra's eyes told me it was worse than just a simple case of mistaken identity, but I didn't want to press, not where others could hear.

"Come on, let's get you settled. Have you come to stay, or are you headed elsewhere with Lightning Strikes?" The organization Tigra had worked for was under Gaia's direct authority and kept a watch out for any resurgence of the Weather Wars.

"That's another thing, but it needs to wait until we can speak privately."

We settled Tigra and Carson in, and then we all met in one of the council chambers. I asked one of the servants to bring an early supper. Once we were settled and the doors were closed against prying ears, Tigra and Carson told us why they were there.

"The quake that happened a couple days ago? Lightning Strikes traced it back to something in this area. It wasn't Lyon, unless he snuck out here. But it wasn't natural, either. The epicenter was pinpointed in Willow Wood."

I stared at her, dumbfounded. "That's impossible. Nobody here has any artifacts. At least that we know of." I paused. "We don't really know, do we? But who would want to destroy the village?"

"Somebody who doesn't like you. You've taken in a number of people from Seattle, haven't you? Have you vetted every one of them? What if there's a spy from the Order of the Black Mist in your midst? You know that Lyon has to be keeping an eye on you, Fury. You're his biggest enemy right now." Tigra shook her head. "This wasn't random happenstance. The quake was triggered from this village, and Lightning Strikes—which is now loosely held together, who knows for how much longer—was able to verify that it wasn't caused by natural forces. We don't know *what* set it off, but we know that it wasn't just a fault rumbling."

Damh Varias spoke. "We should clear Under-Barrow of strangers, Your Majesty. We can't take a chance on anyone targeting you or milady Fury from within the Barrow."

The thought made me wince, but I had to agree. "He's right."

After what Shay had done to Tera and his niece, I had lost any residual naiveté about trusting strangers. I had lost most of it watching my mother be tortured by the Carver.

Tam was in immediate agreement. "I don't like

turning them out, but Willow Wood has space enough, and if we speed up the crews building cottages, there will be shelter for all by winter. Those who are in critical condition may stay—but keep an eye on them. Everyone who wasn't living in the Barrow when we arrived must move to the village. Damh Varias, instruct the guards to begin the transition. I don't anticipate it will take a long time, but best to start immediately."

I folded my arms across my chest. "How many days till Heimdall's done with the explosive?"

"Explosive?" Tigra asked, looking alarmed.

I explained what we were planning. "I will have to sneak back into Seattle, into the Sandspit, and find the gate on the Tree. Once we destroy that, the Order of the Black Mist can attempt to cause all the chaos they want, but they won't be able to bring in the Elder Gods through the portal. And I'm sure they've tried magical means, but it obviously hasn't worked yet."

"Twelve days yet," Jason said, staring straight ahead. He had been awfully quiet lately and we hadn't had a chance to talk for some time. We had both been so busy.

"Twelve days. Does anybody in the village know about our plans? That's the most dangerous scenario—that someone will find out what we're planning and tell Lyon. As long as he thinks we're just futzing around in the woods, then he'll probably be focused on other things." At first, I had thought the idea of a spy in the village was a little too paranoid, but now that Tigra had brought it up, a cold ripple raced up my back.

"Just those of us in this room, I think," Jason said. "Oh, Kendall and Tyrell as well. I don't know if Shevron knows, but she wouldn't tell anyone."

I paused. "Is there a way to tell if we've got a turncoat in our midst? A truth spell?"

"I suppose there is, but right now I suggest we just keep our eyes peeled and keep as tight a ship as we can." Tam pushed back his chair. "Tigra, does Lightning Strikes have any way of finding out what kind of artifact we're looking for? Would it be like the Thunderstrike?"

We had chased down the Thunderstrike, an artifact from the Weather Wars, and managed to steal it away from Lyon's group. At least we had known what we were after and who was carrying it.

I broke in to answer that one. "No, we gave it to Jerako, remember? He destroyed it, I believe."

Tigra pulled out a folder and opened it. "There were only so many weapons made that were like the Thunderstrike and each was unique. Ten of them were destroyed. Two...we have no clue of where they are. The Thunderstrike is now gone, but that leaves one other."

She slid a photo to the center of the table. "This is the Earthshaker. It, too, focused on wind and earthquakes. We believe it was what the Order of the Black Mist used to set off the quake that engendered the tsunami. And yes, we think it was used to set off the most recent quake. If we don't find it soon, whoever has it in their possession could easily destroy this entire area. It would be a suicide stunt, but if they're loyal enough to Lyon, they might try."

With that thought, we moved on to other subjects.

Chapter 8

OVER THE NEXT five days, we managed to secure UnderBarrow and erect large, temporary shelters for those who had lost their homes. Tam ordered all those who were able and not involved in gathering food for the winter or tilling our gardens to help with building sturdy structures to replace the flimsy ones that had been lost. We decided to build several large dormitories for the single men and women, and later on they could build their own cottages if they wanted.

As the building continued, Elan, Jason, Tyrell, Kendall, Tigra, and I tried to keep our eyes open for anybody suspicious, who might possess the Earthshaker. I had my doubts, though. Oh, it would be wonderful to magically run across the spy but the reality was, although things like that happened on occasion, it was too much to expect. Finally, after several fruitless days of trying to gauge who might be our hidden enemy, we gave up.

"This isn't going to work." We were sitting around one of the conference tables. I pulled the calendar to me and stared at the date. In one week, Heimdall would have the explosive ready for me. "We should decide who's going with me and how we're going to get in."

"Who do you want on your team?" Tam asked.

"Jason, Hans, Greta, of course. Tyrell—you and Kendall if you're willing to go." I couldn't ask Tam. UnderBarrow relied on him, and so did Willow Wood.

He seemed to understand, because he gave me a grave smile. "I'd like to come with you."

"Your Majesty—" Damh Varias began, but Tam waved him off.

"I know. I'm needed here."

"I'd like to help, but I think I'd be more of a hin-drance," Tigra said.

"I appreciate the offer, but this is going to be a rough trip." I didn't want to tell her I didn't think she was physically up to the challenge, but the truth was, if she came, I'd be concerned about pro-tecting her and it would cost me my focus.

"I get it. Don't worry about me. I think I'm more useful right here." She winked at me. "I'm strong and sturdy, but I wasn't trained to fight."

"And that's what we will probably have on our hands. We'll be going into zombie territory, and who knows what else. I wish we could teleport there, but I don't know anybody who has that abil-ity besides the gods, and they don't seem inclined to use it to help us." But then I snapped my fingers. "Of course, I know one way we can get there in minutes, but it's draining."

"How?" Jason gave me a suspicious look.

"Through the Crossroads. I wonder if I can get tokens from Hecate?" I hadn't considered it before because the Crossroads was my territory and I wasn't used to other people being there, except for the rare souls I met at the juncture. But it would answer our needs if Hecate thought it possible.

Hans looked slightly nauseated. "I don't think I want to head out on the Crossroads. The mere thought makes me queasy. But I have another idea, though again, it depends on the goodwill of the gods."

"What's that?"

"I can ask Thor if he'll take us in his chariot. That thing can hold a small army—it's like some weird black hole that expands to fit whatever you try to shove in it. It can travel through the astral, so he might be able to take us all."

"I like that idea," Greta said. She and Hans had been married six months and the Valkyrie had really blossomed into her own after getting her wings at her flying-up ceremony, as well as marrying the love of her life. I tried not to think about their wedding because I had been an unwilling volunteer to witness the consummation of their marriage. It had been...eye-opening, and I had been forced to congratulate Greta. She was a lucky woman with what Hans had to offer her. And I had seen *every-thing* he had to offer.

"Can you go ask him now? The sooner we figure

out all of these details, the better. But don't tell anybody else what you're asking. We still have no clue who is hiding the Earthshaker, or whether they're even still here."

"I'll return as quickly as I can." Hans excused himself.

For all we knew, the spy could have been passing through. In one way, I hoped that would be the case. Then again, if they were still out there somewhere with a weapon that could level a city, it meant every city was a potential target.

Elan held up her hand.

"I want to ask you something, Lord Tam."

He inclined his head. "Go ahead."

"I'd like to request sanctuary. I don't intend to return home to Verdanya, even though my father requests that I do so. By refusing to obey, I'll be cast out from my people. May I formally pledge myself to the Bonny Fae and to UnderBarrow as a permanent resident?"

Damh Varias cleared his throat, speaking before Tam had a chance. "Are you sure you've thought through what this means, Elan?"

Elan nodded. "I have. I've been thinking about nothing else for days now. I've considered the consequences, and I want to move forward."

Tam rubbed his head, pinching the top of his nose. I knew what that gesture meant. It meant he had just been jumped by a massive headache. He let out a long, slow, breath before answering. "You realize that this will set your father and me at odds, if I agree?"

"I know it's a great deal to ask. I know that I'm

causing trouble by asking. But I can't bear to go home. If you can't agree, I do understand. I can leave and find another village." Elan's voice was calm, but I knew that beneath that cool exterior, she was treading water, trying desperately to stay afloat. One thing our friendship had taught me—just because she was reserved, didn't mean she was devoid of emotion. Her doe eyes were soft and shimmered in the Barrow light.

"This can't be an easy decision for you," Tam said. He finally let out a slow breath. "You may pledge to the Bonny Fae, and take your place as one of my people. But you *must* inform your father that this is *your* decision. I will not have a war break out if he thinks I'm refusing to let you return home."

Elan leaned back in her chair. "Thank you. I will send him a message. I will make it clear this was my decision, and mine alone."

"Then Damh Varias, will you begin the process of sanctuary?" Tam glanced at me.

I stared at him, clueless.

"Fury, this will be something you'll also have to deal with in the future. So while we wait for Hans to return, let me explain. Whenever a member of the Woodland Fae Court asks to join the Bonny Fae, and vice versa, it's considered a traitorous act. While we act as allies as much as we can, the Woodland Fae and the Bonny Fae have been at odds since the beginning of time. We were once known as the Dark Fae, or the Unseelie Court. Also—the Winter Court. The Woodland Fae were known as the Light Fae, the Seelie Court, and the

Summer Court."

"So you're natural enemies?" I was beginning to see why Elan's request was so daunting.

"Let's say we are not the best of friends, though we don't actively seek out confrontations. At least we don't *now*. There was a time when we were at war and I expect such a time to come again." Tam shrugged. "It is what it is."

"Elan, I will come with you if you want to return to Verdanya." Jason leaned forward, looking like he, too, had a massive headache.

"No. I won't allow my father to cart me off to a secluded existence, and that's what would happen. He'd just stick you amongst one of any nameless nobles—connected to the court by our marriage but nothing else." She turned to Damh Varias. "Please, make the arrangements. I will send a message to my father. There will be no going back."

"As you wish, Elan."

There wasn't much to say after that. Tigra told us about their harrowing journey and how the Lightning Strikes team had been caught by the tsunami, stranded on a rooftop for several days first by the water and then, after the waves retreated, zombies waiting below.

"We lost three members, sadly. We weren't prepared for the secondary wave rolling in. Headquarters hadn't been able to notify us. We scrambled to the top of the tallest building we were near, but three of our team didn't make it," she said. "It was harrowing. I'll never forget Matt's screams as the waters sucked him under. There was nothing we could do. No way we could reach him."

"What did you do after that?" Jason asked.

"We managed to make our way to Bend, where we stayed with my brother until we knew what was going down. Unfortunately, the organization couldn't come get us. Also, the main headquarters in Atlantea went down. Radio silence, as the Order of the Black Mist moved into the capital. We've been able to receive scattered reports from our people in Bifrost—that's how we got the report about the Earthshaker—but it's random. We're doomed as an organization, and it won't be much longer before we'll only be a memory, like so many other things in this world."

As we absorbed that somber piece of news, Hans returned, followed by Thor.

I tried not to laugh. The massive Norse god looked out of place in the chamber council. Thor had also let his beard grow over the past six months since he first joined us, and now it reached his belly, making him look like a gorgeous but scary bogey.

He pulled out one of the chairs and gingerly sat on it, as if he expected it to give way under his weight. "So, Hans has been telling me that you are requesting that I ferry you to Seattle in my chariot."

I almost choked on my coffee. "I didn't exactly ask."

"No worries, girl. I like helping out." The rumbling god actually did seem pleased at being included in the plans.

I zipped my lip and graciously accepted. "Thank you, then. How long will it take us to reach the area near the World Tree?"

"Oh, with my chariot, a couple of hours, depending on what turbulence I find in the astral plane. Of course, my chariot can hold up to about fifty people, so if you want to go en masse with a contingent of guards, I say the more the merrier." He seemed absolutely jolly about the idea.

I glanced at Tam. "What do you think? Go in with a force?"

"I think taking a few extra guards would be a good idea. Not fifty, but maybe five to ten extra?" Tam's eyebrow was twitching and I had the feeling he was trying to suppress a laugh. Before I could answer, Thor set his hammer on the table. It immediately broke through and landed on the floor next to his feet. Hans jumped back, narrowly escaping his toes being crushed.

"Oops, sorry about that," Thor said. He hefted the hammer and sat it on his lap. "Didn't think the table would give way."

"No problem," Tam said, staring at the hole. "They don't make them like they used to."

"So when do we leave?"

"Next week, as soon as Heimdall finishes the explosive. So we go in your chariot. Jason, Kendall, Tyrell, Hans, and Greta are coming with me along with five extra guards. We need to plan on Lyon meeting us there. I'm *hoping* he won't catch word of our plans, but given the fact that we think there's a spy in our midst, I wouldn't be surprised."

"I'd mark it as a sure bet," Tigra said. "I don't buy the premise that the spy's left Willow Wood. And my guess is that they haven't used the Earthshaker again not out of any kindness, but because they can't."

She cleared her throat. "The ancient weapons from the Weather Wars required a great deal of energy. One use would expend it until the weapon was recharged. Most of them were recharged magically. That means that if whoever has the Earthshaker *isn't* a magician, he's going to have to find a different way to siphon energy to fuel it. But the moment he manages to recharge it, my guess is that he'll use it again, and probably with a worse effect. Actually, there's another factor that could wipe out your village and it wouldn't even require the artifact. I highly recommend you keep a double duty of guards watching out for any signs of it."

"What's that?" Tam asked.

"Wildfire. We're in high summer and it's dry enough that a forest fire could take out everything here without the proper means to fight it. Well, except for UnderBarrow proper—you can keep that safe, I assume. But a fire could wipe out the village and a lot of people along with it. And all it takes to start a fire is some kindling, a dry patch of under-growth, and a spark."

Tam's eyes grew wide. "I hadn't even thought of that. Damh Varias—go now, and set an extra watch for fire. Beef up the guards and tell them to watch for anything suspicious. Also, make a rule—no fires outside the village. And a burn ban on fires in private dwellings. People can eat communally for the time being and can bring their foods and cook them at the central grill pits."

Damh Varias nodded. "Yes, Your Majesty."

"Fire is a deadly weapon and too easy to use, especially now that we're out of the rainy season." I frowned. "Maybe we should create a firebreak around the village. Take down all the potential fuel for fires before anybody else gets the idea."

"Another good idea. Damh, set that in motion as well. Make certain the guards keep water on hand at their stations."

By the time we finished our meeting, we were all feeling the strain. I caught up with Tigra as she headed back toward her chambers.

"Do you have any clue who might have the Earthshaker?"

She shook her head. "No, unfortunately, or I would have told you immediately. And it's fruitless to go looking for it, unless you plan to search through every shelter. Even then, chances are the spy would hide it somewhere else before anybody reached them."

"Unless they were surprised. We could ask everyone to gather and then, keeping them ringed with guards, go through the dwellings." But even as I said it, I knew that wasn't a viable plan. "What can you tell me about the artifact? Does it look like the Thunderstrike?"

"No, this is more like a little black box. It has a field of hidden buttons, but it looks like a cube about the size of small box of chocolates." She rested a hand on my arm. "There's no way to know what it is by simply looking at it. You have to see it in action to know that it's anything but a shiny black cube of metal."

"At least that gives me something to go on." I

paused. "I'm sorry I can't take you with me."

"I'm not cut out for it. I know that and it's all right. I don't expect to go, though I'd love to see the end of this. At least the end of the threat from the Elder Gods of Chaos. The Order of the Black Mist can still try to open other gateways, but things are breaking down so much that I predict within another six months, even their organization will fall into the very anarchy it seeks to instill on the world. They didn't consider that by destroying the communications infrastructure, they also destroyed their own ability to communicate with their various cells."

"Small favors, I guess." I stopped at the intersection of passages leading to Tigra's guest quarters. "I'll leave you here, then. I have a few errands to run."

"I'm tired, anyway. I think I'll take a nap."

As I headed back down the corridor, she slipped into her room. The world had shifted a hell of a lot since we had first met some eight months back.

A COUPLE DAYS later, I was looking all over for Jason. I finally found him by the lake. He was flying over the water, soaring as the updraft caught him under the wings. Another hawk came into view, and circled him, playing. A noise from the water startled me. Leonard popped his head up, surfacing as he stood on the shoal that led up to the shore.

"Hey, Fury," he said. He wiped the water out of his eyes and squinted against the sun. Then, pointing at the two hawks, he said, "That's Mom and Uncle Jason, in case you didn't know."

"I figured one of them was Jason. Somebody told me he was out flying over the lake. I didn't know your mother was with him." I sat on one of the driftwood logs that lay across the beach, providing a handy seat from which to watch the water. I patted the seat next to me. "Come, sit down. We haven't had the chance to talk for a while."

He shook himself off like a puppy dog, splashing water every which way, then padded over, wincing as he crossed the pebbles.

"Damn, those are rough on the feet," he said, sitting next to me. "So, here we are. Miles from nowhere." Leonard was going through another growth spurt. He had added another four inches over the summer, and now he was almost as tall as Jason and definitely taller than me.

"You're growing too fast." I winked at him. "I remember when you were a baby and I babysat you. You loved your crib and never wanted out of there."

"Oh, no. Not you too. Mom never lets up on how big I'm getting." He licked his lips, staring at the ground. "I wish I was an adult."

"Don't wish away time. It goes too fast as it is."

"I suppose, but I just want the freedom to go after what I want. But my life isn't going quite the way I thought it would."

I patted his arm. "None of us are going to live the lives we thought we were."

"Yeah…" He paused. "Do you miss it? The city?"

"Yeah, I do. But it's gone, and all that's left there is death and decay. And zombies."

"And zombies." Another pause. Then, "Fury, can I ask you something?"

I nodded. "I don't promise to answer, but of course you can ask."

"You were younger than me when you first came to live with my uncle, right?"

"I was thirteen." I glanced at him. He looked like he was debating asking something. "What is it, Len? What do you want to know?"

"I just… When my mom starts bugging the hell out of me, I guess, I think about you. You don't have a mother. You lost her when you were barely a teenager. Do you think I'm a bad person because sometimes I wish I didn't have a mother?"

The angst of youth. It never failed to raise its head, whether in the inner city or out in the wilds. I tried to hide my smile. Leonard and Shevron had a volatile relationship. It hadn't always been that way, but as he hit his mid-teens, he had been trying to stretch out toward adulthood, and the ways in which he attempted to grow hadn't always been the wisest.

"No," I said softly, thinking over my words. "I think that I even felt that way at times, before I lost Marlene. But there's a difference between the occasional thought and the wish for harm. I take it you feel guilty because of feeling this way?"

"Well, yeah, I guess. I mean, your mother was…"

"She was killed by a serial killer, Len. She was tortured and murdered. Do I think that I caused that because of my anger at her? Not in the least. If I had known what was going to happen, I probably would still have had days where I wanted her out of my life. It's a normal feeling for a teenager. But don't nurse the anger, and don't let it linger. Enjoy what you can because someday, she may not be there for you. And you don't ever want to regret destroying a relationship that means so much."

He brought his feet up on the log, stretching out so he was lying on it with his head by my side. "I know you're right. And I'm not as angry as I was six months ago. That's one thing Verdanya did for me—they taught me to channel my frustration into work. But I can't wait to grow up and start my own life."

"Hey," I said, brushing my hand over his forehead. "You already have. Even though she still can tell you what to do, the fact is, you started your own life the day you were born. Remember this, and it will make it easier: no matter who you are, or how old, there will always be somebody who can tell you what to do or not to do. For me, it's Hecate. For Tam, it's the High Queen and King of the Bonny Fae. For your uncle, it's the Cast. And for your mother, too."

He was silent for a moment as we watched the two hawks gliding side by side. They were making synchronous turns, diving and pulling out at the same time. It looked like an exhilarating freedom.

"I wish I could fly. I wish I had inherited my mother's nature rather than my father." Len rolled to a sitting position, gazing up at the hawks. "I don't belong in the Cast, Fury. Uncle Jason wants me to pretend I do. My mom tells me not to worry about it. But I'm not *like* them. I can't fly. I don't know what it means to have the bond they do. How can I be part of something when there's no connection?"

I thought about his question. It was a valid one, and eventually he'd have to make a decision. The Cast was introverted. They didn't open to strangers easily, and while they would accept Leonard if he played by the rules, the fact was he would never be at home among them.

"What do you want to do? I know things have changed so drastically since we lived in Seattle, but given where we're at now, what do you want to do with your life?"

He worried his lower lip for a moment. "Honestly? I want to become a guard. I want to join Lord Tam's guard. There are people who aren't Bonny Fae living in UnderBarrow. Heck, you're going to become queen there—so it's not quite like the Cast, where you have to be one of them to really be accepted, is it?"

"No, actually it's not," I said. "Let me talk to Tam, and then to your mother and uncle. Maybe I can figure out something. You're not too young to start training."

"You'd talk to them for me?" His eyes lit up.

"Yes, but you have to promise to let me do it in my own way. If you push Jason and Shevron before I've had a chance to talk them into thinking about it, they'll resist and you won't have anything to show for it. I know them—and trust me, what you are asking them won't go over well. If I make the suggestion, they may actually give it consideration." I gave him a stern look. "Promise you'll keep your nose clean till then?"

He laughed. "I promise. And Fury, thanks." He glanced back at the lake. "They're coming in to land now."

Jason and Shevron arced gracefully in the air, spiraling lower with each circle. Then, as if they were mirror images, they landed on a nearby log and, in a blurry shimmer, transformed back into their human forms. All Jason would ever tell me about their clothes disappearing and reappearing with them was that it was hawk-magic.

Shevron stretched, yawning loudly as Jason let out a resounding laugh. Flying always seemed to calm them down.

"Fury! Hey, what's up?" Jason jogged over and, after high-fiving Leonard, sat down beside me. "Is anything wrong?"

"Nothing more than usual. We haven't had a chance to really talk for a while, and before we head into Seattle, I thought it would be nice to catch up."

Shevron joined us, but she declined to sit. "I need to get back to the village. I'm on KP duty tonight. Len, you too, son."

He started to grumble but, with one look from me, shrugged. "Sure thing. Bye, Uncle J. Bye, Fury."

"Make me something good to eat," Jason called after them as they headed toward the trail. He closed his eyes. "Listen to the waves on the lake. I love it out here, you know. The rest of the Cast is thinking of moving up here. They may start their own village nearby. We never thought about that in the past, but now, it makes sense."

"Seattle's a ghost town, but when you think about it, it's seeded so many enclaves and villages." I paused. "Hecate and I are talking about opening a training center. I'd train those who have the talent how to hunt down and kill Abominations. Right now, I'm one of the few who really know how to attack them. They're coming through a lot of the World Trees now, Hecate found out. So I'll be Queen of UnderBarrow, and the sensei of a movement."

Jason blinked. "Really? So you'll be like the founder. What does Tam think about this?"

"He's down with it. Hecate will be meeting with him soon to discuss what sort of structure we'll need. It will need to house students, and we have to figure out how to get the word out. Hecate's taking care of that part. I'm supposed to start figuring out a lesson plan, once I'm done with the little matter of destroying the portal to Chaos, and then my coronation and wedding."

"You really love Tam, don't you?" Jason picked up a rock and chucked it at the water, skipping it across the surface.

I watched the ripples spread out in concentric rings. "More than I thought possible. You know, when I had a crush on you all those years, I thought love was...something it's *not*. There's a big difference between infatuation and love."

Jason lowered his gaze, staring at his feet. "I still feel horrible about not telling you about your mother and me. But Fury, even if that had never taken place, you know that we never would have worked. We're too different. I could never look at you in that way. I admit, I never expected Tam to slip in and win your heart. He's good at keeping his feelings masked. But I guess we've ended up with the people we need to be with."

"Oh, I know. I adore you, but sometimes I want to beat some sense into that thick head of yours. You and me? We make good friends. I'm glad you and Elan found each other, by the way. You're happier with her than I ever thought you were with Eileen."

"Eileen—I would have been a good husband to her. But being a *good* spouse doesn't necessarily mean being a *happy* spouse, you know?"

"I know." I leaned back, resting my head against a curve in the massive log. "So, good flight today?"

"The best. Good wind, good weather. It's nice to be able to get out and fly more. Shevron and I are making a habit of doing so regularly. Len likes to come along. I wish the kid could join us," he said wistfully.

"Hmm, about that." Now was as good a time as any.

"What? You have something you need to tell me about him?" Jason instantly assumed his stern-uncle look. I knew that look from when I was a kid, and the lectures that followed had never been pleasant.

"Nothing bad, so chill out. In fact, Len and I had quite the talk while you two were up in the sky." I waited for a beat, then said, "He wants so badly to find his own way in life."

"I know, but his place is with the Cast."

"The Cast isn't anywhere near here, and you know as well as I do that he'll never fit in there. You just don't want to admit it."

Jason frowned, staring at the rocks beneath our feet. "I owe my loyalty to the Cast."

"Yes, but you also have a responsibility to your nephew. Your responsibility—as well as his mother's—is to see that Leonard becomes the happiest and most productive young man he can be. And you know as well as I do that he can't do that in the Cast. You think it's none of my business—gods know, you've told me that before—but he lives in Willow Wood, so he *is* my business. I'm going to be queen over this little plot of land we've staked out as home. Tam's people will be my people, and that includes everybody who lives in the village."

If what I said offended Jason, at least he didn't show it. He narrowed his eyes, but finally let out a deep sigh. "What are you thinking?"

"Len told me what he wants to do. I happen to think it's a good idea."

"And what is that? Because he hasn't told his mother or me."

"That's because he knows you don't want to hear it." I paused. "Even Shevron knows he doesn't fit in with the Cast. What do they hold for him, Jason? He can't fly, he's not a hawk-shifter. He'll become a second-class citizen. You know that I love you and Shevron, but let's face it, the Cast is exclusionary. You exclude anybody who doesn't meet your standards. And even if he tries two hundred percent, Len will never be a full member of the Cast."

A pained look washed across Jason's face. "Do you see us as that cruel, then?"

"You aren't, but your social structure is."

"What does he want to do? I'll listen." This was the first time Jason showed any interest in discovering what his nephew's hopes and dreams were, and I sure wasn't going to waste it.

"He wants to join Tam's guard, like Elan did."

I expected an explosion, but it never materialized.

After a few minutes, Jason cocked his head to the side. "Really? He told you that?"

"Yes, he did. But he's scared to tell you and Shevron, because he doesn't think that you'll care for the idea. He can make a contribution to UnderBarrow in a way that he couldn't if he joins the Cast."

I hung my head. "When I first came to live with you, it became very apparent, very quickly, that I could never fully be a part of your world. I was a Theosian, not a hawk-shifter. At times it hurt and I felt excluded, but I shrugged it off because I had a destiny. I belonged to Hecate, so it didn't matter so much. Leonard needs something of his own. He needs something that doesn't feel like he's just marking time, tolerated because his mother is Cast."

We watched the water as the wind picked up, rippling waves toward the shore. Jason finally turned to me. "He really wants this?"

"Yes. I heard it in his voice."

"Then I'll talk to Shevron and Tam. Because

I don't want him running off or sliding onto the wrong path. I guess I should thank you, even though it rankles to think that..."

"That being part of the Cast can't solve every problem?"

He snorted, flicking my nose gently with his thumb and forefinger. "No, dork. It rankles me because I want so very much for him to feel part of the bigger family. But I guess that's never going to happen." He paused. "You and Elan are getting closer."

"I like her. She's honest and she's smart. And I'm glad she's staying, to be honest. Are you happy about that?"

"I'm not happy it will strip her away from her family, but she's not a princess to sit in an ivory tower and be waited on. And I doubt they would ever agree to let her be anything else now that her father is king. So, yeah, I am happy. I want to be with my child, and..." He paused.

"What?" I recognized that "aha" look.

"And I wouldn't have a place in their culture. Even though they would make space for me, I'd always feel on the outside."

I smiled softly. "Like Len and the Cast?"

He exhaled a soft breath. "Yeah, like Len." After a pause, he said, "Shall we get back to the village?"

I shook my head. I loved the peace and quiet, especially when I was near the lake. "You go ahead. I think I'll stay for a while longer. To breathe for a time."

With that, Jason pressed a quick kiss to my forehead and headed back to Willow Wood, and I returned to watching the lake, letting the sound of the lapping waters gently cushion my nerves.

Chapter 9

BY THE NIGHT before Heimdall was supposed to deliver the explosive, Leonard was ready to begin his training with the guard. Shevron had strenuously objected, but Jason and I overruled her and she finally backed down. I joined them to watch his formal induction.

Leonard was there in full uniform—a blue tunic over a pair of black trousers. He looked scared, but eager, and was standing in a line with four other young men and two young women. All six of the others were Bonny Fae.

Jason was talking with Elan, off to one side.

The chambers housing the guards were spacious, with the barracks at the end of the passageway. There were several training rooms, the armory, and the Guard Hall—where we were. The chamber was huge, filled with tables and benches for the guards when they came in from their shifts to eat. The tables had been moved to the side, and the benches were lined up in rows for those of us who came to witness the induction. Several other families were here, milling around, no doubt the parents and siblings of the other recruits.

In the front of the hall was a large throne, though not as large as Tam's main seat in the throne room. Four members of the guard surrounded it, one to each corner. As we waited, Shevron swung around, confronting me.

"This is your fault," she said, keeping her voice low but steady.

Shevron had been angry at me before, mostly when I was in my teens and doing stupid things, but she had always laced her words with love. This time, all I heard was hostility.

"I knew he didn't belong in the Cast, but I never wanted my son to wield a *weapon*."

"I understand your feelings, but Shevron, like it or not, he's going to grow up and do what he wants. Leonard has a lot of energy. He can harness it in a productive manner instead of running off half-cocked to join a vampire's nest, like he almost did last year. Or instead of charging out to fight lycanthropes like he tried when we got attacked a few months back."

"He's *my* son! You don't get a say in his life. Jason has the right, but you don't. *You're not Cast.*"

"No, and neither is Len, as you admitted a few minutes ago." I shook my head. "Be angry with me all you like, but Leonard is fifteen and in the world we live in now, that makes him a man. Soon enough, he'd feel useless and run off on his own, probably get himself killed. Would that be better than seeing him in uniform?"

A bitter note filled Shevron's voice. "I wanted him to go to the university. To study and make something of himself. Now, he's just going to be another servant, cannon fodder. And it will be your fault. Jason told me that you talked to Len about this."

"University? What world are you living in? There *is* no more university. No more life the way we knew it. There's nothing but a harsh world out there now, Shevron. Leonard told me what he wanted to do and I told Jason. Will he learn to fight? Yes, but he'll also be taught to reason and to think. You know perfectly well that Tam doesn't keep an army of hooligans. You know that. Every one of his guards can read and write. That's as close as you'll get to sending him to the university."

Her glare was steady, though, and I realized I wasn't getting through her anger. She only saw me as interfering with her parenting, not being a voice of reason.

I paused, then softly said, "Shevron, the world's changed. Seattle is dead. Hell, the entire country is dead. And if you wanted him to go overseas? How would that happen? We don't even have rudimentary communications with the nations across the ocean. We're lucky to hear anything out of the Canadian Empire."

She wavered for a moment, then deflated, as if all the anger and worry had suddenly drained from her body. "I worked so hard to build my business.

I tried so hard to give him a steady footing. And now, all of that's gone. Everything I built was for nothing."

I realized she wasn't just mourning her son taking up a trade she didn't like, but her own business. She was a single mother, and it must have felt that everything she had built had been swept away with the tsunami. But even if we were able to destroy every last zombie in Seattle, the city was a pile of rubble.

"Why don't you start a bakery here? There's nothing to stop you. We can surely salvage enough supplies for you for a year or so, until we have our own crops."

She paused, glancing at me. "You think that would be possible?"

"I know it. I'll talk to Tam. We'll make it happen. Unless you'd prefer to work in UnderBarrow with the bakers there. But I think Willow Wood could use a dose of your sweets. I know I could. This isn't an easy change for anybody. It might go down better with a spoon or two of sugar on top."

She frowned. "I'll need to figure out how to bake on a wood stove, but it can't be that hard. I'll need a stove, in fact. Do you think that the next raiding party could possibly bring me back all the equipment I need?"

I didn't want to promise anything, so I just said, "Let me talk to Tam. We'll figure out how to get you situated, but as for learning to bake on a wood stove, I know just the woman to teach you—Memy Pendrake. I'll introduce you later. After we're done why don't you take a walk through the village and find a spot for your shop? Up-Cakes doesn't have to be a memory."

She laughed. "I think I'll be baking a lot more bread than I did. That's more important than éclairs."

"Yeah, but don't skimp on the cupcakes, all right?" I pointed toward the front, where Damh Varias had appeared from the door to the left of the throne. "They're about to begin."

We settled down as Jason and Elan joined us.

A loud trumpet sounded from near the throne. The herald was announcing Tam's arrival. My breath caught in my throat as he entered in full dress regalia. Tam wasn't just Tam today, he was the Lord of UnderBarrow. I had seen him in dress uniform before, but today he wore the colors of the guard, with a flowing blue cape that billowed out as he walked, and he was carrying his ceremonial sword—an antique that looked ancient and ornate. Tam wore his power today, and I felt a welling up of awe and nervous joy when I realized that he was going to be my husband. He approached the throne as the herald announced him in.

"Stand for Lord Tam, Prince of the Bonny Fae Nation, King of UnderBarrow."

A fleeting thought crossed my mind. UnderBarrow was returning to a more formal approach. Tam had always been well loved as the ruler, but now, it was as though the formality had increased, and the attention to tradition was stronger than I had seen before.

We stood until he ascended to the throne and turned. Then he waved for us to sit as he did.

"Welcome, families and friends of our newest guard-elect members. Today you will see your loved ones sworn into the Guard. This is a momentous occasion in their lives. Today they will pledge their honor, life, and blood to the throne and to UnderBarrow, to serve and protect UnderBarrow and all of its citizens. They will no longer belong to your families, but to the Court. This is a joyous occasion. They are starting a glorious adventure, and it is my honor to welcome them," Tam said, his voice reverberating through the room.

He motioned to the head of the Guard—Lt. Dashell—who was standing near. Dashell approached the throne and knelt. Tam bade him rise.

"With Your Majesty's approval, may I present the newest recruits requesting to become members of the UnderBarrow Elite Guard?"

"Proceed." Tam stood, unsheathing his sword. It glistened in the light of the hall.

Dashell motioned the seven teens to move forward. One by one, they approached the throne, where he introduced them, and they knelt. He came to Len.

"Leonard Aerie, of the Hawk-shifter Cast."

"Your Majesty," Leonard murmured, going down on one knee like the others. They all remained in front of Tam, on bended knee.

Tam nodded to Dashell. "Administer the oath."

"Recruits, I present to you the oath of allegiance. Repeat after me." As he administered the oath, he paused after each sentence and the recruits answered in unison. They must have been practicing because even though their voices were shaking, they didn't miss a single word.

"I swear, upon my life, to honor UnderBarrow as my nation, and Lord Tam as my King. I pledge my life in the service of the King and the Nation. I leave my family and my former life to enter the service of the Guard. I will listen and learn, and obey my superiors without question. I will remain vigilant and watchful, and protect UnderBarrow and its people, enforcing the laws and regulations with my very life. By my blood, I bind myself to the Guard until the day I die, or until I petition for release, and receive my freedom from Lord Tam himself."

As they finished reciting the oath, Tam descended the steps of the throne and walked to the first youth. He tapped her lightly on the shoulders and head with his sword.

"I accept your service. Rise now, as a member of the Guard. Do not dishonor your uniform or your oath."

He made his way through all seven of the teens, ending with Len. As Leonard rose, Shevron choked back tears. But he was beaming when he turned with the others as all the families erupted in cheers. I nudged Shevron with my elbow, and she stood with Jason and me, cheering even though I could tell her heart wasn't in it. By the time Leonard was allowed to come over to speak to us, she had managed to wipe away her tears.

"You do what you're told, son." She stared at him, reaching out to straighten his tunic. "No more rebellion."

He nodded. "I will, ma'am." A tinge of pride

filled his voice, and he broke out into a wide smile. "Thank you for letting me join. I know you don't approve, but I'm going to make you proud."

Shevron let out a long sigh. "Make yourself proud, son. I'm already proud of you. Be go—" She had started to say "Be good," but she stopped herself. "Be careful. Do what you're told. I expect you to visit me when you're allowed time off."

For the first six months, Leonard would be totally immersed in training and we had been warned that he wouldn't be allowed to visit family until the training was over, not even during his downtime. The only time he would be allowed to talk with us was if there was an emergency, or when we were in passing.

"I will. I promise." He gave her a long hug and a kiss on the cheek. "This is what I want, Mom. Please don't be mad at Fury and Uncle J. They were just helping me feel like I have something of my own."

Shevron closed her eyes for a moment, then opened them. They were watery—I could see the tears close to the surface, but she plastered a smile across her face. "I'll support your choice, Len. You know I love you. Never forget that."

A whistle blew and he quickly gave Jason a hug, then me. He whispered, "Thanks, Fury. This wouldn't have happened without you. I owe you one." And then, before we could say anything more, he hurried back to Dashell and the other recruits, and they filed out of the room, off to their new lives.

The other families were mingling, but Shevron

turned to Jason and me. "I think I'll go for a walk. Then, since you're so good at making dreams come true, Fury, maybe you can help me pick a spot for my new bakery."

I pulled her to me and gave her a long hug. "You're going to be fine, Shevron," I whispered. "And Leonard will be fine, too. New lives. New paths."

TAM AND I were in his chamber, snuggling under the covers. He ran his hand over my bare shoulder. "I'm terrified, you know. Tomorrow, you head into danger and I'm so afraid that you'll be hurt. I'd lock you up here if I thought I could get away with it, but I know that this is something you have to do. Not just for yourself, but for the world."

"Heimdall will be here in the morning," I said, rolling to a sitting position. I wrapped my arms around my knees and Tam pulled me into his embrace, holding me against his shoulder. I hesitated, then said, "I'm afraid, too, and not just of what lies ahead in Seattle. I'm afraid of seeing what's become of the city. It's been six months. While the raiding parties have told us what to expect, seeing it is going to bring it all home."

"I know." Tam's hair tickled my shoulders as he pressed his lips against my temples and then said, "*Iya eser ovair fre saswen. Thia ayr ais thogham.*"

"I love you too," I said softly. "And I'll come

back. I promise." But my voice was shaking as I thought about Lyon and the remains of Seattle, and what we were setting out to do. Hecate had trained me hard over the past six months and I was in possession of a great deal more power. My fire burned strong within me, but we had no clue what to expect.

"The world is such a big place." I turned my head to gaze in Tam's eyes. "And sometimes I feel like such a very small part of it."

"We all are just dust specks in the scheme of things, but what we do matters. Every person who has ever lived matters because we *all* affect the world, whether in good or bad ways. Whether we only live for a day, or for a thousand years. History remembers those whose actions affected millions, but each family remembers their own. Parents remember their children. Victims remember their attackers. And lovers remember their loves." Tam pulled me down into his arms, laying me back.

"Do you?"

"Do I what?"

"Do you remember all of your loves?" I wanted to hear him say "Yes." I wanted to hear that he never forgot those women whom he had loved and left behind. Because even though I was a Theosian and was looking at a vastly longer lifetime than I would have had as a human, the Fae were even longer lived and I knew that one day, Tam would remember me with his past loves.

"I do," he said, his hand moving to stroke my breast. "I remember them all. I remember their names, and the sounds of their voices. And I still love them, like I'll forever love you. But Fury, it's been a long, long time since I've loved anybody the way I love you. You're my heart song. You're my passion."

I kissed him, then, pulling him close to me. We had made love twice already, but I felt like I couldn't get enough of him. I wanted to feel his body under my fingers, I wanted to feel his hardness inside of me, moving and shifting. I wanted him to take possession of me again and again, to ride me until I couldn't walk, to own every inch of me.

"Make me yours," I said. "Make me yours, with every touch and movement."

He kissed me, and he went on kissing me, deeply, long and dark and pulling me into his world with the brush of his lips. He kissed me, and I fell into the dark brilliance of his alien nature. The Bonny Fae wore passion like I wore my fire, and when Tam's passion met my flame, they ignited like wildfire, crackling as the glowing sparks showered every inch of skin, every place he touched me. Every nerve trembled as he worked his way down to my breast, and lower.

And as I cried out, he returned to lean over me, working his way inside, spreading my thighs with his weight, moving at first so slowly that I could barely feel the wave. Then he drove faster and faster, carrying me with him as we tumbled into a flare of hunger and need. Another moment, and sweet relief showered through me, holding me taut, until the wave crested and then, slowly, receded. Tam cried out as I held him to my chest.

Wishing the night could never end, we fell into that soft afterglow, and then, into a deep, dreamless sleep.

MORNING ARRIVED AND, after an early morning reprise of the night before, Tam let me get out of bed. I bathed, then kissed him before returning to my room to suit up for the journey. Heimdall had left word with the guards he would meet us for breakfast with the explosive.

Patrice was waiting for me. She had my leather shorts ready, and a leather corset. It would be warm, but protective. I suited up, staring at myself in the mirror. "Braid my hair, if you would, Patrice."

"Yes, milady." She paused. "How long till you return, milady?"

"I'm not sure, Patrice. We're hoping it won't take too long. Or be difficult." I didn't want to think ahead. Not when we were so close to going in. Nothing else had happened in Willow Wood since the earthquake and I prayed nothing more would.

Patrice seemed to sense my reticence, and she fell silent as she braided my hair and helped me on with my boots. She brought out my sword and dagger while I focused on centering myself.

"Thank you." I slung Xan over my shoulder and belted my dagger to my thigh. "I guess it's time to go meet them in council."

"If I may be so bold, good luck, milady. And

please be careful. I love being your maid."

I smiled then, and pulled her in for a hug. She looked startled, but happy. "I'm glad. You'll be my lady's maid, you know, when I wed Lord Tam. Meanwhile, watch over things here. Keep an eye on Elan, if you would."

"I will."

As I left the room, I prayed that I would be returning to it. But so many variables were at play that I didn't want to jinx the future. I headed toward the council chamber.

EVERYBODY WAS WAITING for me. I entered, and immediately my gaze fell on Heimdall, who was sitting beside Thor and Hecate, chatting amiably about something going on at the Temple Valhalla.

"Fury," Tam said as he stood. "My love, please sit by me."

I walked over and slowly sat down after slipping Xan off my back. I had learned that lesson the hard way. "Everybody's here already. I'm sorry I'm late."

"Not a problem." Tam cleared his throat. "If we could begin."

"Of course," Heimdall said, setting something on the table that looked like a tray with nine children's blocks in it. "Here you go. Nine charges. It was all I had time to make, but it should be plenty."

I stared at the gray cubes. Each one would fit

in my palm, and the tray itself was square, fitting three across and three down. The entire thing was about six inches wide by six inches long, and about three inches high. Small and compact, it was capable of destroying a magical portal. Shivering a little, I started to pull it toward me, then paused.

"Tell me what I need to know. Tell everyone, because that way if something happens to me, then somebody else can set the charge. I may be the only one who can find the portal, but we need to have backup to set the actual explosion. Just in case."

"First, you can put it in your pack and carry it without worry. I have the triggers here. They have to be affixed into the holes on top of the blocks. The only caveat I'll give you on that is do not allow the holes to get clogged. Keep them in a protective bag so they don't get any dirt or mud in them. Keep the triggers separate until you're ready to use them. Once you plug them in, you'll have one minute to get away."

"In other words, I probably shouldn't just throw them into the portal and run?"

"No, because if the chargers come loose, they won't work. You need to set them up, all together, right at the base of the portal. Then jump back through and get the hell away from there. Thing is, you have to set them up *through* the portal—on the other side, not on this side. They will only work from the inside of the realm you're attempting to close off."

I frowned, mulling over the info. "Which means, I have to actually *enter* the realm of Chaos in order to destroy the portal. And I will have one minute to exit after setting the explosives."

"Correct." Heimdall shrugged. "I wanted to give you a longer escape time, but the Horn Resounding was firm on that. You see, the horn, when blown, can topple mountains if it so chooses. I asked it to create a concussion to destroy the gate, and this is what it gave me for the magic. I would go with you, but it's not my battle to fight, other than what help I was able to offer. Use them wisely—I won't be allowed to make another set. That, too, was made clear."

I lifted the tray and set it in front of me. The nine blocks looked innocuous enough, but together, they could bring down a vortex. "Where are the triggers?"

Heimdall placed a bag on the table. "Here. But I caution you again, do not carry them in the same bag with the explosives."

I picked up my pack and tucked the explosives in one pocket, and the triggers in another. "All right. So, Thor, you're taking us?"

"Yes. I can take you as far as the edge of the Bogs. I'll wait there for your return. Odin has proscribed me taking you any farther in this matter. You see, we're interfering with something Gaia created and we can only intrude so far before the Norns bar our attempts. Like the Fates, they limit what and when we can interfere."

I frowned, and not at his comment about the Norns. "The Bogs? That doesn't make sense. They're on the opposite side of the Sandspit."

"Not anymore," Thor said. "Remember? They've

expanded. You'll find a great deal has changed since you were there. Getting through the Bogs won't be easy. Take weapons with you and be prepared to use them."

My heart sank. If things had changed that much, we weren't going to be able to just march in and get this over with. "Anything else we should know?"

"Not that I know of, but I'm sure there is. Best to just be prepared for the unexpected." He leaned back, his arms folded across his burly chest.

"Then the sooner we get moving, the sooner we get this over with." I stood. "Are we ready?"

"I've had provisions set for you, and we've included everything we can think of that you might need to make the journey," Tam said. "I wish I could accompany you."

"You're the King—" Damh Varias began, but Tam waved aside his protest.

"I know. We're all aware of that."

We had been preparing for this for a month, and there was no going back now. Tam stood, holding out his hand to me. I took his fingers in mine, bringing them to my lips.

"I love you. Please, take care of yourself," he said. "*Thia ayr ais thogham.*"

"I'll come back to you. I promise you. I love you."

I leaned in and kissed him, trying to keep decorum, but he pulled me to him and pressed his lips against mine in a dark, passionate kiss. I felt a rush of strength fill my body, and realized he was sacrificing energy to shore me up. I accepted his offering, drifting as his power merged into mine. We stood, frozen, creating a loop of energy, a circle running from him into me back to him again. After a moment, I finally broke away and, without a word, turned back to the others.

When I could find my voice again, I asked, "Hecate, are you coming?"

"I will be on the Crossroads, waiting should you need me. Queet will go with you." She shimmered out of sight.

Elan and Jason spent a moment in the corner of the room, saying good-bye. I saw him press a ring onto her finger, but said nothing. It was a private moment, and they would announce their engagement when they were ready. But I understood the need to formalize things. What we were about to do felt a lot like a one-way ride.

After saying our good-byes, Thor led us out of UnderBarrow to where his chariot was parked. The goats looked as excited as dogs waiting for a walk. They were bouncing around, straining at their harnesses.

Thor motioned for us to file into the chariot, one by one. I waited till last, and then, with one last look at Tam, Shevron, Elan, and Damh Varias, who were standing to the side of the chariot, I entered the vehicle, ducking my head to enter the storage area. It felt like I was in the belly of a great ship. The next moment, Thor stepped aboard, and we were off and running, crossing the worlds as we headed back to Seattle and to the World Tree.

Chapter 10

RIDING IN A chariot was odd enough, especially one that felt like a battleship. But riding in a chariot drawn by Thor was like riding that battleship through a hurricane. Thunder and lightning crashed around us nonstop, and the hairs on my arms stood up, thoroughly electrified by both the storm raging around us and our proximity to the thunder god. My own fire crackled in response. While I worked with flame for the most part, fire and electricity went hand in hand and where my flame was, the other—whether in the form of forks or sparks—followed.

The others huddled on the floor. Finally, realizing we weren't going to be there in seconds, I sat next to Jason.

The chariot reminded me of the hold on Laren's boat—bigger inside than out and able to hold a massive amount of people and items given the apparent space. It would be so handy, I thought, for me to have a purse or backpack with a pocket extending into the astral realm like this. Maybe not one big enough to hold people, but to hold all the supplies we needed and weigh no more than the average handbag.

"What are you thinking about?" Jason asked.

"Purses." I grinned.

He blinked. "That answer I did not expect."

"I'm a conundrum." I laughed. The combination of the approaching danger and the energy surrounding us amped me up like I had drunk too many glasses of wine. I leaned against the side of the chariot, listening as the massive hooves of Tanngrisnir and Tanngnióstr thundered through the woods. Or the sky. Or wherever we were racing. I thought about peeking outside to see where Thor had taken us, but something whispered, *"You might not want to do that. You might not live to regret it,"* so I restrained myself.

"Elan and I are getting married." Jason abruptly broke into my thoughts.

Hans, who was sitting on his other side, clapped him on the shoulder. "Good man. Stand by your woman and child." He looked giddy.

"What are you so happy about?" I asked.

Hans laughed. "I'm in my Lord's chariot, riding through the ether. Is there much better than that?"

"Yes, old man of mine," Greta said. "Riding with the Valkyries with Freya at the helm!" She was sitting opposite us. She was laughing too. I had the feeling they sparred this way quite a bit.

Tyrell and Kendall, who were sitting by her,

looked vaguely uneasy. The guards, further inside the chariot, remained stoically silent.

"You asked her before we left, right? I saw you putting a ring on her finger."

Jason nodded. "She said yes, as long as we remain in UnderBarrow. I have no objections to that. I'll run my shop, she'll work for Tam. The world will continue as it is." He broke out into a broad smile. "And you, my ward, will become queen over UnderBarrow, wed to one of my best friends, and I will kneel at your feet. Talk about events I never saw coming."

"Neither did I, and you'll only kneel at official events. My first decree."

Bantering over daily life and simple things felt good, and took my mind off what we were about to face. My nerves were on edge as it was, and the jolts from the storm raging around the chariot didn't help. Every few seconds, thunder let out a rolling rumble, and even though we couldn't see outside, the lightning was so bright it seemed to illuminate the inside of the chariot right through the burgundy walls. The storm seemed endless.

"How long has it been since we started? Thor said it should take an hour or two, and I don't have a clue how long we've been on the move."

"I don't know," Jason said. "It seems like hours, but...I have no idea, to be honest. When you think about the distance, a car could make it in an hour before everything went to hell, but given a chariot driven by goats, over broken roads? And are we even riding through the physical plane? I suppose I could figure out how long it would normally take us if this were a regular chariot and those goats weren't some form of mutant monsters."

"Never mind. It will take as long as it takes. I think, as with UnderBarrow, you'll find that time on the outside of the chariot passes far differently than time inside," Hans said. He pointed to my backpack. "You have the explosives, right?"

"For the fifth time, yes. I checked and double-checked." Even though I had already done so twice since we started, I slipped off my backpack and opened it to make certain that everything was in order. Which it was.

I sat back against the inner wall of the chariot, trying to focus on a positive outcome. For a month, I'd played over how this would go, visualizing getting in there and out with a minimum of fuss. But the truth was, in my heart, I was afraid. It wasn't the same type of apprehension that I faced with Abominations. There was so much more riding on this, and it rested on my shoulders, because I was the only one who could find the damned gate.

After a while, the chariot suddenly slowed, then came to an abrupt halt. I stiffened as the doors closing off the inner chamber opened.

Thor's voice rumbled out. "We're here. Come on out."

I was nearest the door and as I cautiously crawled out, then straightened, I realized that I had no clue where we were in conjunction to Seattle. Ahead of me was a vast marsh, stretching farther than I could see. The foliage—nettles, poison oak and ivy, tangles of brambles and swamp grass and vines and cat-o-kills so high they were over my head—stretched out in an unending line to both the left and right. It was thick and cumbersome, and we were on a road that led into it, but the road didn't look all that safe, and the asphalt had been broken in numerous places as it intruded into the swampy marsh.

Stunned, because I had only known the Bogs when they were a contained section of lower Seattle, I turned to Thor. "Where are we? What's this road?"

"This is the road that goes past Glass Lake, the road leading to Bend. We're standing on the border of what used to divide Seattle from the Edge." Thor gazed straight ahead, a perturbed expression on his face. "I would ferry you further, but my goats don't want to enter the Bogs and Odin forbade it. To your right, to the north, is where the Metalworks used to be. Follow this path and it will take you to the south of the World Tree. The pavement will end soon and a trail will take over. It's rough, though, and there's a lot of quicksand in there. Be prepared for hard travel."

The reality began to hit home. Seattle *really* wasn't Seattle anymore.

"What else should we know?"

"The Junk Yard's nothing but a tangle of twisted metal. The structure folded during the second wave of the tsunami. There's a small town called Shanty Town out toward what was the Peninsula of the Gods. It's filled with the dregs of those who survived from the Junk Yard, so be cautious. Lyon is holed up in Old Seattle, which is northwest, around where Uptown and North Shore used to be." Thor shook his head. "All of this is subjective knowledge, though, provided by raiding parties. But follow this trail about three miles, then turn into the Bogs themselves, off trail, and head north. That should take you into the Sandspit and the World Tree."

By the time he finished talking, everybody was out of the chariot. Thor pulled off the road, parking to the side on a stretch of grass. "I'll wait for you here."

I looked at the pavement that stretched out behind us. Patches of grass were beginning to break through the asphalt. Another six months and the entire road would be hidden by the overgrowth of vines and plants. Nature was reclaiming what we had once taken from her. The only sounds around us besides our own voices were the clicks and buzzing of insects, the constant bird song that filtered through the air, and the whistle of wind. There were no traffic noises, no sounds of electricity or civilization.

The sun was starting to creeping over the skyline. We had set out at dawn, and now the day promised to be uncomfortably warm. I shaded my eyes as we gathered together.

"I suppose we should move out. If we're careful and focused, I hope to make it to the World Tree by early afternoon, but that depends on how friendly the Bogs are. Three miles can seem like thirty in conditions like these. So be cautious. We don't want to stumble into any patches of Wandering Ivy or the like." I glanced around. "We should take walking sticks. The Bogs are marshy and there's quicksand throughout them. You do *not* want to take a wrong step."

The guards headed over to a stand of new willow saplings and quickly cut and stripped long, sturdy branches for everybody. We adjusted our packs. With no excuses left, we headed into the Bogs.

I BROUGHT UP my Trace and took a look around. No Abominations within our immediate vicinity, at least.

Queet, you with us? The spirit had been supposed to travel with us, but he had been quiet for a while and I wondered if he was still around.

I'm here. I've just been meditating.

I didn't know you needed to meditate once you... I paused, not wanting to be too blunt, but the thought of a spirit meditating seemed almost like an oxymoron.

Just because I'm dead doesn't mean I don't get stressed out. Queet sounded ready to laugh.

True. Okay, keep your eyes open and tell me if you notice anything you think we should be aware of. I'm not sensing any Aboms around, but that doesn't mean there aren't zombies at play.

I've got your back.

We plunged into the Bogs. There was room for two to go abreast, so Vis—one of the guards—took the front. After him, came two more guards—Mara and Shend. Then Jason and me, and after us, Greta and Hans. Tyrell and Kendall came next, and finally, two more guards—Ki and Rally. We used our walking sticks to prod the ground. Every step was suspect, and even if someone was directly in front of us, it didn't follow that we stepped in the exactly the same formation. One step to the left or right could be a plunge into quicksand.

Because of that, the going was slow and itchy, with the tall marsh grass brushing against us with its razor sharp edges. By the time we had edged in a few hundred yards, I had a dozen stinging cuts and was brushing away the skeet-flies who were looking for a good feast off my blood.

Twice, I almost stepped on a snake that slithered past. Though venomous snakes were rare in our area, there were still a few—rattlesnaps and copperbacks were the two most common. The rattlesnaps we could hear if they coiled near us, but copperbacks? Not so much.

It quickly heated up as the sun beat down, accentuating the fetid stench of the marshes. I grimaced. It smelled like we had stepped into an algae-filled pool, or an outhouse that had been sitting too long in the sun. Though this patch of the Bogs was still too young to have any of the ancient yew trees or cypress that the original patch held, there were saplings of the two trees, along with a number of willows. Something had sped up their growth, and it wouldn't have surprised me if some of the rogue magic from the Sandspit had filtered in through here.

Ferns were already waist high, and the cat-o-kills towered over our heads, a good six or seven feet tall. The scent of bog-water was ripe, and I thought I detected the smell of rotting flesh inter-mingled with it, but I didn't want to say anything.

We came to the end of the asphalt road. It had become so broken by then that—trail or road—it really didn't matter. I stepped off the last remnants of the pavement onto the spongy dirt. Here, the danger of quicksand increased. We'd have to be extra alert.

"We should have thought about this back in the village. I don't know why we didn't think about how rough going through the Bogs might be."

I kept my voice low, not wanting to alert any-body or anything that might be in the area. The Bogs had always held dangerous creatures, and I didn't expect that to be any different now. In fact, they were probably rife with zombies as well as bog-dogs and the other fauna that had evolved in marshy patches.

Jason shook his head. "Honestly, doesn't matter. So the Bogs are a lot bigger than they were. If not Bogs, we would be picking our way through rubble and scorched land. That might have been easier, but who knows what we'd be facing then? Really, it's six of one, half-dozen of the other. There are al-ways going to be wandering hazards. We have our ropes and lights and all the other gear we could think to bring."

Fury, up ahead to your left about a hundred yards from here—tell the guards to watch out. There's a bog-dog nest. Mother and bunch of pups. She'll probably leave you alone if you don't disturb her. Your party is large, but you should be aware of her anyway.

Thanks, Queet.

I relayed the information to the others. "Don't disturb her. She's with a litter of pups and frankly, if we don't bother the mama, she probably won't bother us." It wasn't that I had any love for the mutants, but the fewer fights we had to engage in, the better.

I could hear a low growling as we passed the area where she was making her nest, and part of me wanted to take a peek, but mama bog-dog wasn't poking her nose out of the thicket of reeds, and I wasn't going to poke my nose into it.

As we continued, I cautioned people to keep their voices low, but that didn't stop fate from stepping in. We were probably two miles into the trek when the rustling of marsh grass alerted us, and we froze. I slowly reached down to draw my dagger. My whip wouldn't be much use in such tight quarters. The guards quietly drew their swords. We waited and I brought up my Trace, but still no Aboms in the general vicinity.

Another moment, and the reeds parted as a group of five men broke through. They were dressed in leathers. Rough around the edges, they all sported beards that looked like they hadn't seen the edge of a razor in months, and scruffy hair and various bruises and scars lacing their faces and arms. They were carrying weapons—a few blades, a nasty-looking ax, and several large hammers.

They stared at us, pausing. Then, one—I assumed he was the leader—stepped to the front. A good six feet tall, he had dark hair and even darker eyes, and he was missing a front tooth.

"You're in our territory. Pay the toll or turn around and leave." His voice was rough, sounding like he had laryngitis. An angry scar on the side of his throat still looked fresh. It was a dangerous place for a wound and, whatever had happened to him, it had probably affected his vocal cords.

"We're just passing through. We want no trouble." I stepped forward, keeping a firm hold on my dagger but not lifting it.

"Girl, you obviously have a hearing problem. I said pay the toll *or leave.*" His eyes narrowed as he tightened his grip on the blade that he was carrying.

I let out a sigh. Even if we paid him whatever he wanted, chances were they wouldn't let us alone. "What kind of toll are you talking about?" They didn't look underfed, so I doubted if they wanted foodstuffs. And what use was money now?

"Give us your weapons and your jewelry." He motioned toward my sword. "That's a pretty bauble."

Xan trembled in her sheath. I could feel her wanting out, to take a swing. My sword was sentient, to a point, but we hadn't yet established any major communications. But sometimes, I would sense a movement or feeling from her. Now, she wanted a little taste of blood.

I backed away a step, using whisper-speak to talk to Queet. *Are there any more of them? What do you think they're up to?*

They are, but they're far enough away that they won't be able to get here for a while. As to what they're up to, they're bandits. They're probably from Shanty Town.

That's what I thought. I brought my dagger up. "I'm afraid that's not going to happen, boys. Why don't you just back off and let us pass and we won't give you any trouble."

"You had your chance," the leader said, and brought his sword to bear. "I guess we'll just have to take them from you by force."

He took a swing at me, but Vis jumped in, bringing his sword to deflect the bandit's. I moved back as our guards took the lead. We stood ready, but they were prepared for this—trained for battle—and so we let them move in.

Our opponents were well versed with their weapons, though, and the fight quickly became a deadly dance. I tried to gauge what might help the most. I thought about starting a fire, but even though the weather was hot and the sun overhead, there was enough moisture in the Bogs to fizzle out my flames.

Hans and Greta moved forward, Greta's wings brushing against me as she engaged the leader, giving the guard a chance to back off and rest for a moment. Hans put his own hammer to good use and broadsided one of the men who was focused on driving Ki back. She had been dodging an increasingly quick barrage of swings. Hans yelled for her to get out of the way as he landed his swing against the thief's side. We could hear the crunch of bones and the thief shrieked as several ribs snapped. Hans landed another blow before he could react, this time hitting him upside the head to knock him off his feet. Then one final blow to break the man's skull.

Shend let out a yelp as his opponent sliced him along the leg, drawing a sudden spurt of blood. Stumbling back, the guard dropped his sword as he frantically tried to control the bleeding. Kendall raced over to him as I pushed into place, deflecting the bandit from finishing off the guard.

I managed to swing around behind him. The moment I was close enough, I thrust my dagger into his back, right into his kidney area. He screamed and I twisted my blade, driving it deeper.

My opponent tried to reach behind in order to grab my blade, but I didn't give him the chance. I slid the dagger out of the wound with a twist. The bandit let out another curse, but he was bleeding out by now. I had managed to stab something vital.

I pushed in, not wanting him to escape into the thicket. He stumbled as I crowded him toward the marsh, and then he began to flail, dropping his own blade. He was sinking fast, and I realized that I had pushed him into a patch of quicksand. While I was taking stock of what had happened, he lunged forward, already mired up to his knees. He managed to catch hold of my right arm and tried to pull me in with him.

Instinctively, I stabbed at him with my dagger and managed to catch his shoulder with the blade. But as I struggled to get away from him, I slipped on a wet patch of marsh grass and lost my footing. I stumbled forward, landing on top of him. That made him sink all the faster, but he tightened his grasp, dragging me with him so that I was caught by the floating sand as well. His head was below the surface and he was struggling wildly.

I didn't want to lose my dagger, but I couldn't take the time to try to find it, and I sputtered, now waist deep. My opponent had lost the fight, but he still had hold of me and it was apparent that he would go to his death holding onto my arm. Using my left hand, I frantically tried to grab hold of the nearest vegetation on the edge of the pit, but as the thief sank further, the edge grew further out of my reach.

"Help me!" I was chest deep now, and though I was trying to kick his body, to make him loosen his grip on me, I was sliding into a panicked haze. Within another moment, my head would be under the sand, too. Behind me, the sounds of fighting continued, but I couldn't see who was winning, and all I could do was hope that somebody would notice what had happened to me.

"Grab hold of the rope!" Kendall was by the edge of the pit, tossing me a rope.

I thrashed around, trying to grasp the end of the rope with my left hand. Finally, on the third toss, I managed to catch it. I was chin deep in the liquid sand, and I looped the vine around my wrist. I gave one final kick and the drowned bandit finally let go of me. I brought my other arm up, out of the muck, and took hold of the rope with both hands, holding it tightly as Kendall dragged me out.

"Oof, you might as well be dead weight, woman," she said. Then Jason was beside her, helping to pull me out. The moment I was half over the edge, he raced forward and grabbed hold of my arm, pulling me the rest of the way.

I rolled over onto my back, gasping as I tried to catch my breath. I felt like I could barely move. "I can't sit up."

"That's because the quicksand numbs your body. Remember, everything in this area is laced with magic." Jason knelt by me, helping me roll into a sitting position. I squinted, trying to make out what was going on.

"Are there still—"

A cry rang out and Jason sat back. "That's the last of them. Mara's wounded, as is Shend. Everybody else is all right." He slipped off his backpack and rummaged through till he found a towel. He handed it to me. "I'm afraid we don't have enough water to wash you off, but wipe off what you can."

I tried to take the towel, but my fingers still didn't want to work, so between Kendall and Jason, they wiped me down as much as possible. By that time, the feeling in my limbs was returning. I was able to bend my fingers and my joints no longer felt like they were frozen.

"Damn it, I lost my dagger." I wasn't happy about losing Xan's companion, but there wasn't much I could do about it. I couldn't go diving back into the quicksand after it. And there was no way the marsh was going to hand the blade back to me on a silver platter. "Fuck. Well, at least we're all in one piece. How badly injured are Shend and Mara?"

"Shend took a couple nasty bites of the blade, and he's sick from it. Mara broke a wrist when she fell over a pile of debris that was hidden by a patch of vegetation. But all the bandits are dead."

Queet, are the others still too far away to be a threat?

Queet wafted around me. *They're still a good distance from here. You can escape them with plenty of time if you don't sit around too long.*

"Let's get moving. There are others out there, but they're still far enough away that we can escape them. Can Shend walk?"

"Yeah, though Shend's gash is deeper than I like to see. We need to make sure an infection doesn't set in. Do you have any antibiotic salve?" Greta was examining the guard's wound.

"Yeah, in my pack. I brought a jar, thinking it might come in handy."

I shrugged off my pack, grateful that it was waterproof. Sure enough, when Greta had wiped off the outer surface of the pack and opened it, everything was cozy and dry. I was still mourning my dagger as she found the salve and applied it to both Shend's and Mara's wounds.

"That should put an end to any possible infection. Let me wrap it up and see if you can walk on that leg." Greta tended to the guard, then strapped up Mara's wrist as best as she could.

I wearily sat my ass on the ground. The struggle in the quicksand had left me tired and achy.

"Are there other pathogens that could be inside that sand? I'm feeling achy in a way I don't normally feel after a fight." My stomach was roiling, since I had swallowed a couple mouthfuls of the sand as I struggled to get away from it.

"That's because the chemical that causes the

paralysis also seeps into your muscles. Prolonged exposure can lead to arthritis and neuromuscular diseases." Jason dug into his backpack and pulled out a vial filled with capsules. "Here, take one of these. It will help your muscles warm up and settle your stomach."

"I guess we need to be on the watch for more than just bog-dogs and Wandering Ivy," I muttered as I accepted the pill and his canteen.

"We need to be prepared for anything. But the good news is, we're only about a mile from where we turn straight north. Then it shouldn't be too far until we reach the World Tree." Hans slid the blade of his ax against the marsh grass, trying to wipe off the blood. "I'm sorry you lost your dagger."

"Yeah, that's a painful loss. Anybody have a spare? I have a feeling I'm going to need it. I have Xan, of course, and my whip, but I like having a weapon for close quarters as well."

Mara handed me her spare dagger—she wasn't going to be able to use it, after all. I slid it into the sheath, mourning the loss of Xan's companion. But if the dagger and the guards' wounds were the worst we encountered on this trip, it would be a small price to pay.

We set to march again, and Queet kept an eye out. I scanned the area again with my Trace, but so far there weren't signs of any Abominations. I whispered a prayer to Hecate that it would stay that way.

BY THE TIME we turned north, off the path, the sun was creeping just past noon. We had made good time and, with the exception of the bandits, had managed to avoid any other encounters. I had grown used to the rhythm of the Bogs. They were different than they used to be—the feel was more feral and less malignant. In fact, it felt like their increase in size had decreased the sense that they were waiting for their next victim. But the difference didn't stop me from starting at every noise that sounded remotely out of the ordinary.

Once we turned north, the going grew rougher because we had absolutely no trail to follow. More than once, we nearly stumbled into quicksand pits. We skirted the edges so many times, I was worried that we might be getting off track. But Mara carried a compass and assured me we were staying on course.

"Milady, no worries, please. We're heading in the direction that we need to go."

I nodded. "Good. Thank you, Mara."

Another hour and we broke through the edges of the Bogs. We were staring into the Sandspit. In the center, we would find the World Tree.

I stared at the unending patches of reddish sand. "Gear up, boys and girls. It's time to rock 'n roll."

Chapter 11

SUDDENLY, I REALIZED Tyrell wasn't with us. I was about to send Vis back into the Bogs to look for him when he popped out from between the reedy grasses.

"Sorry, had to take a piss."

"Hurry up," I said, frowning. "Next time, warn us you're going to step to the side so we don't get worried."

As we stepped out of the Bogs into the Sandspit, I felt a swell of relief. The Sandspit, I was familiar with. Though we could see from the edges that the tsunami hadn't left it alone, either. The fences the government had put up to encase it were gone. Huge boulders lay strewn around the Sandspit as though giants had been playing a game of dodge-ball. At least I *thought* they were boulders till I took a good look and realized they were chunks of concrete and steel. Debris from broken buildings, I thought, as my heart sank.

Rusted cars were half-buried by the sand, and even from the edge we could see a number of skeletons and bones. They weren't walking or animated, which actually made it more horrific as it hit home that they were the bleached bones of victims caught in the massive tidal wave.

We were all silent as we stared at the expanse. The waters that had engulfed the area were long gone, but the aftermath would last for centuries.

I checked my Trace. A faint blip from the other side of the Sandspit. An Abom, but since it was moving the other way, out of range, I let it go. Our mission was more important.

"All right, let's get moving. It's about twenty minutes' walk to the Tree from here. Keep your eyes peeled for patches of rogue magic." Even facing the possibility of the wandering magic—the very magic that had turned me into a Theosian—I was relieved to be out of the Bogs. I wasn't looking forward to returning through them, though.

"Fury, when we get there, I want to help you with the explosives," Tyrell said, catching up to me. He thrust his hands in his pockets. "I mean it. I'll do whatever you need me to."

Something about his eagerness irritated me. I chalked it up to being on edge already. "Thanks. I'm going to need everybody's help."

"Yeah, I figured as much, but I'm ready to do whatever you need. Just point me in the direction you need me to go and give me marching orders."

When I didn't reply, he stared up at the sky. "No clouds today."

"Given we seem to be in the middle of a heat wave, that doesn't surprise me."

I wasn't in the mood to chat about the weather. My mind was racing over the steps we needed to take. And I was also deep in thought about the streets beyond the Sandspit. Once we were finished, at some point I needed to return to Seattle and walk through the streets to face what had happened to my beloved city. I needed to say good-bye and put the past to rest.

The blip signaling the Abom began to move and I watched it closely, but it remained heading in the opposite direction, into what was left of the city itself. After a moment, it vanished off the Trace, which meant that it had moved out of range. I let it go.

As we moved further into the Sandspit, our pace picked up. The debris from the tsunami reminded me of when we had gone out on the Tremble, without the weird warping of reality. That brought to mind the question of our friends, the Mudarani. Had they survived? Was the Tremble even worse?

Up ahead, a swirl of mist flared up, bringing me out of my thoughts. I motioned to circle around the patch of rogue magic. The wind had died down and it was stationary for the moment, and we managed to pass by it without incident. I let out a breath of relief. When rogue magic hit, you never knew what was going to happen. I brought up my Trace again. Still no Aboms near. I waved my hand and we continued on in silence.

TWENTY MINUTES LATER, at around 3 P.M., we were standing on the edge of the crater in which the World Tree had grown. A hundred feet deep and just about as wide, the pit had dug deep into the earth. The massive oak had been born at the bottom. Its upper limbs stretched above the top of the pit, a lacework of boughs and branches. The Tree exuded a pale green glow.

As I peeked over the edge, I expected to see Lyon's guards, or the Devani, but I saw neither. But we were facing a definite problem.

The pit was filled with debris. When the tsunami had swept through, it must have filled the pit. When the waters receded, they had left a massive tangle of remains. Cars, chunks of stone, all manner of debris cluttered the base of the World Tree.

My heart sank. The tree was beautiful and the debris surrounding it felt sacrilegious. But an even more dangerous situation waited at the bottom, and that had to be why there weren't any Devani or other guards watching the pit.

"Zombies." Hans leaned on the handle of his ax. "How many do you think there are?"

The pit was swarming with zombies. There had to be at least seventy to a hundred down there. Some had been cut in half and were dragging their torsos around with their arms. The lower halves were twitching, a few walking around, lurching into things because they had no eyes with which to see—or heads or anything else. Others were intact, though looking more like walking skeletons.

"They probably got trapped in there when the tsunami hit and haven't been able to get out," Jason said. "So how do we work this? If we go anywhere near the bottom of the crater, we'll be targeted by the entire group. I don't think we can withstand that many coming at us at once. I can fly over to the tree, but Fury's the one who needs to be there."

I eyed the tree. There were a few zombies in it, though most seemed to be on the ground around the base. I searched for the staircase leading down into the crater, wondering why they hadn't made use of it to get out of the pit, but the steps that had once led to the base of the trunk—and to Under-Barrow—were gone.

"I'm not sure what's going on," I said. "The steps are gone. I don't know if that happened when UnderBarrow moved or if it was the result of the tsunami. Probably the wave, or Tam would have warned us. I'll have to find another way over into the tree."

"Jason can fly over with a rope and tie it off to a branch. You can zip line into the tree," Hans said.

I nodded. "It would seem that's about the only way I'm going to manage it. I sure as hell don't want to end up at the bottom. Even with as much fire as I can control, I wouldn't be able to get out of there."

Nobody else had a better idea, so Jason agreed to carry the rope over. He slid off his pack and shifted into hawk form. As he took the rope in his beak, Hans held onto the rest of it, doling it out as Jason flew into the upper branches of the oak, away from any zombies that were climbing up the tree from below. He found a sturdy limb, and then—after transforming back—tied the rope to a thick branch that looked like it could bear a lot of weight.

I wasn't relishing the trip over, but there was nothing else to do. Hans found a nearby boulder that wasn't going anywhere—it actually looked like part of a pillar from some building—and he looped the rope around the girth a couple times, then tied a knot that any sailor would be proud of. As he fashioned a harness, I tried to calm my nerves.

Vis barked out orders. "Shend, you and Mara stay here. You're both injured. Rally, stay with them. Ki and I will zip over first, before her lady-ship goes. We'll stay with her at all times. Lord Tam expects us to bring her home alive and unin-jured."

I turned to the others. "Greta, you and Kendall stay with the guards. We'll need everybody else."

Greta nodded. "We'll come over if you need us. Just call."

I slipped into the harness, making sure my pack was firmly on my back. The rope angled down, so I had some momentum, but I still had to pull my-self along hand-over-hand on my way across the chasm. The zombies were watching, I could see that at a glance below. They were milling around the base of the tree, no doubt hoping that I would fall off the rope and land in their midst. I tried not to think about what would happen if they started up the tree after us. Some of them could, theoretically. After all, Lyon had first brought them in through one of the portals.

He had opened a vortex and they had streamed out. I had managed to close the gate, albeit too late. But looking at these zombies and the way the remnants of their clothes hung on them, I thought they were most likely former city folk, turned by the hordes that had crowded through the streets, attacking anybody they could get their hands on.

Pacing myself, I inched across the rope to land on the branch next to Jason. He helped me get out of the harness and then, as I waited, he detached the rope harness from the zip line and flew it back to the edge of the pit, then returned to me. One by one, Vis, Hans, Tyrell, and Ki made their way over, and each time Jason returned the harness to be used again. He took it back one last time, handing it to Greta, should we need help from those staying on the other side.

We had waited a month for this, and now the time was finally here.

I searched my memory, focusing on the vision that Gaia had given me. Then I began scanning the tree, looking for the gate. It took a while, but finally, I saw it.

Fainter than the others, the gate shimmered in a pale light, but I could see its outline.

Even though Lyon had been searching for it, I realized that, with the dozens of other portals on the World Tree, the gate to Chaos could easily be overlooked. The oak was so massive that it glowed with the energy from all of the portals. Not all were easily accessible, and sometimes, one would form, then vanish, and then reform elsewhere. For whatever reason, Lyon had managed to miss this one.

"I see it," I said, pointing in the direction of the gate. "That one. That leads to the realm of Chaos. Come on, let's get this over with."

As I set off, cautiously climbing up the branch toward the inner well of stairs that encircled the tree, Tyrell followed me. Jason, Hans, and the guards fell in behind him. We were about fifty feet off the ground, and below us, some of the more intact zombies were attempting to climb the steps from the base of the trunk. If they had been held captive since the tsunami, chances were they were ravenous. My stomach lurched when I looked down at the wave of walking carnage.

Vampires were bad enough, but zombies? So not my choice of enemy. For one thing, most of them were probably pretty decent people when they were alive. They hadn't chosen the change, and chances were, if their spirits knew what had happened, they would probably be horrified. I hoped they had moved on and couldn't see what their bodies were doing.

The bough we were on was slippery with moss, and while it was wide, with a number of handholds, it was still a dangerous climb. I rested my foot on a burl the size of my head, reaching for the next limb that looked sturdy enough to hold me steady. I was about ten feet away from the inner stairwell, which was dangerous enough on its own, but at least the steps would be less problematic than trying to cross moss-covered bark.

Finally, I reached a point where there was only

a five-foot distance to cross in order to stand on the steps. I considered my options. I could swing over by tossing a rope over a bough that I gauged capable of holding my weight, or I could jump. Either way had its downside, and either way would expose me to the chance of falling.

I scanned the trunk and saw a fairly thick branch jutting out from above the stairs, right above where I wanted to land.

Turning, I said, "Jason, can you take a rope up to that branch and tie it off, then fly it back to me? That way we can wrap it around our waists, swing over, and lessen the chance of falling."

"Sure thing. I have a spare rope in my pack."

Jason squatted on the branch, holding on precariously as he transformed into his hawk shape. He flew to the branch I had indicated and, shifting back, straddled it as he tied the rope off. He tossed the end my way and I managed to catch hold of it.

I wrapped it around my waist and then, taking a deep breath, swung across the distance. Five feet sounded like an easy hop, but when you were fifty feet up with a horde of starving zombies below, it became a gaping chasm. I landed on the step, teetered and almost swung back again, but Jason grabbed the rope and held it taut, steadying me.

Panting, more from anxiety than exertion, I leaned against the main trunk before climbing a couple of stairs. Untying the rope, I let Jason swing it back to Tyrell. The gate to the realm of Chaos was about twenty more feet away from me. There, I would need to step about two feet over onto another bough, then scoot toward the trunk where the portal glimmered against the bark.

When everybody was safely on the staircase, I began the trek. Twenty feet wasn't far, but given the slick stairs I was cautious. There was no sense in rushing when we were so close. Finally, I was staring at the gate. One more step, then ten feet in, and I'd be there. I turned back to the others as they joined me.

"Who wants to go with me? I don't think that bough will hold more than two or three."

Jason almost cut off my words. "Me. I'm going with you."

Tyrell was quick on his heels. "Me too."

"All right, if you're both sure. Come on." I began to edge out on the bough, with Tyrell close behind me. I had made it about halfway across when he was suddenly pushing against my back. "Slow down, Tyrell. You're crowding me. Give me a little space."

"Sorry, Fury," he said. "I'm really sorry."

But instead of pulling back, he lunged forward, shoving me.

"What the—" I wasn't prepared to deflect a body slam, and found myself flailing as I listed to the right. I tried to squeeze my knees around the bough, but the moss was so slick that I was having a hard time keeping my hold.

"Back off!"

He laughed, then. "Sorry, again, Fury." But there was no apology in his voice. Instead, he gave me a brutal shove.

"What the hell are you doing?" Jason shouted as I fumbled to keep my grip.

"What I need to." Tyrell elbowed me sharply in the left hip.

As the jab ground into my flesh, I lost my balance and found myself dangling from the bough, holding on with fingers that were rapidly losing traction on the moss. I tried to swing my legs up to catch hold of the bough and would have been successful, except that Tyrell brought his fist down on the fingers of my left hand.

I screamed, not expecting the blow as the bones of my pinky and ring finger cracked. Adjusting more of my weight to the right hand, I tried to move my left hand out of his way, but before I could, he brought his fist down again. This time, I lost hold as the pain laced through my hand.

Jason was yelling and there was the noise of a scuffle overhead, but my focus was entirely on trying to keep hold of the bough as I dangled from one hand.

A glance below told me there were several branches I might be able to land on if I fell, but there was also a good chance I could slip through them and land in the waiting crowd of zombies below. They would break my fall, but that didn't say much for my chance of survival, given they were growling and moaning as they scrabbled around the trunk of the World Tree.

Before I could make up my mind what to do, a blow hit my right hand. Tyrell had managed another hit, even though it sounded like he and Jason were fighting.

I tried to keep hold, tried to reach up with my injured hand, but the moss was too slick and the blow had managed to dislodge my grip. I dug in, but as I began to fall, the nail to my right index finger got caught and ripped off as I plummeted.

Ignoring the pain, I looked down to see that I had one chance. I was going to be falling right past another big branch. I bent forward, extending my arms just in time to clip the bough. I had managed to land on my stomach, which brought another world of pain into my life, but at least I wasn't in freefall. I was about fifteen feet below the branch I had been on. I swung my left leg up, groaning as I managed to catch hold of the limb with my foot. I shifted, struggling up to straddle the branch.

My left hand was swollen and bruised, while the index finger to my right was bleeding heavily from where I had ripped off the nail. But my pack was still on my back, and I wasn't zombie fodder. *Yet.* I looked up, trying to see what was going on above me.

Jason was grappling with Tyrell, as was Hans. The next moment, Tyrell shrieked and went hurtling past me as Hans decked him, knocking him off the branch. Unfortunately—at least for Tyrell—he wasn't able to catch himself on the way down. He landed square in the middle of the zombies. They swarmed him, and his screams echoed through the pit as they began to feast.

I grimaced. What the hell had happened? But I had no time to spare. We'd sort out why Tyrell had tried to kill me later on. I needed to get back up to the portal.

"Stay put," Jason called. "I'm coming down." Sure enough, as soon as he had spoken, he shifted into hawk form and flew down to land on the branch next to me. He shifted back as Hans dropped a rope down to us.

"Let me see your hands," Jason said. He stared at them, shaking his head. "Oh, Fury. Let me bind them up and I can give you a minor healing spell that will at least take away some of the pain."

"We don't have time to bind them. Just cast the spell and then get me up to the gate. If Tyrell was in cahoots with Lyon, then Lyon has to know we're here."

I held out my hands and, without protesting, Jason took them, whispering softly. The pain died down to a dull ache, but my left hand was too badly hurt for me to use it at all. The blood seeping from the right index finger slowed, though, and Jason tied the rope around my waist. As Hans and Vis pulled me back up, Jason shifted back into hawk form.

WE STARED AT the gap between us and the next branch. It was only two feet, but with an injured hand, I didn't trust myself. Jason flew over, shifted back, and then between him and Hans, they eased me across and back onto the stairs. Vis and Ki joined us. We were mere feet away from the gate. It was time to end this now.

I asked them to take the charges out of my backpack and loop the handles of the bag they were in over my right arm, along with the sack containing the triggers. Ready, I advanced on the portal.

"I have to go through, set the charges, and then jump back before they go off." I paused, realizing that I needed help. "I need two hands." I wasn't ready to order anybody to join me, but Jason gave me a smile.

"You know I'm with you, Kae." He stared at me, a soft glow in his eyes. "I'll help you."

I held my breath. "Are you sure? This might be—"

"Don't even say it. I'm sure." He stared up at the gate. "So what do we have to do first?"

"We go through the gate, then set the charges and get our asses back over here." I inhaled slowly, then exhaled in a slow stream. "The sooner we get this over with, the better."

Jason gave me room as I headed toward the gate. I was about to enter it when there was a shout from above. I glanced up to see one of the sky-eyes, a policing drone modified to be a hover platform, spiraling down. As it headed directly for us, I realized there was someone riding on top of it. And that someone was Lyon.

"Jason, hurry!" I dove for the portal, not wanting Lyon to get there first. Jason followed, pushing me through the gate. As we tumbled through the vortex, all I could think of was if I allowed Lyon to summon the Elder Gods of Chaos, the world would be lost.

THE REALM OF Chaos was worse than the Tremble. We were on solid ground, but it felt spongy and every movement made the ground shake as though we were caught in an earthquake. All around, a dark gray mist roiled, boiling through the silhouettes of shadowed trees. The stench of bog sand was near, a putrid, fetid scent that permeated the air. I wanted to cough but that would require a deep breath, and the last thing I wanted was for the scent to settle deep in my lungs. I glanced around. It was impossible to tell if there was anything hiding in the shadows. There could have been monsters only feet from us, but it would be impossible to tell unless they came out of hiding.

Once I realized we weren't going to die from lack of oxygen, I shook the bags off my arm and struggled to open them to get to the explosives.

"Help me."

Jason grabbed the bag with the blocks and spilled them out onto the ground. As I used my right hand to set them upright in the tray, he opened the bag with the triggers and lined them up by the blocks.

"We have to hurry. The others will do their best to keep Lyon from getting through the gate, but I'm not going to lay odds they'll be able to stop him." I glanced over at Jason. "Tyrell was on his side. How did we not know that?"

"Don't even worry about it right now. We don't have time to speculate. Here, hold the blocks while I set the triggers."

I grabbed up the first block and held it out, wincing as my nailless finger twinged.

Jason picked up one of the triggers. Thin wires fit into a small hole atop the blocks. The triggers would automatically arm the explosives once they were firmly set.

"You do realize that, once set, we have one minute to get back through that gate." I stared at him. "Move closer to the gate. We have to be within jumping distance."

The portal shifted at that moment, like the iris on a camera, swirling counter-clockwise. From here, we could see the sparks and crackles of the energy as it whirled in a crazy kaleidoscope, the patterns fracturing and bending as we watched them. The aperture opened again and Lyon jumped through.

He sized up what we were doing and dove toward us. Jason and I rolled out of the way, scattering the blocks as Lyon caught hold of me. He thrust his hands around my neck and started beating my head against the ground, slamming it against the spongy soil.

Fearing he would break my neck more than crack my skull, I tried to push him away but my left hand was still useless. I reached down with my right to where he was straddling me and grabbed his balls, squeezing as hard as I could. He shrieked, rolling off me into a fetal position, and I struggled to my feet, bringing a fresh jolt of pain to my left hand.

Jason was on top of him then and the two rolled, grappling one another.

For a moment I thought about helping, but

decided to gather the blocks from where they had scattered. I managed to get them in the tray and then searched for the triggers. I found three, then another three, and finally the last three as the men continued to fight. As long as Jason kept Lyon occupied, Lyon couldn't use any spells against us. But it also meant that Jason couldn't help me.

Shaking, I fit the first trigger in the first block, then quickly followed suit with the others. Once all nine were set, we'd have one minute to get out of here and it was my intention to leave Lyon behind. But as I finished the sixth one, Lyon landed a blow to Jason's stomach and was quickly on his feet, bearing down on me.

I held out my hands, ignoring the pain, and summoned my fire, wondering if it would work while we were in the realm of Chaos. But sure enough, there it was. Glowing, waiting, and I brought it to bear, channeling it as quickly and as hard as I could. The backlash as the flames shot through knocked me off my feet, but the resulting ball of fire that flew toward Lyon was brilliant white, scorching him square in the chest. He let out a scream, then fell back.

I returned to setting the triggers. *Three to go.*

Jason staggered to his feet and was heading over to help me when Lyon once again managed to stand. He brought up his hands.

"You want to play with the elements? Let's play," he shouted as a massive rush of wind and cloud boiled up behind him. I realized he was creating a twister. If he managed the spell, it would undo all of our efforts.

"Jason! Stop him!" I continued to fumble with the last blocks, shaking as I forced my left hand to close around one of them to keep it steady. The pain seared through me, stripping me of any focus save for getting the explosives set.

Jason landed on Lyon again, taking him down to the ground. He pulled out his dagger, but Lyon grabbed hold of his wrist and squeezed so hard that I could hear the crack from where I was kneeling. Jason dropped his blade, backhanding Lyon. The twister vanished.

"You have to hurry, Kae—he's too strong. I can't keep him down much longer." Jason groaned as Lyon did what I had done—drove his fist into Jason's balls. But he managed to keep the magician on the ground.

Shaking, I held the last trigger. "Get ready to run!"

"Set it and get the hell through the portal, Kae."

I set the last block and, putting it back in the tray, scrambled to my feet and headed toward the portal. "Jason, move! We have less than sixty seconds!"

Jason looked up at me from where he was straddling Lyon, who was still flailing, trying to get in a punch. "If I let him go, he'll destroy the blocks. We can't chance it now that he knows where the gate is! Go, damn it. Go."

I stared at him. He meant to stay behind. "No, Jason, get the fuck over here!"

"Go! You have to go back. Get your ass through that portal. Tell Elan I love her. I'll try to find a way home!" Jason was struggling in earnest now.

Lyon was starting to throw him off.

I calculated—less than ten seconds remained. If I jumped through now I could make it, but even if he let Lyon go at this point, Jason had no chance. I could disarm the triggers, but I couldn't do that. I couldn't let Lyon have free rein to bring the Elder Gods of Chaos through the vortex.

"I'll find you. I promise," I shouted at Jason.

"Just go! Go now!" He was losing his grip.

Sobbing, I closed my eyes and jumped for the vortex, leaving behind the man who had saved my life when I was a child.

Chapter 12

I LANDED ON the branch hard, wavering as I started to slip over the side. Hans caught me by the elbow, yanking me back, but for all of his efforts, he couldn't help me when the tree itself started to rock. The gate in front of us flared, a brilliant blue flash that showered us with sparks as it went into a manic spiral. Then, with a rattle that sounded like the last gasp of a dying man, the gate vanished. Only smooth bark against the tree remained.

Hans let out a soft curse. "Fury—where's Jason?"

"Lyon—he was fighting Lyon while I set the charges. He told me to go. I tried to make him let go and come back with me. But he said...Lyon would have..." I stopped. My heart was as numb as my hand. I stared helplessly at the tree. "I left him. I left him behind."

"You did what you had to."

"I didn't want to. I was going to disarm the explosives but Lyon would have broken free and he would have—"

"It's all right, Fury." Hans gathered me to his chest, holding me tight as I started to sob. "We know how tough Lyon is. He killed Ki."

I jerked around, looking frantically for the guard. Vis was standing beside Hans, his expression grim.

"Where? What happened?"

"She's below, with Tyrell. Lyon managed to throw her off the tree. She probably died before she hit the ground—one small mercy," Hans said. "Lyon nearly took out both Vis and me, too. He's crafty strong."

I pressed my lips together, unable to speak. My heart was breaking and all I could think about was that I had let Jason down. A glance over the side sent my stomach into spasms as I caught sight of a zombie holding up an arm. The shreds of sleeve were all too familiar. It was Ki's. Shivering, I turned back to the trunk.

"Milady, we should get off the tree. There are zombies trying to climb it, and they might very well succeed." Vis pointed toward a low branch where a group of zombies were making their way up.

I stared at them, suddenly exhausted. The pain from my broken hand was returning in spades. Defeated, I let the guard lead me back. I couldn't hold on, so between him and Hans, they managed to help me through the branches. I wished we could just climb up and crawl off the top of the tree, but we were too far from the edges of the pit.

We made our way back the way we had come and finally reached the rope leading to the other side. I stared at it. "I can't do hand over hand."

"Let me take you, Fury." Hans motioned for me to drape my arms over his shoulders from the back, and Vis tied us together. "Just don't strangle me on the way over."

"I'll try to avoid that," I said, but I felt like anything but smiling.

He grunted the entire way across the rope, but was able to carry me across with him, using his massive arms to pull us up the incline to the edge of the pit. Vis followed suit, and we cut the rope loose so nobody else could get over there.

"Hold on," I said once our feet were firmly on the other side. I crept to the edge of the pit, staring down. My fire wouldn't hurt the tree, and there wasn't anybody down there alive to worry about. I summoned up a ball of flame in my hands, ignoring the pain as I stretched out so that my head and arms were leaning over the edge. I cried out as the fire licked against my fingers, warming the bones as the flame flowed through my body. I willed it stronger, drawing on the deepest part of my core, where I was bound to the element. Then, in one massive rush, I expanded it, driving it through my fingers to pour into the pit. The blaze fell onto the mass of zombies, a liquid rain of fire and sparks, drenching the mass of writhing bodies below. They shouted as the flames caught hold. The walking torches stumbled back, spreading the flames, and soon the entire base of the World Tree was blazing like a bonfire gone mad, raging out of control, feeding on what little fat the zombies had left in their bodies.

I watched for a moment, silently, and then turned to find the others staring at me.

"Fury…" Kendall stopped. "Where's Tyrell?"

"Tyrell tried to kill me." That was all I needed to say. She held my gaze for a moment, then nodded. "Ki's dead. Lyon was there. Tyrell let him know. I don't know how, but he let him know. Jason is trapped on the other side of the portal, along with Lyon."

Actually saying the words aloud was as hard as pulling teeth. I just wanted to crawl into a bed somewhere and cry until the tears were gone. Vis tapped me on the shoulder.

"May I speak to you, milady?"

I nodded, following him to one side. "What is it? I'm sorry about Ki, by the way. I liked her."

"I'm sorry about her too, but she was doing her duty. It would be fitting to award her a medal for bravery posthumously. Milady, I know you're in pain and in shock, but times like this will happen. If I might make an observation?" He looked pained, as though he really didn't want to be the one offering me advice.

"Go ahead."

"You're the queen-to-be. Even though you're in shock, and hurt, it's up to you to take charge now. To claim the victory. For you did what you came to do. Even though your friend sacrificed himself, you have to give others hope. In the future, when there are other disputes, you have to be able to stand on the ashes and raise your hands over your head in a victory salute. You will be the heart of UnderBar-row, and it's your job to carry us through sorrow."

He dropped his eyes to the ground, as though waiting for me to smack him for speaking so forth-rightly.

I let out a long sigh that was part sob. I didn't want to be strong, I didn't want to carry the day forward, to pick up the banner and march on. But Vis was right, and I knew it. Even though I hoped to hell we'd never go through anything like this again, I knew that at some time in the future, we'd face another enemy, another gate, another battle. And if Tam and I didn't keep up morale, who would?

"You speak wisely, Vis. Thank you for remind-ing me of who I am. Of what duties I'm taking on." I shivered, more from exhaustion and pain than anything else. "And please, feel free to speak to me in the future. I'm going to need all the help I can get when I marry Lord Tam."

"I think you'll learn quickly, milady. You have the makings of a fine queen. I'm proud to serve un-der you, and I pledge my life in your protection." With that, Vis led me back to the others.

I let out a long sigh, then forced myself to smile through my tears.

"Jason's sacrifice and Ki's, sacrifice were great prices for us to pay, but I won't dishonor it by mourning. We lost two good people today, but we managed to close off the portal that the Order of the Black Mist has been seeking for months now. Come what may, they won't be able to use it to contact the Elder Gods of Chaos. And closing it off in this World Tree, we sealed it off in all the others. We've accomplished what we set out to. It's time to go home."

"Let me bind up your hand first, milady," Kendall said. She was crying as she spoke. "I can't believe Tyrell was one of the enemy."

"None of us suspected it. Somehow, he kept it from the Dagda, as well. The Order of the Black Mist is a powerful organization. But as communications degrade, they'll be cut off from their other cells. Maybe they'll fade with time." I didn't know if I really believed that, but for now, I had to. And while Jason was caught on the other side of the portal, so was Lyon. Trapped away from Seattle, away from this world.

Kendall bound up my wounds and we headed back toward the other side of the Sandspit, back to Thor. Back to our home.

WE MADE IT back through the Bogs without incident, though both my hands were hurting like hell. I marched on sheer will alone. I wanted to lie down and sleep, but finally we stumbled out of the briny marshes and there was Thor, waiting. He scanned the company and set his jaw.

"Three missing. Did you complete the mission?"

"We did. The portal to the realm of Chaos is gone. The explosives Heimdall made worked." I paused, not wanting to go through it all again. "We

lost Jason—he's trapped in the realm of Chaos—
and Ki was killed. Tyrell turned out to be our spy."

Thor let out a great sigh. "I'm sorry, lass. I'm
truly sorry. I know Jason was like a brother to
you." He opened the chariot. "Get in. Rest. That
hand looks like it needs attention. We'll be back to
Willow Wood forthwith."

We entered the great chariot, and Thor handed
us water bottles and sweet buns, then shut the
doors. As the chariot began to roll, I leaned back
against the side and closed my eyes. Even with the
pain in my hands, I fell asleep, drifting off as the
vehicle rocked from side to side.

WE PULLED INTO the village near midnight.
I didn't want to see Elan just yet. I couldn't face
her. Instead, I asked Vis to immediately take me to
Tam, and to bring a healer. Tam could heal some
of my wounds but he couldn't set bones, and I
needed someone to splint up my fingers.

Tam was waiting for me in his chambers.

I stood for a moment in the door, staring at him.

He searched my face, then opened his arms
and I raced over. He wrapped me in his embrace
as I buried my face against his chest. He asked
no questions, just stroked my hair as we stood
there. All the pain from losing Jason and from
my wounds drove themselves into my tears and
I broke into sobs, crying so hard I could barely
breathe.

Tam rocked me, kissing the top of my head, kissing my forehead, just murmuring my name over and over again. Finally, I hiccupped and shaking, stood back, unable to cry another tear. But I felt no joy in knowing that we had succeeded.

"Tell me everything while she binds your wounds." Tam led me over to the table where the healer waited. I held out my hands and she began to work on them, washing the wounds, setting the bones to heal straight, then binding them in a soft silken wrap that proved to be much more compressive than I thought it would. She cleaned off my other hand and cast a healing spell on the nail bed. Then she motioned for me to undress.

Patrice entered the room—I wasn't sure who had sent for her, probably Tam—and she carefully helped me out of my clothes. I glanced down to see the multitude of bruises that I had gotten from falling through the trees. My body was a patchwork of black and blue, and my ribs were aching. I had hurt them before, and apparently, I had again.

As the healer silently moved from bruise to bruise, spreading salve on the contusions, I looked up to see Tam staring at me, a worried look on his face. Patrice waited till the healer was done binding me up before helping me into a loose nightshift. Taking my clothes with her, she vanished out the door.

"You'll have to keep that hand splinted for at least four weeks. No more fighting until it's fully healed, which I estimate to be another month. Your nail will start growing back soon, so just keep the nail bed clean and covered. I'll come check on you tomorrow, unless you have any troubles during the night, milady." The healer gave me a quick curtsey, then packed her things and exited the room, leaving a draft of pain medication on the table.

Once we were alone, I turned to Tam. I wasn't sure how much he knew. As I slid into a chair by the table, I realized just how utterly exhausted I was.

"Tell me what happened, love."

"We lost Jason. He's trapped in the realm of Chaos and I have no clue of how to help him." I rested my elbows on the table, burying my face in my arms, the smell of the medicine making me queasy.

Tam took the seat opposite. "Tell me everything."

I poured out everything that had happened, from the trip to finding the tree, to Tyrell's betrayal, to Lyon's appearance.

"Jason knew that Lyon could have disarmed the explosives if he got loose. I knew it too. Jason told me to leave. He sacrificed himself to prevent Lyon from accomplishing his plans. I don't know if the explosion killed him or if he's alive—I don't know how to find him. It's not exactly like when you were lost on the Tremble. I just destroyed the only portal over to Chaos."

"You did what you had to. You very likely saved this planet. I doubt if many people will ever know about what happened, but you and Jason prevented a nightmare of epic proportions. Jason volunteered his life for the cause. Don't blame yourself.

He knew what would happen."

I didn't want to hear it. I needed somebody to blame.

"Tyrell kept asking to go with me when I set off the explosions. Now, I realize he wanted to prevent me from getting there."

Tam's expression grew dark. "The man is lucky he's dead. If he came back here alive, I'd have him flayed alive." By his tone of voice, I knew he meant it.

"The question is...what next? I just shut down the realm of Chaos. Lyon's trapped there. So where do we go from here? It feels like saving the world should be a happy thing—something to celebrate. Saving the world shouldn't mean trapping a friend in another realm."

"Shush, love. We'll figure it out tomorrow."

I nodded, thinking. "I want to go back to Seattle—not to stay, but to see the city. To see what it's like beyond the Sandspit. I need closure, Tam. I need to say good-bye in order to let it go." I looked up at him, holding his gaze. "In order to let Jason go. I need to put the past to rest in order to face the future."

"It will happen," he said. "And we'll mourn the city together. And then we'll be free to build our kingdom in the forest."

After that, he held me all night, just rocking me gently when I woke, screaming. My dreams were filled with ash and fire, with zombies and Jason's desperate face as he yelled for me to run. My dreams were a cacophony of tidal waves, and the cries of a golden-haired maniac, out to raze the world. Finally, toward morning, I slipped into a deep sleep and didn't wake till noon.

ELAN TOOK THE news with her typical reserve. There was no way to soften the blow, so Tam and I just told her outright. She excused herself and we didn't follow, though I wanted to.

"No, let her go." Tam refused to let me run after her. "She's Woodland Fae. She needs time to process the information. Leave her be and when she's ready, she'll come to us. Meanwhile, you need to talk to Hecate."

I took another step toward Elan's retreating back, but Tam stopped me firmly.

"I said, leave her be. Trust me on this, Fury."

I let out a bittersweet sigh. I didn't want to believe him. I wanted to run up to her, to beg her forgiveness, but he was right. The Woodland Fae were reserved, and they mourned in private. Shevron was another matter.

I was on my way to tell her the news, but she found me first.

"First, you tear my son away and encourage him to join the military. Now, you trap my brother in a realm of horrors with a madman. What do you have planned for me? Why are you trying to hurt the family who took you in when you were in desperate need, gave you love and a home?" She lashed out, her anger biting through any reserves I had.

"I didn't force him to stay. Jason saved me over saving himself," I said, trying to get through to her, but apparently it wasn't working.

She spat on the ground at my feet. "I'm moving back to Verdanya. I never want to talk to you again. Until you got mixed up in his life, Jason was on a focused path—"

"And how long would that have lasted? Whether I showed up on his doorstep or whether the Carver killed me too, Lyon would still have stolen the Thunderstrike and all of this would have happened. And you and Jason would have been stuck in the city with zombies. Leonard probably would have run away to join Kython. So how the hell has my existence hurt your family?"

I hadn't planned on lashing back at her, but I was tired, and it felt like the fact that her brother had helped me stop a catastrophe ricocheted off her and all she could see was her loss.

Shevron's cheeks flared bright red—brilliant against her pale skin. She held my gaze for another minute, then shook her head and turned. "My son's gone and my brother might as well be dead, if he isn't already. I'm not letting you finish us off."

She walked away, shoulders slumped. I watched her go, realizing that no matter what I said, I was the messenger and she was blaming me.

My heart sinking even more, I made my way out to the gazebo to find Hecate sitting on a tree stump, staring at a fistful of flowers in her hand. She looked up as I entered the clearing and scattered the petals on the ground, then gave me a wide smile and patted the stump beside her.

"Come and sit, Fury."

I sat.

"What a morning. The World Tree is safe now, at least from the realm of Chaos. The birds are singing, and I know where a honey log is. The bees are in full swing, but we can siphon off enough for UnderBarrow until autumn." She paused, and after a moment where I said nothing, added, "Tell me."

For what felt like the twentieth time, I told her what had happened, ending with, "I feel like we lost. I feel like we won the battle, but we lost so many things."

"There's no fanfare. No trumpets and not all of the heroes came marching home, is that right?"

I nodded, somewhat ashamed to realize that I had wanted a fanfare of some sort. But mostly, I was just missing Jason.

"How many wars have you been through, Fury?"

"None, I guess."

"No, you've been through one now. The battle against the Order of the Black Mist—the struggle to keep them from wrenching open the gates to Chaos, correct?"

I shrugged, picking a long blade of grass and whistling on it. "I guess, yeah. I suppose that was a war."

"It was a war, all right, and you won. There could have been a lot more little battles, each one ending a step closer to their goal. But you went straight for the heart and won. And all you have to show for it is a missing friend, a betrayal, and a dead guard."

"That's about the size of it," I said.

"Something you need to realize, Fury, is that every day, in every corner of the world, battles are being played out. Most of them are small, most aren't over anything huge, but when you look at all of them together, war takes on a massive scope. A fight against injustice here, against petty tyranny there. They add up. Now Lyon—that was a big one. He could have destroyed the world if he opened that gate. You managed to close it. And at the end, Jason gave himself to the cause when all seemed lost. He's a hero, Fury. He stepped up when the world needed him to."

"Shevron won't speak to me."

"That's because she's mourning her brother. You can't expect her to take his death—"

I jumped in quickly, cutting her off. "We don't know that he's dead, do we?"

"No, I suppose we don't. In any case, you can't expect her to take his disappearance...his *sacrifice*...with good graces. She'll come to appreciate his bravery in the future, but right now the only thing she knows is that she lost a brother. And Elan, even though she'll come around, she lost the father to her child. You can't expect her to swallow that easily."

"No, I know that." I paused. "So what's next? What do I do? How do I move on from this?"

"We find out what we can about the Order of the Black Mist. You marry Tam. You learn to be a queen. You and I set up our school to train others to hunt down Abominations. Elan has her baby, and tells him—or her—stories about her *oh-so-very-brave* father and how he sacrificed his life for others."

"I just feel at loose ends. We managed to stop the Order of the Black Mist, but nothing changed when we did that. Nothing went back to the way it should have been. It's not like I feel like we should have saved Seattle by doing that."

Something still didn't add up. But I had been expecting more.

I felt stupid. I realized that I'd expected once we overthrew Lyon, it would be like a stack of dominoes and one change after another would topple, returning us to where we were a year ago, before the Thunderstrike had ever appeared.

"But you thought there would be some magical shift."

"I don't even know if *I* understand what I'm feeling. We just accomplished a major feat. Now, the next day, we're sitting here in the woods, chatting."

"Yesterday the world was in danger from Lyon and his dogs loosing the Elder Gods of Chaos on the world. Today, that threat is gone. But there's no big parade, and the world moves on, and everything seems the same, even though nothing is the same. Is that it?"

I nodded. "I don't know what I expected. Nobody ever threw me a party for killing the Aboms and I never even thought of it that way. That's my job. I hunt them down and kill them. And then, the Thunderstrike happened, and Lyon happened. And then came the zombies and tsunamis and... now..." I looked around and shrugged. "Woods."

"What would you say if I told you that a few hundred years ago, another Theosian of mine also

saved the world? In a different way, but he par-
ticipated in a strike that took out a shadow corpo-
ration intent on taking over, and that prevented
nationwide slavery."

I blinked. "Really?"

"Yes, really. His name was Sargino, and he
worked with the element of earth. He saved the
world from a dictatorship that would have made
the Conglomerate look like your best friend. And
the day after he and his friends destroyed the up-
start emperor, he sat beside me and said the same
thing you are saying to me."

"What did he do after that?"

"Returned to his other duties. Lived out his life
until he accidentally fell into Pacific Sound and
drowned. He thought he had also missed out on a
grand party. But Fury, here's the thing about being
a hero: *Only a few ever make it into the history
books*. Every day, people do heroic things. Every
day, people save others and change the world.
Maybe it's a small change, or maybe a big one, but
they all have ripple effects. What you did changes
the future. Will others know it? Probably not, because right now there isn't anybody writing history
books about this time. But the important thing is
that you did what you had to. You may not see it
now, but you have transformed the future."

I searched my heart, looking for some feeling of
peace. But even with her reassurance, all I found
was cold comfort. "I'm not sure if I'm even asking
the right question. I'm not looking for parties and
parades, but it feels like something's missing."

"I think what you mean is that it feels like *some-*

one is missing, and you're correct. Jason's gone. You saved the world, Fury, but you couldn't save the man who saved your life. And you blame yourself."

I broke down again. "How could I have let that happen?"

"You aren't invincible—none of us are. Not even the gods. You can't read minds. You had no idea that Tyrell was playing for Lyon's team. Fury, you're used to putting yourself in danger, but you never expected to leave Jason behind." She paused. "Like you had to leave your mother behind when you fled the Carver."

I paled, realizing the connection. "Jason and my mother loved each other. And I'm the common factor."

"The Carver killed your mother. Not you. And Jason volunteered to stay in order to help defeat Lyon. You didn't force him to stay."

"I could have stayed with him." I finally put my finger on it. "I feel like a fraud. I left him, just like I left my mother. I returned through the portal and left him behind. I feel like a coward."

"In time, you'll realize how absolutely wrong you are. But for now, Fury, you need to just accept my reassurances. You couldn't save your mother. You couldn't force Jason to let Lyon go free. If he had, neither one of you would have returned, that much I can foresee."

I thought about it for a moment. She was right— I still felt like a coward, but I knew she was right. And in time, I'd be able to face Jason's loss.

"Is there any way to save him? I told him I'd

come back for him." I was afraid she was going to say no, and in fact, expected it, so her answer surprised me.

"There might be a way, but I'm not sure how yet. And it may not be for some time. If we can find him and bring him back, he won't ever be the same after being locked in that realm. But I will look for answers. That's all I can promise you." She leaned forward, picking a flower off a nearby wild rose bush. "Meanwhile, you have to move on. Don't try to forget him, but accept that for now, he's no longer a part of your path."

The heaviness in my chest moved. "When Jason took me in, it took me years to stop having nightmares. The first year, it was a struggle to get through the day. Then it slowly got easier. After five years, I wasn't panicking every time a car slowed down near me. I don't want to live in sorrow and fear like that again, Hecate."

"You won't—not the same way. For one thing, we don't know that he's dead."

"I hate myself for saying so, but it would almost be easier. But you're right. And I'm no longer a teenager." I licked my lips. "I should still marry Tam, right? I should go on with my life? I can't go back to living in anger like I did for so long after Marlene died."

"You don't have to, Fury. Jason wouldn't want you to. This isn't the same sort of situation." She glanced at the sky. "I think we're due for a sprinkle later on. Why don't you go take a walk down by the lake? I think it would do you some good."

I nodded, silently taking my leave. Hecate

watched me go, but I felt her with me every step of the way.

ELAN STOOD THERE, waiting for me as I approached the lakeshore. I wanted to ask her how she knew I'd be coming, but it didn't matter. I joined her, and we silently circled the lake on the trail that led around it. It was a long walk, but I needed to work out my aching muscles, and she seemed to need the companionship.

After a while, she slid her arm through mine. "I have a favor to ask of you."

"Anything I can do, and I mean that." I studied her face. There were no signs of tears, and her eyes were cloudless and clear. Whatever demons she had wrestled with, she seemed resigned to Jason's loss.

"Help me raise my child. Be his aunt. Jason and you were best friends."

"We were like sister and brother. I know." I swallowed hard. I hadn't expected her to be so open. "Of course. Tam and I'll do everything we can for your baby. And for you. I'm so—"

"Don't say it." She held up her other hand. "Don't apologize. He went on a dangerous mission, and he didn't return. He helped you stop Lyon. He helped you stop the Order of the Black Mist from achieving their plans. My love was a hero." She held up her hand, looking at the ring on her left finger.

"Will you wait for him? To see if we can find him?"

"I will wait as long as it feels correct. I will love him always, and forever see him reflected in our child's face." She led me over to a bench. "Don't blame yourself. Don't let Shevron make you feel like this was your fault."

"Hecate just told me the same thing." I paused, then asked, "Will you stand with me when I get married? Shevron's turned her back on me. I have no other family."

"I will, and I'll dance at your wedding if you can spare the bridegroom for one waltz." She smiled, and as she smiled the sun broke through the clouds for just a moment, and then, it once again vanished.

Chapter 13

THROUGHOUT THE REST of the summer, we focused on harvesting crops and putting them up for the winter. Crews worked around the clock, building houses by daylight and lamplight. Autumn would be intense this year, with making sure the food stores were plentiful and that everyone had sturdy shelter. We found the residual components to Tripwater among Tyrell's possessions, along with the Earthshaker.

"So Tyrell was against us longer than we thought." I stared at the artifact and the herbs, feeling heartsick all over again.

"Yes, but we found him out before it was too late," Hecate said. She took the artifact. "I'll turn this over to Jerako." And that was the last we spoke of the traitor. There was nothing more to say.

IN EARLY SEPTEMBER, six weeks after Jason vanished, we needed to send out a raiding party again. Now that Lyon was gone, I felt comfortable going in as long as I had a strong contingent of guards with me. Hans and Greta came with me, and Kendall, and Vis and Mara, both of whom had asked to be part of my personal guard. Elan was too pregnant to make the journey comfortably.

Before we left, I stopped in to check with Hecate. We were half-done with our training center, and hoped to have the doors open come mid-October.

The gazebo that she, Athena, and Artemis had been using was now dismantled, and a sturdy structure built from old slabs of stone had been erected as the new Naós ton Theón. It wasn't nearly as grand as the temple had been on the Peninsula of the Gods, but it felt true to heart. It was still a work in progress—they were adding on as they needed. Sure enough, the rest of the Elder Gods had returned and even Coralie was back as the receptionist, though now there was no air conditioning or soft electric lights.

I quietly entered the temple, smiling at the bustle and sense of activity that permeated the building. In Seattle, the hush had been almost voluminous, like a swell or a wave, but here, the Elder Gods were active and busy. And Theosians from all over the world were doing their best to converge on the temples and barracks for them were being built.

I waved at Coralie and she motioned for me to head back to Hecate's office. As I followed the brilliant gold rug that ran along the hall—they had managed to scrounge it, along with furniture, from the temple in Seattle—I was grateful for the little touches that reminded me of what life had been like. They had also retrieved the tapestries that were still usable, and those hung along the walls. There was an odd, rustic majesty to Naós ton Theón now that it had never fully had before, now that I thought about it. It felt more *temple* and less *office building*.

Hecate was adjusting the drapes to let in the early morning light. The temple was long and narrow so that the gods could have windows to let in the natural light, given that the only other choice was lamplight or magical charms.

"Fury, how are you?" She turned, and I noted that she was wearing her long indigo-colored dress. Sometimes the Elder Gods dressed like we did, but now they seemed to have returned to a different time for their clothing and they no longer assimilated into our culture quite so thoroughly. I privately thought that was a good thing. People didn't take them for granted now.

"I'm fine. I'm heading to Seattle with a raiding party. We're taking guards so it should be safe enough." I slid into a chair opposite her desk. "Is there anything you want me to look for, for you? To bring back?"

She thought for a moment. "We could always use training jackets and clothes for the new recruits that are coming in. We actually have fifteen signed up—three of them from Verdanya. So our first class will be a busy one. Oh—and mats. If there's any way you can bring back training mats so nobody breaks their skull, it would be a good thing."

"I think Thor is coming along with Hans and Greta, so maybe he can fit them in his chariot. Anything else?"

She furrowed her brow, then shook her head. "I'm actually happy with the way things are." As she took a seat behind her desk, she laughed. "I never thought I'd say that, not six months ago, but honestly, Lyon may have done this world a big favor. Though the cost was great, and too many lives were lost."

"It's an adjustment, all right, but I think I'm finally starting to find the rhythm."

She caught my eye. "Do you think, given what you know now, that you would have changed your mind when I offered you the chance for a different life?"

I thought over her question carefully. Even though my first inclination was a resounding "No," I wanted to know in my heart that I meant it. I didn't expect a do-over, but I just wanted to hear the truth of what my heart was telling me.

Would I have changed? We had had a rough six months, and lost Jason. I lost Shevron when Jason vanished. Leonard wasn't talking to me much, either. But we had stopped the Order of the Black Mist. We had closed the portal to the realm of Chaos. We were building a village where people relied on and trusted each other. I was learning what I would need to know to be a queen. And I was about to start teaching others how to destroy the Abominations that still infiltrated the world. And all of those things mattered more than any loss I could imagine.

"No, I'd make the same choice again." I smiled. "I'm a minor goddess, and so often, I forget that. But it comes with responsibility. It comes with a price. And it comes with rewards. I'd never choose a life in which I wouldn't make the difference in the world that I already have, and that I expect to continue making."

"Good. I'm glad. I want you to be happy, Fury. I take my responsibility for my Theosians seriously, and who knows how many of those will come along from now on, with the destruction of so many cities? The Sandspit is still there, and the patches of rogue magic elsewhere, but the population dynamic has shifted, and I have a feeling there will be far fewer Theosians born than there were the past few hundred years."

"I'm part of a dying breed, you mean?"

"You were always part of a rare breed, Fury. Remember that. Now, you'd better go so you can leave before noontide hits. The nights are coming quicker, and autumn is marching steadily toward us." Hecate stood, crossing to her window, which overlooked a lovely patch of freshly tilled ground. The kitchen garden was one of hundreds that had been planted.

Lettuce and carrots were growing, and cucumbers, and other foods that were quick to harvest. In other patches near Willow Wood the potatoes and turnips and squashes were fat and ripening on the vine, and scouts were looking for fruit to harvest, and young fruit trees to transplant.

"I'll see you when I get back. I'll try to bring the mats and clothes." As I left, I wondered again at how things had changed. Hecate seemed more like an old friend rather than the goddess who held my yoke now. And that was priceless.

THE RAIDING PARTY traveled in Thor's chariot to the north side of Wild Wave Inlet, and from there, Laren met us with his boat and ferried us across the water to Old Seattle. I hadn't been in this area since before the zombies invaded.

As we scrambled off the boat, I caught my breath. North Shore—the richest area in Seattle a year ago—was now a wasteland of rubble and ruin. The vast skyscrapers had mostly toppled into dust and debris. The roads were broken, though we could still follow the general trail that had been a major highway. Foliage had begun to creep in again, and Wandering Ivy was growing rampant over the blocks of stone that littered the landscape. Everywhere, there was a feeling of watchfulness, and I couldn't get away from the sensation that we were being observed as we began to make our way south, into the heart of what had been North Shore and Uptown.

Our raiding party was fifteen strong—starting with Hans, Greta, Kendall, me, and Tipton and

Journey—two of Willow Wood's best trackers and scouts. Nine guards chosen for not only their skill with the sword and bow, but their strength and ability to haul the goods for which we were searching. Since the roads were a mess of cracks and stones, there was no way we could commandeer a car, so Thor's chariot would ferry our loot back to the boat, where Laren and his crew waited to stow away the goods.

The smell of Seattle now was fetid and sickly, a toxic combination of mold and maggots. One hundred thousand dead had been trapped in the city, and while some of the bodies had already decomposed, others were still in the process. Everywhere we looked there seemed to be a living, thriving ecosystem of bugs and vermin. I thought about plague and disease, and decided that this would be the last time I'd return until the bones of the dead were bleached and nature had cleansed the city streets.

We headed out, picking through the rubble, looking for shops and buildings that had survived the flood and the quakes and everything else that had beset the city. Row after row of buildings had managed to stay intact, mostly the ones that were single or double story, but whether we would find anything of use in them was hard to tell. All had been swamped by the tsunami and chances were, whatever treasures they held were unusable. But there were some on the higher hills that had gone untouched, and we struggled up one of the steep slopes, fighting off the smells and the heat as we went.

Thor finally took mercy on us. "Come, get in the chariot. I'll take you up to the top of the street. Honestly, humans and Fae and..." He shook his head, but a twinkle in his eye told me he was enjoying himself.

We arrived at the top of the street to find several shops that hadn't been touched by either the waters or looters. As we headed toward what had been a drugstore and, next to it, a general department store, a noise sounded from between the buildings.

I slapped my thigh, bringing my whip to bear, and put enough distance between me and the group so I could use it. The guards immediately armed themselves, as did Greta, Hans, and Kendall. Thor hoisted his hammer. Mjölnir let out a loud *zing* as he swept it overhead.

Four zombies stumbled out from between the buildings. They were so ripe they were gooey, and I grimaced, not wanting to get close to them. Thor sent Mjölnir singing through the air and it struck all four, and they all went down, flat as pancakes before the hammer flew back to the thunder god. The guards dove in, hacking away until there was nothing but slime and tissue left on the sidewalk. I cringed, but slowly put away my whip, realizing that this wasn't my battle. In fact, unless an Abom came along, I probably wasn't going to end up in a fight any time soon. Feeling both oddly useless, and yet relieved, I turned toward the drugstore.

"Wait, milady. Let us make certain that everything is safe." The guards pushed in and again, I moved to the side.

I turned to Hans. "I feel..."

"Like royalty?" Hans laughed. "The look on your face, Fury—it's almost like a puppy dog that lost its chew toy."

I rolled my eyes. "And I'm going to whimper about it. Speaking of dogs, how's Geekly doing?"

"Geekly is quite happy and healthy, thank you. He loves being out in the woods, and he's turning into quite a happy hunting dog." Hans winked. "Thank you, by the way, for letting me take him. I've never thought much about Geemo dogs, but they're handy."

Geekly was a Geemo dog—genetically modified— that had belonged to my neighbor. We found him hanging out with her corpse when we fled Seattle, and Hans had taken him on. They had rapidly become inseparable.

"I wish we could have found her cat." Fursia had been nowhere in sight when we picked up Geekly, so we had emptied the bag of cat food on the counter so she could get to it.

"You want a cat?" Greta said. "How about this one?" She had been poking around in the bushes near the drugstore and now turned around with an armful of kittens.

I groaned, staring at the armful of gray and white striped babies. "Is the mama there?"

"I don't see her. But the kittens are crying for dear life." She buried her face in their fur. "I want to take them home."

Thor snorted and sorted through his chariot, popping back out with a large basket that had a lid. He poked a few holes in the lid and then opened it.

"Into the basket. Then you sit by the chariot and keep an eye on it until we're ready to head back to the boat."

Greta laughed and deposited all ten kittens into the basket, carrying it over to the chariot. At that moment, a very loud and obviously lactating mama kitty came racing over, frantic. Greta snatched her up and slipped her into the basket with her babies. "We need cats around the village to stop any rodents from getting into the foodstuffs."

I couldn't argue with that. "All right, but I get my pick of the litter."

We—sans Greta—entered the drugstore and began to search through the shelves. The guards had determined there were no zombies or bandits inside so we went hog wild, pulling a huge haul of bandages and medications and supplements. Most wouldn't expire for a year or two and we had enough people in the village that they'd be used up by then. We stuffed sack after sack of goods into the chariot. Again I marveled at how it never seemed to fully fill up. I knew there was a finite amount of space in there, but it was deceptively massive.

After the drugstore, we hit the department store. I found athletic wear and confiscated a variety of styles and sizes for the training center. We also raided the housewares section for pots and pans and anything we could find that would help out in the village. There was a lot of tinned and jarred food that was still edible, and that went along with everything else.

"You need cows," Thor said.

I happened to be standing next to him and I jerked around, staring out him. "What? Why do I need a cow?"

"I mean the village. You need livestock. Cows and pigs, goats and chickens. We can take care of that, as well, though not today." He rubbed his chin through his beard, a gleam in his eye. "Come now, get a move on. We don't want to be trapped in the city when it's dark. The ghosts are thick here, and I doubt if you want to be fighting them."

"Speaking of which." I pulled up my Trace. No Aboms nearby, thank goodness. But Queet suddenly wafted around me.

He's right, Fury. The city is laden with ghosts. So many died here and they're trapped. I'm not sure what Lyon did, but most of the dead haven't left and I'm not talking zombies. You don't want to be here after dark, when they come out to play.

That gave me the shudders. I called for the guards to hustle, and we swept through the store. I found several exercise mats and Thor made room for them, taking everything back to the boat and returning for one more load. We finally had wiped out a lot of the shelves and were standing outside, staring at the rubble by then. I walked to the corner, staring down the street. It was broken and cracked from the quakes that had hammered the city, and Wandering Ivy and nettles and brambles were growing through the cracks to uproot more of the pavement. In another year, we wouldn't be able to see the road through the tangle of undergrowth.

"It's gone, isn't it?" I breathed a soft sigh. "It's

well and truly gone."

Greta joined me. "Yes, the city is decaying. It died, and now the flesh falls from its bones as sure as flesh falls from a corpse. Soon, only the skeleton will remain to remind the future that we once lived here."

I thought about the remnants of the past we had encountered in the woods. Rubble and twisted metal from the past. Time was on a perpetual cycle, it seemed, with history returning again and again on itself.

"I wonder what will happen to the Tremble. Will it grow? Will the walls that kept it walled off come down? And Kython and his nest of vampires, what about them? Will they shed their civilized manners and spread out as the predators they really are? What will this all become in a year—five years?"

"I guess we'll just have to wait to find out. Willow Wood is growing, and I'm pretty sure we'll be returning here from time to time, looking for materials to build with, if nothing else." Greta's wings fluttered. "There are ghosts on the wind. Thor is right. They're here even now, thousands who perished." She paused, then shuddered. "I think Lyon somehow managed to bind them to the city. This is truly a ghost town, Fury—waiting to pounce. And they're hungry. The spirits want to feed. We should leave before they grow too restless. The living are no longer welcome here. I doubt if there are many who could survive long in this area."

The look on her face was enough to make me turn tail. We returned to Thor's chariot and I was about to step in when the ground reeled beneath my feet.

"Quake!" I went down on my hands and knees, holding on as the road buckled beneath us. The rolling felt like it would never stop, but then—abruptly—it did. The roof of the drugstore rumbled and then imploded, crashing in on itself.

"Thank gods we're out of there," I whispered as Vis held out his hand, helping me to my feet. "Is everybody all right?" But as I steadied myself, I heard Jason's voice, echoing around me.

"Kae...Kae...can you hear me, Kae?"

"Jason?" I whirled, looking for him. "Jason, where are you?"

"What are you talking about, lass?" Thor said.

"I heard Jason, clear as day. I know it wasn't my imagination. I heard him! I know it." I quickly began to scan every direction, squinting as I tried to figure out where the voice had come from. "Jason? Where are you? Say something!"

Fury, stop. Queet was beside me, misting around me like a cloud of smoke. *Jason's not in the city. He's trapped between worlds. He's out on the Crossroads, running through the mist.*

I had to help him! Frantic, I headed for the middle of the intersection nearest us. "Queet says Jason's on the Crossroads. I need to head over there and see if I can find him."

"We have to leave soon. We don't want to be here after sundown," Vis said. "The zombies come out then and so will the ghosts."

"I don't care. I'm not leaving without trying to save him." I glared at the guard. "You just sit your ass down and wait for me."

Thor coughed. "Hurry, then. The guard is right. This is a dangerous place for all of you when the sun sets, and we don't have long."

Queet, I need you to rush back to Hecate and tell her I'm looking for Jason on the Crossroads. Tell her that I'll need a token for him in order to bring him out of there. I can't bring him over my-self—or maybe I can, but I'd rather be sure than to take chances.

I'm on it, but Fury...it's dangerous, and he's been in the realm of Chaos. You don't know what you're going to be facing.

Maybe so, but how can I live with myself if I don't find out? And with that, I stepped into the middle of the intersection, clasped my hands above my head, and vanished onto the Crossroads.

I WAS BY the cauldron again—that's where my landing point was—and it took me a moment to register that a funeral procession was making its way through. Papa Legba was at the front—it seemed most of the funeral processions that came through here were under his guidance—and I slipped back away from the road as the train of mourners and attendants carried the coffin through. I wasn't sure how all of these people made it to the Crossroads, but every one of the Elder Gods had Theosians with differing powers. Come to think of it, I wondered where the Elder Gods of Santeria, Voudou, Chinese, and Japanese pantheons were going to make their new homes. But right now, that wasn't my concern.

I wanted them to pass so I could be free to start hunting for Jason. I could go running off now, but I wasn't stupid. I knew full well I needed to try to contact him first. If I couldn't, then there was another way I could make a deal to find him, but I was hesitant to try that. Hecate's cauldron wasn't exactly the safest route to take, even for one of her own.

Finally, the procession was gone and I was free to come out into the center of the juncture. The mist was rolling along. It was hard to see the plains that stretched down the roads to the left. The Y-juncture was a triple meeting place, and I had never been far from the center of the fork. I was hesitant about the road to the right because every time I had seen one of Papa Legba's processions, it led in that direction.

I closed my eyes, listening to the eerie calm that descended around me. Finally, when the last strains of the jazzy march had faded, I called out in a loud voice, "Jason? Jason!"

My voice bounced through the air, reverberating off the trees and through the mist like a dizzying echo. As it faded, I listened.

Nothing.

"Jason? Where are you? I know you're out here!"

Again, the echo and then, stillness. The Cross-roads were eerie in their desolation. They were full of emptiness, connected to the Void in ways I didn't understand. They were a hop and a skip from the center of the wheel around which our lives revolved. Even those who couldn't land on the Crossroads in-body like I did had to face them at some point. Every person who ever lived had a moment when their energy took over and forced them to ask, "Should I do this—or should I do that?"

"Jason? Where are you? It's me, Fury!"

And then, slowly, as if rising from deep within the ground, I heard, "Kae? Is that you? Kae?"

My stomach clenched. He was out here. He was trapped somewhere and I didn't know how to reach him. I began to cry.

Queet? Queet! I need you. Jason's out here. I need your help. Damn it, Queet, where the hell are you? Get your ass here now!

Frustrated, I kicked the ground and stomped over to the cauldron. I had no choice. I needed to find Jason and free him. I held my hands over the cauldron and said, "Help me find Jason and bring him off the Crossroads, back where he belongs."

The cauldron seemed to exhale a deep breath, and I heard a low laughter rise out of its cast-iron belly. *Strike the flame,* it whispered. *Strike the flame and seal the deal. Make the deal and promise me bones and blood. Promise me a day of your life. Promise me your next-born child, your peace of mind, the heart of your dreams. Promise me anything. I'll make a deal you can't refuse. A drop of blood. A flicker of flame. That's all you need to seal your claim.*

Shivering, I stared at the empty vessel, and yet, I could not see the bottom. I couldn't see how deep it was, or what was in it. A black void, whirling with stars, filled the center. The stars rippled as though they were waves, a pond of sparkles caught by a stiff breeze.

Something stayed my hand as I waited. I wanted to—it would be easy enough to prick my finger and drop my blood in the cauldron. To strike a small flame and add that. But something inside recoiled from making the deal, and as I stood there, trying to force myself to act, a soft swish behind me sounded. I whirled to find Hecate staring at me.

"Have you—" She nodded toward the cauldron.

"No, damn it. I wanted to. Jason's out here and I need help to find him, but something—something is staying my hand. I don't know what's going on, Hecate. Why can't I act to help my friend?"

I was near tears, ashamed of the fear that wove itself through my veins. It was as though the fear was a dam, keeping me from letting go and doing what I needed to do.

"Good," she said, letting out a deep breath. "I will help you, but never like this. Never through the cauldron."

"Why?" I asked. "It's yours, isn't it?"

"Yes. One of my aspects owns this cauldron." She backed away. "You know me as your patron. As Hecate, the Elder Goddess who watches over you. But Fury, there are sides to me you haven't seen." She stepped back and raised her hands.

"Behold, Hecate the Crone Mother, the Mistress of Magic, the Keeper of the Cauldron of Change! Make a deal with me, and let me weave the threads of your web and your life!"

Standing there before me was an ancient crone, with hair as silver as the starlight, and her face a map of wrinkles so deep they were furrowed into her skin. Her eyes, though, were clear and brilliant and cruel, and she was dressed in a gown as black as the night with a silver belt and silver snakes that writhed around her arms.

I fell to my knees, afraid. I had never met this Hecate before, this ancient hag who embodied all the power of the night within her very essence. She was Queen of the Night, Queen of Nightmares and Dreams, Queen of the Dead, Queen of Phantoms, and around her, ghostly images flooded in, swirling like smoke rising from her hem. She caught hold of one and bit into it, draining the spirit dry as it screamed and fought against her.

"I am the Keeper of the Cauldron. Do you dare to make a deal with me? Or do you stay Fury, beloved of Hecate, the Goddess of the Crossroads?"

I hid my head as her voice thundered around me. "No—no—I don't want to make a deal!"

"Then stand, my Fury, and let your fear go." The thundering voice was gone, soft again and modulated. As I glanced up, she was back, the Hecate I knew and loved. "You do not have to make deals with me, Fury. You are my Chosen, my Theosian. You are mine already. Don't bind yourself to the Cauldron Keeper when you don't need to."

I stumbled to my feet, feeling shell-shocked. Even though Hecate was back to herself—the *her* I knew—I would not forget the fear that had raced through me, and from now on, I thought, I'd be a damned sight more respectful. Maybe there was such a thing as being *too* comfortable around the gods.

"Hecate, I didn't know."

"Remember this: Always come to me, always be patient enough to wait for me. Don't make decisions lightly. Now, you said Jason is out here?"

"I heard him, yes." I told her what had happened. "Can you help me? How could he have gotten out on the Crossroads from the realm of Chaos?"

"Every realm has a connection to the Crossroads. Jason must have managed to find it. Let's hope Lyon hasn't." She held out her hand. "Come, Fury. Let's go find Jason and bring him home."

As I touched her fingers, we were off, racing into the fields, and my fear was forgotten as I raced through the Crossroads with my goddess.

Chapter 14

WE WERE IN the middle of a barren field when I heard Jason again. He sounded lonely and desperate. Hecate motioned for me to be quiet, and she cupped her ear to the wind, listening. After a moment, she relaxed.

"He's trapped in the stream that flows between the different realms. He didn't quite make it over to the Crossroads, but he's no longer in the realm of Chaos. You might say he's in Limbo."

"What can we do to help him?" I was ready to jump through any portal to help him the moment she gave me the order.

"We go over and bring him back. You need to be there because he'll respond to your voice. Chances are he's confused and dazed from being lost in Chaos. The moment we get out of Limbo, I'll take him back to the village because he'll need a lot of help. I'll bounce you back with your friends so they don't worry." She held out her hand. "Don't be frightened. Limbo's overwhelming, but if you keep hold of my hand, you should do fine. Don't let go, though. It's too easy to get lost. Close your eyes."

I did as she asked. As we shifted, my stomach lurched and I felt like I was dropping from a great height. I almost let go, trying to steady myself, but she held tight to my hand and I tried to stop fighting. We dropped, dropped, dropped a long way and I wanted to open my eyes but was afraid of what I might see. I fought back the impulse to scream, clenching my teeth. After what seemed like a long while, we slowed, and then—we were settling in on what felt like an uneven surface, and Hecate let out a long sigh.

"Open your eyes, but keep tight on my hand." Her voice whistled by, then vanished as if it had been snatched away by an angry wind.

I slowly opened my eyes. We were standing on a mist-shrouded plain, and everywhere there seemed to be a gray boiling fog racing along across the ground. I looked up, but immediately shifted my eyes back down to the ground again. Overhead, stars wheeled, turning as though we were in a kaleidoscope, shifting positions with no thought to any pattern.

I paused and, in that moment, realized that it felt like we were whipping around and around on some carnival ride. Oh, we were standing still, but whatever plain we were on felt like it was moving and taking us along with it at a tremendous speed. I wasn't sure I trusted myself to take a step for-ward without lurching to the ground.

"What *is* Limbo?" My words tumbled out of my mouth and—like Hecate's—echoed for a brief second and then were gone, ricocheting away from me, yanked out of my lips by some unseen force. The faintest hint of an echo reverberated behind them.

"Limbo is a place where everything waits in stagnation, and yet nothing is still. It's a contradiction, a paradoxical realm where nothing moves and everything changes."

Her words whipped by so quickly I had the impulse to duck.

"How do we find Jason in this? I don't know if I can even move."

She cocked her head, looking around. I still kept my sights on the ground—it helped me feel less queasy. I hadn't felt this nauseated in a long while. It made traveling on a boat seem like the steadiest motion in the world.

"Call him by name. Tell him who you are. With a little luck, he'll hear you and follow your voice."

I tried to catch my breath and realized I wasn't really breathing. Or it didn't feel that way. Panicking, I gasped for air and Hecate's firm grip on my hand tightened even more.

"Stop. You're breathing. It just doesn't feel the same here. Close your eyes again and steady yourself. Search for that inner fire but don't summon it. The glow will warm you and help you feel more like yourself."

I did as she suggested, closing my eyes and summoning the fire within. There, I felt a soft glow. It strengthened as I centered my attention on it, and after a while, it grew to life, warming my body and core, and I felt stronger. I opened my eyes, strong enough to focus on what I needed to do. I ignored the feeling that I couldn't take a deep breath and, instead, thought about Jason.

"Jason! Jason! It's Kaeleen. Follow my voice. We're here to help you! Jason!"

My words echoed around us, skipping off like stones across the river. Another moment and I repeated the call, and then a third time. We waited for a time, and Hecate urged me to try again. She seemed confident, so I called for him a fourth time, and a fifth.

I was about to lose heart when—on the sixth call—I heard his voice, faint but sure.

"Kae, I'm coming. Keep calling, please!"

"Jason. We're here. Follow my voice! Jason, listen to me and focus on the sound of my words. Come here, Jason—we'll get you out of here and home! Elan is waiting for you! She loves you!" I kept up a string of chatter, wrestling to control my voice as the wind tried to snatch it away before the words were fully out of my mouth.

"Keep talking. He's on the run. I can sense him. He'll be here soon. I'm going to have to let go of your hand when he arrives in order to catch him because otherwise, he'll overshoot the mark. Do not fall, do not move, stay completely still and you'll be all right. Do you understand?" Hecate whispered fiercely, her grip starting to lessen.

I nodded, continuing to call Jason our way. I could sense him now, too—he was running toward us at full tilt, as though he were being chased by some creature. He was wild-eyed and terrified, and I realized that Hecate was right. He wouldn't be able to stop himself in time. I closed my eyes to make the transition easier, and then, as he neared, Hecate let go of my hand.

I lurched, but managed to keep myself upright as the world began to spin at a dizzying rate. I tried to ignore the sensation, to focus on the soft glow of the fire within. I whispered to it, asking it to keep me grounded. Without Hecate's hand holding on to mine, the power of the realm fully enveloped me and I understood why Jason seemed so frantic. There was nothing here to hold onto, nothing to offer a sense of stability. Everything was moving and shifting, and yet, there seemed to be no end to the realm, and nowhere to go.

It reminded me of the Tremble, only far worse, and I had a sudden thought that perhaps some of the energy from the realm of Limbo was seeping into the Tremble. Or perhaps from the realm of Chaos? But if that was so, why didn't Lyon go up to the Tremble to try his plan from there? I focused on the thought, narrowing my attention and suddenly realized that I wasn't quite so afraid. But I wasn't feeling secure enough to open my eyes.

A few moments later—I actually had no frame of reference for time but it seemed like it might be that—Hecate took hold of my hand again and we hurtled through space. Before I could catch my breath, we were standing back at the Crossroads.

"Where's Jason? Did you get him?" I stumbled to my knees, all the *oomph* knocked out of me.

"Yes, I did, and I took him back to the village. I

need to go there now, so that we can care for him. He's alive, that's all I can tell you, and he's unhurt physically. We'll have to see what we can do to repair his mind. Now, go—you've been out here too long, and the realm of Limbo saps your energy so no trying any magic for a while. I'll see you back at the village. Be safe."

Before I could say another word, she waved her hand and I found myself back in the intersection, on my knees, groaning as I realized I'd landed right in the middle of a fight.

THOR WAS KICKING ass on a group of zombies to my left. To my right, Vis and Hans were fighting more of the same. Greta was fighting something with her sword that I couldn't see. Dizzy, I staggered to my feet, shaking my head as I stared at the brawl.

Greta motioned to me. "I need help. Ghosts—a big bunch of them. Fury, do something!"

It was then that I saw the misty forms writhing in the dusk that had fallen. I must have been away for the better part of an hour. I started to summon up my fire but it wouldn't come—wouldn't spark and I remembered what Hecate had said. No using magic for a while.

I slapped my thigh, bringing my whip to bear and Greta fell back. The fire of the whip wasn't something I had to summon, and it could affect creatures of all types, including the incorporeal.

I brought it crackling down on the form that was trying to choke Greta and there was a hiss as the spirit backed away, turning toward me instead.

"Crap—there are too many! And on top of zombies—we can't fight all of them."

Nobody paid attention to what I said, which wasn't surprising given everybody seemed to be caught up in the massive brawl. No matter what Hecate had said, I had no choice. I had to use what magic I could manage to give us the chance to escape. I didn't have the time nor my tools to summon a Psychofágos demon, which could have helped corral the ghosts.

So I searched for my flame, searched for the inner core of the fire, and then, when I found it, I whispered to it, asking it to ride me hard and wild, to take control given I couldn't nurture it with my own energy. At that moment, an elemental rose up with a deep laugh, and dove toward me. I screamed as the sheer force and flame overcame me, burning every nerve raw.

Then, as the flame entwined with my muscle and bone, I rose up, a living pillar of fire, the fury of the flame incarnate. I could see through the haze of white-hot tongues and I realized that the elemental and I had merged into one. Its hunger and desire to feed threatened to overcome my control, and I battled back. The elemental didn't care who its targets were, only that it found sustenance. I focused on the zombies and ghosts and, by sheer willpower, forced the creature of fire to turn in their direction. As I walked toward the guards who were fighting the creatures, they fell back, leaving the zombies and spirits open to me.

I held out my hands and a spray of fire came shooting out, like ten thousand sparklers. The zombies fell, consumed by the flames the moment they hit, and then the ghosts backed away as they, too, begin to explode in a vapor of smoke. I raged on, burning the stone rubble in front of me, driving the fires toward whatever could take flame and burn.

Burn. The hunger to burn brightly, to see the world alight in a crackling blaze…

I couldn't fight the impulse much longer as I attempted to wrest control from the elemental and keep it from turning on my friends. I let out a scream, loud and primal and the sound of a thousand wildfires converging. As I turned my fire spray toward Greta and Hans, my consciousness fading, a crack of thunder split the sky and rain began to pour down in a deluge. The water washed through the flames from the elemental, extinguishing them on impact.

I clenched my teeth, holding on to the last shreds of awareness as the water began to wash away the hold the elemental had on me. It struggled, trying to hold on, but as the flames died back, the creature of fire slowly withdrew. Then, with a last spark and hiss, it vanished, and I collapsed. Everything went black as the cool rain soothed my body and my soul, and I allowed myself to slip into a chasm churning with ocean waves and the howl of the storm.

WHEN I WOKE, my head was resting on Greta's lap, and Thor was kneeling by my side, holding my head, whispering my name. I blinked, feeling charred and yet drenched to the bone.

"What happened? The zombies?"

"Gone. You destroyed them. The ghosts fled too. And now that you're awake, we need to leave this place." Thor lifted me up, carrying me as if I weighed no more than a feather.

I leaned against him, smelling ozone and beer and the musky scent of goat. It was an oddly comforting mix, and I murmured something, pressing my lips to his chest as I closed my eyes.

"Shush, young goddess. Let sleep take you."

The swaying of his walk lulled me into a light sleep, but the next moment, I jarred awake again as I found myself deposited on a fluffy cape inside the chariot. The others crowded around me and Greta stroked the hair out of my eyes. Then the motion began again as we took off. I closed my eyes once more, and the next thing I knew, they were transferring me to Laren's boat, and we were setting sail across the inlet, away from Seattle.

Even in the midst of my confusion and exhaustion, my last waking thoughts were that I would never again walk the streets of Seattle. It was a skeleton of a city, belonging to only the walking dead and the ghosts, and it was truly time to leave it behind.

Chapter 15

Three months later…Winter Solstice

I STOOD IN my bedroom—or what had been my bedroom and what would now become Elan and Jason's room—staring at myself in the mirror. Patrice was fluttering around me, talking up a storm as she tucked a handkerchief in my hand and then moved around to fasten the laces on my corset. I sucked in my stomach.

"Are you excited, milady?" She gritted her teeth as she pulled the laces taut, then let them out just a little before tying them off.

"Nervous, excited. I can't decide which. Both, I guess."

I couldn't take my eyes off my reflection. I had never looked like this before. I was wearing a dress of deep indigo blue, with beading on the corset bodice. The beads—which I had found out were actual diamonds—also studded the waist of the corset and skirt, and a belt that draped around my waist. I had been terrified when Tam told me they were diamonds, but he quickly reassured me that in UnderBarrow, they were mere stones, like any other crystal.

The sweetheart neckline of the dress was strapless, and Patrice handed me long indigo gloves to slide on. They were satin, above the elbow, and once they were on, Patrice fastened a bracelet of pearls and diamonds around my wrist, then a pendant—a large emerald-cut sapphire set in silver filigree—around my neck.

"You won't wear a crown until after you're married—it will be placed on your head at the conclusion of the ceremony," she told me.

Damh Varias had told me the same thing, but I was grateful that Patrice had bothered to find out for me. She held out silver ankle boots—sparkling and with three-inch heels—for me to slide my feet into, and then zipped them up the side. We had designed the dress after getting Damh Varias's approval that it met the expectations of my soon-to-be station, and the raiding parties had scoured Seattle for the proper material that was still good, and boots and other accessories. The pendant had been a present from Tam, as was the bracelet and matching earrings.

Patrice had convinced me that on my wedding day, I didn't need a slit in my dress to reach my whip, and I had given in. Hecate had told me the same thing and I finally let go of being Fury for a day and embraced being Kaeleen—the woman whom I thought I had lost long ago.

"You're so beautiful, milady." Patrice stepped back, offering me a bright smile. "I'm so glad you're marrying Lord Tam."

"Are you ready to be the queen's maid, then?" I turned slightly, trying to get a good look at my back. The skirt swept out, a sheer silk organza overlay covering the satin skirt. The back of the skirt trailed behind by a good two or three feet.

Patrice draped a long velvet cloak around my shoulders. It met in front with a Celtic knotwork clasp. The cloak was a deep plum, complimenting my dress.

She stood back. "There, milady. And yes, I am ready to be the queen's maid." There was a touch of pride in her voice that seemed to spill over into her stature, and she straightened her shoulders, beaming. "You're so beautiful. His Majesty will be pleased, I hope."

"I think Lord Tam will be more than pleased." I stood back, almost afraid to move because I didn't want to mess up anything. My hair was a cascade of upswept curls and tendrils wisping down by my ears.

Patrice answered a knock at the door and Elan entered, followed by another maid. She was lovely, wearing an ice-blue dress that gently flowed over her swelling stomach. Her hair was braided back with holly tucked in through the plaits, and she was wearing a simple circlet of silver around her neck. She broke into a smile as she saw me.

"Fury, you're such a beautiful bride."

"You look good enough to eat, too." I grinned

back at her. "How's Jason doing?"

"He's all right. Still skittish and hesitant, but he's growing stronger every day. He worked so hard to be able to walk you down the aisle. I'm so proud of him." Her eyes clouded for a moment. They had had a rough patch, for sure.

When Jason had returned from the realm of Chaos, he couldn't tell us how he had escaped, or how he managed to find his way into Limbo. As the months wore on, he stopped jumping at every noise, and he was able to carry on more of a conversation than just a few sentences.

Physically, he was unharmed, but his mind had broken just enough to leave him insecure and confused. The healers in UnderBarrow were working with him every day to help him regain his sense of self. Shevron still wasn't talking to me, though she didn't avoid me as much as she used to, and she and Elan took care of Jason and they were doing their best to avoid coddling him—the healers had said he needed to push himself, and be pushed.

He had recently shifted into a hawk for the first time since he returned, and flown for a good half an hour. It seemed to spur him on, and he was making faster strides now.

We had heard no more about Lyon, and in fact, the Order of the Black Mist had fled Seattle, leaving it to the ghosts and the zombies. If they were still active, we didn't know, but communications between countries—and in fact towns and cities— was now spotty at best and we seldom received any news from the outside.

A shadow seemed to fill the room, deepening,

and I shivered.

"What's wrong?" Elan asked.

"A goose just walked over my grave, I suppose." I gave myself one last look in the mirror, and turned. "I'm just jittery. I get to meet my in-laws today. That's scary enough, I guess."

Tam's parents—the High King and Queen of the Bonny Fae—were in the building, so to speak. Or rather, in UnderBarrow. I hadn't had the chance to meet them yet, and the reception would be the first time that I'd greet them. I wasn't looking forward to it, given that I had no clue in the world what to say to them.

"It's a day of change, all right." Elan let out a soft breath.

Today, later after the ceremony, Tam would take her oath of fealty to UnderBarrow, officially severing her ties to Verdanya. Her father had ascended to the throne and immediately cut her off, disowning her for her treachery, and while the two Fae Courts kept civil discourse, we weren't exactly best buddies and visiting between the two nations was highly discouraged.

"How's your daughter?" I nodded to her stomach.

She broke into a bright glow. "She's doing wonderfully. The midwife says I'll be having her near the spring equinox, so she'll be a March hare baby, it looks like. She's kicking up a storm lately. I think she's going to be a little fighter, like her mama." She paused, then added, "Focusing on her helps Jason ground himself, I've noticed. She's helping her daddy heal."

"Then maybe she'll be a healer," I said, winking.

"Maybe. But I like to think she'll join the guard like me. You know, a mother wants her daughter to follow in her footsteps."

Patrice answered the door again as a discreet knock interrupted us. It was Vis and Mara, along with an honor guard, waiting to escort us to the wedding. Captain Varga was there, and Vis helped me up on his back. I would ride sidesaddle into my new life.

As Elan took her place in front of me, and Patrice walked by my side, I tried not to think of the past. The future was waiting, and that was the only direction we were headed in.

TAM WAITED IN the Grove of UnderBarrow—the official grove that was to the west of Willow Wood. Since the entire town, as well as the population of UnderBarrow, couldn't fit in the throne room, Tam had ordered the grove fashioned for court functions where everybody would be present. While our marriage wasn't a must-attend, most of Willow Wood and UnderBarrow were there, milling around, filling the makeshift bleachers even though it was barely thirty-two degrees and there was three feet of snow in the forest. Walkways had been cleared, and a large canopy covered the center podium where we were to be wed, but I still was impressed by the turnout, given the weather.

It was three P.M., and Tam stood on the large

dais, dressed in his royal best. Beside him, Damh Varias and Hans waited, and his mother and father stood off to one side.

In the center of the dais Hecate stood, looking more beautiful than I had ever seen her. She was dressed in soft ivory with a pale plum overlay, and around her head she wore a headdress of silver snakes and knotwork. She was standing next to the Dagda—the official God of Willow Wood. To-gether, they would marry us—much to the chagrin of Damh Varias, who wanted only the gods from the Temple of the Sylvan Woodland. But Tam had firmly negated the idea, claiming that since I was pledged to Hecate, it would be sacrilegious for me to be married without her presence.

As we passed the band I caught my breath and my hand fluttered to my chest. Tommy Tee was there—with the rest of the band. He was playing his guitar, along with a harpist, two flautists, a drummer, and two musicians playing the bowed psaltery.

He bowed as I passed, the musician whom I had only ever known as a sweet-hearted addict. His eyes were clearer than I had ever seen them, and I blew him a kiss as the band struck up a delicate song that reminded me of unicorns and maidens, of doves flying over a frozen lake, of the Frostlings.

In fact, Naia and Derra, the two Frostlings who had guided us to Eleveanor a year before, were in attendance. Their frozen forms looked to be formed of ice, their features etched into their perfectly smooth glassine skin. They were living sculptures in ice, and they waited silently at the edges of the circle of our people. To another side, I saw Zhan—one of the hedgemites who served the Greenlings. He waved, smiling brightly as he saw me. I gave him a little wave back, thinking how strange my life had become. Even Queet was there, swirling in his mist, watching with a thumbs-up.

We were in the middle of a frozen Faerieland, in a forest where traffic and the dirt and grime of the city were only memories. And here I sat on Captain Varga's back, on midwinter's day, ready to wed the man of my dreams who was waiting to make me his queen.

Jason rode forward, astride a black stallion, looking nervous but sure. He leaned across to touch my cheek.

"Oh, Kae, you look so lovely." He paused, his eyes watering. "Did you ever in a million years think…"

I closed my eyes as snowflakes drifted down to dust my hair. "I never really dreamed of any-thing beyond the present moment. I chased down Aboms. That's what I did. I had daydreams, of course, but they were vague. But *this*…this is life. Everything changes and moves on. Life evolves, we evolve, the world evolves. We're witnessing history as civilization crumbles again and…who knows what will replace it? But we'll be here for a long time, watching and helping to shape the future."

"You're going to be a queen. Queen Fury."

"Queen Kaeleen the Fury," I said softly. "That will be my official title. I need to reclaim my past, as well as reach for my dreams. I'm Fury, through and through. But Tam reminds me that I'm also

Kaeleen. I'm no longer just angry and seeking revenge."

"Tam's waiting for you. We should begin," Jason said. "May I escort you to your future?"

As we road down the path, the players switched to an ancient song—the melody haunting and weaving around us. "Irish Handfasting" had been the song played at every Winter Court wedding. I wasn't the only one reclaiming the past. Tam had renamed his court UnderBarrow of the Winter Court, with his parents' blessing. Together, we were blending the past and the present to create a new future.

We rode up the aisle to the dais, and Jason slipped off his horse to lift me down. The music beckoned us on and, when we reached the platform, Jason held my hand as I ascended the steps.

And there he was, Tam, Prince of the Winter Fae, Lord of the Bonny Fae, the keeper of my heart. His hair billowed down his shoulders, black as night, and his eyes were glowing silver as he held out his hands to me. I took them, letting him pull me in.

Hecate and the Dagda bound our hands with a silver, black, and blue plaited cord, and they took our vows. We pledged life, love, and heart, blending our oaths, blending our lives, and the music poured on in the background, sweeping us into our future, as I wed the man of my dreams.

"Take me," I whispered. "Take me, make me your queen, hold my heart forever."

"I pledge to you my life, my heart, my soul, my protection and eternal devotion. You are queen of my world, my Kaeleen…my Fury." And as Tam leaned down to kiss me, the world shifted again.

The Dagda set the crown atop my head and Tam and I turned to gaze out over our people. We were on the verge of a new age, a new era, and together we'd lead them through the ice and snow, through the forest, into the world that was waiting for us.

Three and a half years later…

WILLOW WOOD WAS thriving.

The winter had given way into spring, and Elan had her baby daughter. She named her *Aila*, which meant "from the strong place" and the girl was growing like a weed. She had inherited her father's ability to shift into a hawk, and her mother's prowess and speed.

Elan and I were walking by Reflection Lake, watching as the weavers hunted for the supple reeds that were still pliable enough for basket weaving. I was leading two classes a year at the training center, teaching others to hunt down Abominations, and now there were more than fifty others who had returned to their homes, able to fight against the demons from Pandoriam who drifted in off the World Trees. More were coming for a new class starting in a few weeks, and I was looking forward to the work.

The Devani had mysteriously vanished from Seattle, and we had no idea what had happened to them. Reports filtered in that they were gathering down in what had been Atlantea, but it was impossible to verify them. Seattle was truly a city of ghosts, echoing with the secrets of the past, and becoming more dangerous to enter every day.

I sat on a bench and Elan sat next to me. "How's Jason really doing?"

Jason had reopened his store, and seemed to be healed, though Elan had confided that at times he got night terrors so badly he would wake up screaming. We didn't have much chance to just hang out anymore, but we had reestablished a tradition and now, every week, we all gathered for dinner in a private dining chamber—Elan and Jason, Hans and Greta, and Tam and me.

"He's all right. I don't think he'll ever quite be the man he was, but maybe that's a good thing. He's a lot more flexible now about the weaknesses of others. Leonard, especially."

Leonard had done well with the guards, and Shevron had finally accepted the fact that her son was a warrior—and a damned good one—and she was proud as punch of him. She had warmed back up to me, though I had my doubts we'd ever be as close as we used to. She couldn't quite forgive how much I had played into her son and brother's lives.

I sucked in a deep breath as I looked at the sky. It was the color of pale lemon chiffon, and we would be getting rain later this afternoon. I had learned to read the signs of the clouds as well as any weather prognosticator.

"What about you?" Elan asked. "Do you miss your old life?"

I shrugged after a moment. "Sometimes. But the last raiding party said Seattle's unrecognizable. It's been months since we heard from anybody farther than Bend. Who knows what's happening elsewhere. If Tigra manages to return from her trip, we'll know more."

Tigra and a group of scouts had taken off on a cross-country trip to assess what remained of our nation. Well, *nation* was a misnomer. Of civilization, rather. They had left a year ago, and we hoped to hear from them within the next year. Whenever I thought of her, I felt unsettled, and I wasn't sure I wanted to hear what she'd have to say.

Life now was peaceful, for the most part, with the occasional roust from a pack of lycanthropes or the like. Mostly, we lived our lives day to day, and every month or so, I was even able to kill an Abom that had wandered up this way from the World Tree. But the Greenlings had spread out through the forests, and they kept watch also.

A fat raindrop hit my nose. "We'd better get back. I have to talk to Hecate about the incoming class, and I think you're due on guard duty in an hour or so."

Elan picked up the basket of early watercress she had been gathering. "Yeah, it looks that way."

But as we headed back to Willow Wood, I couldn't help but feel that a force was out there, waiting and watching. And when it broke, I had the sense it would bring a storm such as we had never before seen. But for now, there was work to do, and Tam to love, and UnderBarrow to rule.

And for now, that was enough.

If you enjoyed this book, I invite you to read the other three books that complete this story arc of the Fury Unbound Series: FURY RISING, FURY'S MAGIC, and FURY AWAKENED.

Meet the wild and magical residents of Bedlam in my Bewitching Bedlam Series. Fun-loving witch Maddy Gallowglass, her smoking-hot vampire lover Aegis, and their crazed cjinn Bubba (part djinn, all cat) rock it out in Bedlam, a magical town on a magical island. BLOOD MUSIC, BEWITCHING BEDLAM, and MAUDLIN'S MAYHEM, are currently available, and BLOOD VENGEANCE and TIGER TAILS are available for preorder. And more are on the way!

If you like cozies with an edge, try my Chintz 'n China paranormal mysteries. The series is complete with: GHOST OF A CHANCE, LEGEND OF THE JADE DRAGON, MURDER UNDER A MYSTIC MOON, A HARVEST OF BONES, ONE HEX OF A WEDDING, and a wrap-up novella: HOLIDAY SPIRITS.

The newest Otherworld book—MOON SHIMMERS—is available now, and the next, HARVEST SONG, will be available in May 2018.

For all of my work, both published and upcoming releases, see the Bibliography at the end of this book, or check out my website at Galenorn.com and be sure and sign up for my newsletter to receive news about all my new releases.

Playlist

I often write to music, and FURY CALLING was no exception. Here's the playlist I used for this book:

Android Lust: Here and Now
Arcade Fire: Abraham's Daughter
Arch Leaves: Nowhere to Go
The Black Angels: You on the Run; Don't Play With Guns; Love Me Forever; Young Men Dead
Black Mountain: Queens Will Play
Black Rebel Motorcycle Club: Feel It Now
Broken Bells: The Ghost Inside
Clannad: Banba Óir; Newgrange
Cobra Verde: Play with Fire
Corvus Corax: Ballade de Mercy
Crosby, Stills & Nash: Guinnevere
Damh the Bard: Willow's Song; Gently Johnny
Dizzi: Dizzi Jig
Eastern Sun: Beautiful Being
Eivør: Trøllbundin
Faun: Hymn to Pan; The Market Song; Sieben; Tanz mit mir
FC Kahuna: Hayling
The Feeling: Sewn
Garbage: Queer; #1 Crush
The Gospel Whiskey Runners: Muddy Wa-

ters

Ian Melrose & Kerstin Blodig: Kråka

Jessica Bates: The Hanging Tree

Jethro Tull: Dun Ringill; North Sea Oil

The Kills: Nail In My Coffin; You Don't Own The Road; Sour Cherry; Dead Road 7

Leonard Cohen: The Future; You Want It Darker

Lorde: Yellow Flicker Beat; Royals

Low with Tom and Andy: Half Light

Matt Corby: Breathe

Shriekback: The Shining Path; Underwater-boys; Dust and a Shadow; This Big Hush; Now These Days Are Gone; The King in the Tree

Spiral Dance: Boys of Bedlam

Sweet Talk Radio: We All Fall Down

Tamaryn: While You're Sleeping, I'm Dream-ing; Violet's in a Pool

Tina Turner: One of the Living

Tom Petty: Mary Jane's Last Dance

Tuatha Dea: The Hunt; Irish Handfasting

The Verve: Bitter Sweet Symphony

Wendy Rule: Let the Wind Blow

Biography

New York Times, *Publishers Weekly*, and *USA Today* bestselling author Yasmine Galenorn writes urban fantasy and paranormal romance, and is the author of over fifty books, including the Otherworld Series, the Fury Unbound Series, the Bewitching Bedlam Series, and the upcoming Wild Hunt Series, among others. She's also written nonfiction metaphysical books. She is the 2011 Career Achievement Award Winner in Urban Fantasy, given by RT Magazine. Yasmine has been in the Craft since 1980, is a shamanic witch and High Priestess. She describes her life as a blend of teacups and tattoos. She lives in Kirkland, WA, with her husband Samwise and their cats. Yasmine can be reached via her website at Galenorn.com.

Indie Releases Currently Available:

Bewitching Bedlam Series:
Bewitching Bedlam
Maudlin's Mayhem
Blood Music
Blood Vengeance
Tiger Tails

Fury Unbound Series:
Fury Rising
Fury's Magic

Fury Awakened
Fury Calling

Otherworld Series:
Moon Shimmers
Earthbound
Otherworld Tales: Volume One
Tales From Otherworld: Collection One
Men of Otherworld: Collection One
Men of Otherworld: Collection Two
Moon Swept: Otherworld Tales of First Love
For the rest of the Otherworld Series, see Website

Chintz 'n China Series:
Ghost of a Chance
Legend of the Jade Dragon
Murder Under a Mystic Moon
A Harvest of Bones
One Hex of a Wedding
Holiday Spirits

Bath and Body Series (originally under the name India Ink):
Scent to Her Grave
A Blush With Death
Glossed and Found

Misc. Short Stories/Anthologies:
Mist and Shadows: Short Tales From Dark Haunts
Once Upon a Kiss (short story: Princess Charming)
Silver Belles (short story: The Longest Night)
Once Upon a Curse (short story: Bones)

Night Shivers (an Indigo Court novella)

Magickal Nonfiction:
Embracing the Moon
Tarot Journeys

For all other series, as well as upcoming work, see Website